GUARDIAN'S INSTINCT

CERBERUS TACTICAL K9 TEAM CHARLIE

CERBERUS TACTICAL K9

FIONA QUINN

FIONA QUINN, LLC

THE WORLD OF INIQUUS

Ubicumque, Quoties. Quidquid

Iniquus - /i'ni/kwus/ our strength is unequalled, our tactics unfair – we stretch the law to its breaking point. We do whatever is necessary to bring the enemy down.

The Lynx Series

Weakest Lynx

Missing Lynx

Chain Lynx

Cuff Lynx

Gulf Lynx

Hyper Lynx

Marriage Lynx

Strike Force

In Too DEEP

JACK Be Quick

InstiGATOR

Fear The REAPER

Striker

Uncommon Enemies

Wasp

Relic

Deadlock

Thorn

FBI Joint Task Force

Open Secret

Cold Red

Even Odds

Kate Hamilton Mysteries

Mine

Yours

Ours

Cerberus Tactical K9 Team Alpha

Survival Instinct

Protective Instinct

Defender's Instinct

Delta Force Echo

Danger Signs

Danger Zone

Danger Close

Cerberus Tactical K9 Team Bravo

Warrior's Instinct

Rescue Instinct

Hero's Instinct

Cerberus Tactical K9 Team Charlie

Guardian's Instinct

This list was created in 2024. For an up-to-date list, please visit FionaQuinnBooks.com

If you prefer to read the Iniquus World in chronological order you will find a full list at the end of this book.

GUARDIAN'S INSTINCT

Cerberus Tactical K9

Team Charlie

FIONA QUINN

THE PLAYERS

Team Alpha

Ridge
Ryder
Tripwire

Panther Force

Titus
Thorn
Gage
Nutsbe

Cerberus Team Charlie

Halo St. John

Friends and Family

PROLOGUE

Iniquus' Cerberus Tactical K9 is Building Team Charlie

Mid-August

Shenandoah, Virginia

Basil St. John—code-named Halo—unfolded himself from the back of the gunmetal gray passenger van. For an hour and a half, he'd traveled west with Cerberus Team Alpha from Iniquus Headquarters in Washington, D.C., to the Shenandoah Valley.

"Shenandoah." Halo moved those unfamiliar sounds around his lips and tongue, thinking it had a forlorn kind of feel to it. As Halo set his rucksack on the ground at his feet and sent his gaze up into the hills, he remembered an American Marine from Wyoming he'd met behind the wire of a UN military base back in Halo's early days as an Australian Commando. With his sweat-stained cowboy hat, that Marine sat near the campfire, strumming his guitar, singing about home—lush with prairie grasses dancing under a bright sun during the day and the night's sky a riot of diamonds overhead.

Those moonlit songs painted a picture of the mid-west in Halo's imagination.

The pictures he'd formed of the East Coast, including D.C., the city he hoped to call home, came from the movies. Five days ago, Halo had flown in from New South Wales to interview for a job that had come available with world-renowned Iniquus Security.

Halo's military record stood strong. But that record alone wasn't going to get him a place on the teams. Even with the special operator boxes ticked, the Iniquus hiring process was a thorough one. Halo had spent days moving through daunting security scrutiny, followed by physical, ethical, and psychological tests. Iniquus had a worldwide reputation for integrity and excellence; they weren't going to take on anyone who didn't fit their specs, and that included American citizenship, high-level security clearance, and loyalty to the U.S. Constitution. Lucky for Halo, though, he hadn't been to the United States since he was a month old, he had, in fact, started this life in a New York City hospital.

As Halo stepped off the plane in D.C., he thought his mental pictures had pretty much lined up. But standing here in the parking lot with the sun just breaking over the horizon in the east, sending a golden glow over the height and breadth of the mountain range sprawling across the horizon, Halo had to admit that he hadn't expected *this*—not so close to the capital city, anyway.

Today, Cerberus Alpha was at the base of the mountain, taking on a real-world mission.

The team had invited Halo along. It was a final test to see if he was a good fit for Iniquus's K9 Tactical Team. Just like in all special forces units, only a portion of the job was about skill proficiency and technical knowledge. A big chunk of success was personality. Could you get along? Did you have a team mindset? Did they have confidence that you had their back when things got wild and hairy?

When facing life-or-death scenarios, trust was everything.

And today, there was a life on the line. A woman had wandered from her care facility into the foothills after a delivery man didn't wait to hear the door snick shut behind him.

Throwing his borrowed pack over his shoulders, Halo watched a car park in the back corner of the lot. The driver jumped from the car and ran to the knot of distraught family members huddling close. A high-pitched wail rode the wind, and Halo imagined that it could well be his own family if something like this were to happen to his gramps.

Halo turned to scan the sleepy-looking hill in front of him. It was hard to imagine that someone was out there and would soon be struggling to stay alive if the search teams didn't get to her in time.

The family was lucky, though, in this one regard, trained search teams were amassing.

Max let out a high-pitched bark, looking for Halo and wanting out of his crate. Halo fell in line behind Ryder as the team unloaded their dogs from the follow van. Ryder was an Australian Commando brother. On his recommendation, Iniquus Command extended an invitation to Halo for the interview. And he was grateful.

Ryder tipped his ear toward the family, and Halo gave him a nod of understanding. It was tough to watch that kind of pain.

On the way out here, Ryder had told him that at times when circumstances presented as acutely perilous—be they missing children, someone with a medical condition, dangerous weather, or a suicidal war veteran—area officials often reached out to Cerberus to lend an assist while State resources scrambled.

When the Iniquus search teams were in town, they did their

best to help. But they were often elsewhere—Team Bravo was training in the Caribbean, and Alpha was just now getting back from an Italian mudslide that trapped three contract-protected students for days in the debris.

Team Alpha was jet lagged and exhausted from the physical demands of their time in the dirt but put their personal comfort aside to be here.

Tripwire efficiently unloaded his German shepherd, Valor, from the K9 transport and stepped out of the way for Ryder to get Voodoo.

Today, Halo wanted two things very badly. He wanted Iniquus to offer him a contract, yes. But mostly, he wanted to be a force multiplier as the team worked to save a woman's life.

Halo turned his attention to the van; it was his turn to get his dog.

Max sat proudly waiting, the tip of his tail vibrating with excitement. He knew they were going to work, and Max loved every minute of the physical and mental challenge.

"Ready to go, boy? Today, we're not playing. Someone needs us to be in top form." He unclasped the lock, and Max jumped down, rounding to flank Halo.

When Halo stepped out of the way for the next guy, Max pressed to his side. "Come on, Maxi, let's get you into uniform. Today, you get to wear your helmet and goggles. Let's see what Ryder says is in store for us."

Halo had been training his K9, *Take It to The Max*, since he was about eight weeks old. As they got the call to interview for the position with Iniquus, Halo was celebrating Max's second adoption day anniversary, which launched the Malinois full-blown into his doggy adolescence. And like human teens, that had its challenges.

Back in their early days together, when he was still a K9 handler with his Australian Commando unit, Halo would get home at night and work with his pup, patiently building the skillsets Max would need to reach his full potential. Tactical work, apprehension work, scent work, Max was a nose and a bite. And he enjoyed all of it—especially when he got to wear his doggy goggles. Dressing out in his tactical kit seemed to make Max feel badass.

Clipping the last buckle on Max's borrowed blaze-orange vest, Halo checked his collar with its tracking and comms units affixed. "All's good, Max."

Ryder came over to sit on the bumper beside them. "You're going to need the three Gs here, mate: goggles, gloves, and gators." Ryder opened his pack and pulled those items out. "They'll hand you a can of bear spray as we set out. Powerful stuff, you want to make sure it doesn't leak on you or Max."

Halo opened the loaner pack and pulled out a pair of gators. Just like in the Commandos, every item in the ruck was essential and organized into specific spaces. No matter what went down—no matter the field conditions—an operator could grab up anyone's pack, reach in, and through muscle memory, put their hand on the lifesaving piece of equipment.

Problem was, Halo hadn't trained on the configuration. Handed this pack on the way out to the site, he learned a lot about what he might expect from today's mission just from the equipment inside. Almost all the weight came from the water bladder and climbing ropes. Each tool could serve multiple purposes, and all were special forces quality construction. The wraparound goggles and the thickness of the leather gloves were a bit of a mystery.

Max watched with interest as Ryder and Halo attached the gators to their boots, pulling the thick, water-repellent cloth up over their pants legs, tightening them with the pull cord under their knees. This addition might help to protect from snake bites. More likely, though, they'd be serving to guard against ticks and a bug the Americans called "chiggers." They were "scrub-itch mites" back home, and Halo would go a far piece to avoid those nasty buggers.

Goggles around his neck, gloves slipped into his belt, he squeezed the pocket on the left thigh of his borrowed gunmetal gray tactical uniform pants to double check his first aid kit, then to his lower leg pocket for his emergency sleeve with fire starting materials and signaling backup. With a sat phone in his right pocket, sealed safe with hook and loop fastener, Halo stood and pulled the rucksack over his shoulders as he saw the team heading toward the team leader, Ridge.

With a tap of his thigh, Max plastered himself to Halo's side, and they set off together.

With his K9 Zeus at his side, Ridge had been conferring with the sheriff, but now he strode a distance from the building, and the team formed a horseshoe around him to gather the necessary mission details. The dogs sitting between their handler's feet were ready to spring forward and get on task.

"Gentlemen." After Ridge lifted his phone and swiped, each man reached down to retrieve the pinging phone in their pocket. "The first picture is our lost person. Gloria Haze, female, eighty-one. The only name she will answer to is Grammie. Diagnosed with dementia, she is, for the most part, non-verbal and non-responsive. She's a new resident at this facility and has no history of wandering from here, so there are no historical search finds to check out. She's not from this area, so she won't be trying to return to a place from her past. Five foot two and a hundred pounds, Mrs. Haze is frail. Her carers last saw her in blue striped cotton pajamas and tennis shoes this morning. The camera that monitors the delivery door isn't functioning. A hall camera last recorded Mrs. Haze at zero-five thirty. That means she has a two-hour jump on us. Now, frail and elderly does not always indicate the ability of a missing person." Ridge turned to catch Halo's gaze. "Last year, we were on a search for a man with dementia who was remembering his days on the cross-country team for his university. And every member of special forces knows that the brain can make the body do astounding feats. In that case, he was thirty miles down the trail when our ATV caught up with him. My understanding is that in her youth, Mrs. Haze was an avid hiker, which means we're changing up our search protocol."

Tripwire asked, "Only Mrs. Haze? The other residents are accounted for?"

"When they found the door ajar, they did a census," Ridge said. "Mrs. Haze was the only one unlocated. We're fortunate we aren't looking for more."

"Any information about a shoe tread?" Ryder asked.

"The sheriff is working on that for you." Ridge looked toward the family huddle that had just grown by another carload. "The granddaughter is going to the store when it opens to see if she might recognize the style. If they get anything, they'll send a picture of the tread to our tactical operations center, and you'll get it on your sat phones." He posted his hands on his hips. "On the subject of tracking, in this area, they've had rain showers off and on for the last three days. This might make for good track traps, so while you're watching your dogs, keep an awareness. The ground, being wet, however, poses a threat should Mrs. Haze sit or lie down. With little fat or muscle protection, the ground will quickly wick her body heat away. I want each of you to grab a hypothermia bag from the duffle." Ridge turned to Halo. "Wool socks, fleece hat, four hand warmers, and an extra mylar blanket."

Halo nodded his affirmation.

"Since the time of disappearance, there's only been a light breeze. The scent cones should have held close to the ground for your dogs. Your search areas." Ridge handed out maps, marked in yellow highlighter, to all but Halo. The men looked down at their task sheets and then off into the distance, getting their bearings.

"There are no high-hazard areas in our search perimeters other than the terrain and the weather," Ridge said. "Make absolutely sure that all structures and heavy brush are thoroughly investigated."

"Sir," the team said.

Ridge turned his attention to Halo. "I'll talk to you about your duties momentarily."

"Sir." Halo had assumed he'd be trailing one of the others to learn their methods.

"A Virginia land navigation team is en route. They're about two hours out. They're also mounting an equestrian team. It's going to be an all-hands-on-deck event. We're running against a clock. In three hours, the weather front we were talking about on the way here this morning is going to make Mrs. Haze's survival tenuous. I just got an update from our command center that we should expect sustained, heavy rains that will significantly limit our visual field. The temperature will drop into the lower fifties. So, let's get on task. Blaze orange beanies, team, small game hunting season has begun in Virginia."

Tripwire jogged off toward one of the vans while the others held tight, dropping their maps into silicon sleeves that hung from their packs. Arriving back in the circle, Tripwire handed Ryder one of the duffels. Ryder distributed the hypothermia packs while Tripwire handed out the promised bear spray. After storing the additional support pack in his ruck, Halo clipped the pepper spray on his left, ready for a quick draw.

Tripwire nudged him. "Hey, in case you've never experienced this level of capsaicin, pointing downwind is your friend. If you spray into the wind, and it dowses you, the bear just thinks he's having gourmet for dinner."

"Fair warning," Halo said.

Tripwire caught Halo's gaze. "It's fat bear season. They're getting their last bites in before they settle in for a long winter's nap. They're out looking for food. Keep an eye on your dog."

"Yeah." *Mental note: research American bears and survival techniques.* There were lots of deadly critters in Australia, but bears weren't on that list.

Ridge did a comms check, and the team each took their compass direction and headed out.

Max looked up at Halo expectantly. He got a hand signal that told him to sit and wait.

"Typically, we have our two bloodhounds, Whisky and Chaser, out on a trail," Ridge said. "They weren't available today." Ridge sent a glance down to Max. "Reaper was impressed with Max's stamina while trailing, especially for such a young dog." Reaper was the Cerberus chief training officer. If he was impressed, that was good news. "While the others are air scenting, I want Max working nose to the ground."

"Sir." Max was going to love that. Trailing was one of his favorite things to do.

Ridge bladed his hand toward the building. "The sheriff is beside the door they found open, which he believes was Mrs. Haze's exit point. He has a plastic bag with the subject's scent source—a nightgown she wore yesterday."

"That'll work."

"I know we're throwing you into the unknown," Ridge said, "but that's why we hire special forces. Roll with it. But when you come against questions, I expect you to radio them to the team. The main thing you're to remember is that if you spot our subject, in the civilian world, we treat every find as if it were a crime scene, so minimal trace on your part."

"Sir."

Ridge clapped his hand onto Halo's shoulder. "Let's hope

someone makes that call and makes it soon." Ridge looked up at the sky. To Halo, it looked like a fine day. But Ridge pulled his brow together.

Checking his compass and grid, Ridge and Zeus took off into the woods.

When Halo looked down, Max's muscles were taut, his eyes expectant. He was ready. "All right, Maxi, here we go." Though, their window for a successful recovery was narrow, any anxiety for Mrs. Haze's safety had to be set aside so stress didn't interfere with their task as they worked the problem. "We're going to treat this day like any day we're out there training. Calm and steady, good focus, hey?"

The only thing was this wasn't a typical training day. Ridge trusted them with the trailing task, a position of high importance.

This was Max's first time putting his skills to the test on a mission with real-world consequences. Halo shifted his attention to the family huddled together, arms holding each other tight, the sounds of broken sobs fracturing the otherwise silent soundscape. A family was desperate for the team's success—their loved one's life on the line.

1

As Team Alpha stepped off the blacktop into the woods, Halo and Max accepted the scent source from the sheriff who then removed himself from the scene until Max got onto the trail. Halo calmed his breathing and let go of his stress, thinking of his own gramps, confused and endangered. He let go of the pictures of the granddaughter trying to recall her grandmother's shoe as she frantically looked in the stores trying to get a tread. Other than human eyes and ears and an ability to traverse the mountain, Halo didn't have much to offer here. It was all on Max's keen abilities.

Calm and steady from Halo's leadership was important to Max's success.

Without any equivocation, the reason they were out here was to bring Mrs. Haze home safely.

A distant second was to give Max a career helping others on the Iniquus search and rescue team.

As Halo stood at the doorway with Mrs. Haze's scent in the bag, Max knew what was coming, stomping impatiently, ready to get on the trail.

Halo had needed to run Max through a series of tricks to calm his K9.

When they followed Mrs. Haze's trail, Max and Halo would adulterate the scent cone. They got the one clean shot at this task. Better to wait and get it right.

When Max's posture relaxed into focused control, Halo opened the bag and held it out to Max. "Ready to get at it, Maxi? Scent. Scent. Scent."

On cue, Max lowered his nose into the bag, chuffing the smells left on the nightgown into his olfactory chambers. A canine nose was so discriminating that a dog could detect viruses, cancers, and even how far along a woman was in her pregnancy. Outlandish studies showed time and again how primitive human scent compared to their K9 friends.

Lifting out of the bag, Max had the imprint and was ready to go. Panting with excitement, he caught Halo's gaze, waiting for the command. Two choices could happen here depending on the type of job they were on. "Get it," was the combat command, the "dangerous criminal" command. "Get it," told Max that he was to seek out the source of the scent and then bite it hard. Today, though, Halo called out the other command, "Max, seek. Seek. Seek." Max would go about his business trailing the imprinted scent, and Halo would do his human best to keep up with the prize-winning athlete. When Max found the scent, he'd go back and find Halo and report his findings, leading Halo to the spot.

Max's nose went up in the air. He sniffed over the threshold. After running tight circles outside the door, Max locked in on something and lowered his nose to the ground, chuffing happily. Legs splayed wide to keep his nose skimming the pavement, Max trotted forward in a straight line from the door, into the woods, and up the gentle rise of the slope.

So far, so good, but this terrain was going to present a considerable test, Halo thought as he stuffed the scent source into his pocket and followed Max into the tree line. Squirrels frisking with their playmates and other distractors filled the woods. An unfamiliar environment, the temptation of novel scents, even the feel of the ground underfoot—thick with leaves and slick with wet clay beneath—might be more than a two-year-old's resolve.

Would prey drive overcome pack drive, especially when his pack wasn't in sight? That was the test.

With a sudden jolt, Halo pitched forward. He was quick enough that he got his elbows wide and his hands on either side of his shoulders as he tried to disperse the energy to protect himself from injury.

In the last moment, Halo twisted his head away from the ground, his ear hovering just above the dampened leaves. Halo was grateful he didn't break his nose in a face plant. He wasn't so sure about his leg, though. Giving himself a moment to exhale the pain, Halo pressed himself back up on his feet.

Halo had undertaken his share of searches for people—those desperately praying for rescue and those urgently trying to evade detection—while working in the mountain ranges of the Middle East. But that landscape looked a world apart from this.

Even back home, Halo had been stationed out of Holsworthy, near enough to the Blue Mountains, where he liked to climb the cliffs.

The Shenandoah was part of the Blue Ridge. Those two mountain range names were about where the similarities ended.

The devil, as they say, was in the details.

Here, the terrain confronted the team with a boulder-studded elevation dense with trees. Leaves thickly blanketed the ground, looking like they'd make a soft bed for bivouacking, but could prove problematic when looking for their missing person, especially someone as fragile and endangered as the woman that had gone missing.

As the team got on the trail with their dogs today, they all knew that time was the enemy. For that reason, Halo had started out keeping a steady pace, following closely behind Max. But, very quickly, Halo's foot found the first hole hiding under the blanket of leaves. His weight dropped straight down until he was mid-shin, but his forward momentum propelled him, and he found himself stretched out on the dampened ground. The forest litter hid the dangers beneath—roots that caught the toe of his boot, and worse were the holes that swallowed his leg. Each time he went down, he'd felt the torque and tension on his knees and ankle. Surely, there was a strategy for this terrain. He had a lot to learn.

With an exhale calibrated to reset his system, Halo pulled himself out, checked himself over, and dusted off his borrowed uniform. Made from some lab-created miracle fabric, he still looked immaculate, dry, and mud-free. No one would know how much time he'd spend rolling in the muck.

Halo tipped back to watch angry black clouds amassing above the trees. The rainy mist on his face and the temperature noticeably dropping reminded him that their operational window was narrow. Once that rain started, the scent trail would be challenging, if not impossible, for Maxi to follow. This was their golden hour, and if he broke his ankle, Halo wouldn't be of any help to Grammie, and he wouldn't get the job with Iniquus either.

A phrase that the American SEALs used came to mind: "Slow is fast, and fast is slow." It made all the sense in the world to him under these circumstances.

Halo stepped forward, his foot coming to rest in front of the biggest pile of scat he'd ever seen. He knelt and waved his hand over it—still warm.

Pulling his sat comms from his pocket, he took a picture, sending it back to Cerberus with the text: **Bear?**

Affirmative was the immediate response.

Tripwire had warned him to keep his eye on Max because the bears were getting their last mouthfuls in. He thought Max would try to hold his own, but honestly, other than the movies, Halo didn't have a trained strategy for bears. Images from The Revenant flashed through his memory, and Halo would vastly prefer that he didn't need to face down a bear today.

His phone pinged: **Don't dance with the bears. Get rid of any food. Make noise so you don't startle the bear. If it's charging, get big and loud.**

Big and loud. Halo muttered.

Deploy bear spray if the bear is downwind. Otherwise ...

Halo was gourmet. Yeah, he remembered.

Crouching, Halo looked for tracks to at least get a sense of the bear's direction of travel and saw no disturbances in the leaf litter other than what he had made in his fall.

Halo looked at the tracking readout on his GPS unit, aligning himself with the red dot that represented Max, sniffing his way through the woods. It had been a fairly straight line, so Halo thought Max was still on task and not chasing squirrels. With an adjustment to his pack, Halo paced forward, singing the kind of made-up song he sang to entertain his nieces and nephews. "Hey, fuzzy bear, I mean you no harm. I'm singing out so you won't feel alarmed." Yeah, kids were easily amused. Hopefully, the bear would be, too.

A few paces out, Halo noticed that Max's red dot stopped moving. He didn't know how to interpret that.

As a matter of Iniquus protocol, Max wore a communications collar with a two-way radio system so Halo could command his dog from a distance, and they would have a means for communicating with a lost person. His collar also held a sat camera that was monitored at Headquarters back in D.C. Max was also a moving point on the mission board in the Cerberus operations room as well as a red dot in the tracking app in Halo's handheld GPS unit. It was fumbly to need those three pieces of equipment—a sat phone with video feed for Headquarters, a radio to contact the team and his dog, and the GPS tracking unit with its off-grid memory system—better, though, to have to juggle than to go without the information. As with any mountainous wilderness area, cell tower connectivity was a luxury. And the sat phones were only as good as the weather was clear and the tree canopy was thin.

As he and Max were thrown into today's mission, they at least had the comms part down pat.

Max trained from the get-go in responding to disembodied vocal commands from Halo. It had been an essential skill for the Commandos' dogs to have. When a team sent the K9s in with a camera to give live feed information on the interior of a target location, the handler could direct their dog through the building with "turn left, turn right, hold" commands. This also facilitated recall. A simple "to me" brought Max racing back, twirling to flank Halo, looking up with sharp concentration, waiting for his next command.

Why had Max stopped? Was he off task?

Halo stepped carefully over a fallen log. Ryder had warned him not to step on tree trunks because they often rolled, trapping the hiker underneath. Also, a snake called a copperhead liked to hide out in the space beneath the log. "Copperhead?"

"One of the venomous snakes out here, mate. Not as bad as

what you find out woop-woop at home, but it'll make for a hell of a day."

And just as that thought passed through Halo's mind, his comms broke squelch.

"Bob for Halo."

He pressed the communications tab taped to his chest. "Go for Halo."

"Max has a snake in his mouth, and our AI system is cautioning that it is possibly a rattlesnake."

Rattlesnake. That was out west in the desert where they had cactuses, wasn't it? Cowboys and settlers kind of danger? Cactus and horses kind of danger?

"He's trapped it in his teeth just below the head from what we can see from his collar camera," Bob said. "The head can't reach the skin to sink a bite in that position."

Rattlesnake.

Fear was an ice-blue pulse in Halo's system.

"Command Max to freeze," Bob said.

Halo tapped his radio to access the comms system on Max's collar. "Max, freeze. Max, hold." This was a command they'd been working hard on, though, the scenario Halo had considered was landmines. They had built up time that Max could stand there unmoving, both with Halo in the picture and with distant comms commands.

This present scenario could well have the same devastating effect.

Death was death.

"You're fifty yards away. Straight line," Bob said. "We'll talk you forward."

"Is he holding?" Halo's lungs had tightened down, and he switched to combat breathing, count of four in, hold, count of four out.

"He's doing as asked. We'll let you know if anything changes."

Which was a shite way to deal. Bob would have to perceive, speak, and then Halo would have to, sight unseen, respond with his commands.

"Good boy, Maxi. Freeze. Freeze." Halo kept his tone as light as possible. He wondered if that were the correct command. If Halo gave the chomp command, instead, Max could possibly bite the snake in two.

Halo raced full tilt over the terrain. If he went into another bloody hole, it was a broken leg. Didn't matter. He'd drag himself to Max's side.

"Hold tight, Maxi. Good boy." There had to be an antivenom. But surely the team didn't have it with them, Halo calculated. They were an hour up the mountain. Venom usually worked on weight. Muscle mass might give Halo some advantage if he were bitten, but Malinois were medium-sized dogs. A bite might well prove lethal no matter how fast Halo darted back down the mountain to the Iniquus vans.

Powering up the hill, he could see Max in front of him.

Max widened his field of perception to take in Halo. "Max, freeze," Halo called out, shoving the unit into his pocket to free his hands.

When Max caught Halo's gaze, his tail wagged excitedly.

Now, Halo could hear the rattle of the snake's tail. It sent another burst of blue-colored adrenaline through his veins.

That sound, the wriggling movement, Max must think this was a toy.

Now that he was closer, Halo moved forward crouched and steady, testing the ground in front of himself to make sure he could advance without falling and startling Max into letting go of the snake. The triangular shape of the head chomping at the air with sharp fangs dripping venom just outside of Max's jaw was clearly life-threatening to Max. How could he get the snake safely from Max's mouth?

"Good, boy, Maxi. Freeze." Halo's mind was madly calculating. "Freeze, Max."

Killing the snake, Halo well knew, would not stop the mouth from biting or reduce the lethality of the venom. He had to separate dog from snake.

He couldn't just grab the snake and tell Max to release. That release might not be fast enough, and the snake might turn and get a bite in. It would require split-second timing. But Halo had Max's reward ball in his pocket. And nothing made Max move faster than getting his mouth on that ball.

Would it work here?

Halo slowly drew the ball from his pocket. And Max stomped the ground with excitement. "Max, freeze!"

Sweat slicked Halo's skin. Heart racing, he bent and got his hand around the tail. The vibration of the rattle twitched just below his fist. Twisting his body until his arm was fully extended, Halo prayed that Max would do as commanded the instant the command left his mouth, and Max wasn't going to pull one of his stubborn teenaged tantrums, unwilling to let go of his new-found wriggle toy.

Halo's head was turned to focus unblinkingly on Max.

Here we go.

Halo tossed the ball into the air, calling, "Max, release." And as the S hissed between his teeth, Max opened his mouth and jumped for the ball. In the same instant, Halo whipped the snake through the air.

The snake flew into the distance.

"Bob. Good job, Halo. I have Dani Williams here. She's Team Charlie's assigned vet. She'll talk you through next steps."

Halo looked behind him to make sure the ground was clear,

then dropped his ass to the ground next to where Max was aggressively chewing on his ball.

In that moment, Halo realized his mistake. Sure, he got the instant release he needed to save Max's life. But he'd used Max's reward ball—his "high-dollar" reward—to do it. Halo had just rewarded Max for having a snake in his mouth, reinforcing the very thing that Halo did *not* want his dog to do. That meant Max would look for opportunities to grab up a snake—venomous or not. Halo made a mental note that he needed to undo that training, or Max would be at high risk.

"Dani for Halo. Careful. We don't want to get Max's heart rate up until you've checked him over. Call him into your lap and give him scritches and praise while I give you more information."

Halo held out his arms. "Here, Maxi."

Dani's voice was professionally steady. "We've got this. Rattlesnakes have a low death rate, about twenty percent in dogs. This isn't like some of the snakes in your part of the world. The biggest danger is if Max was bitten in the tongue or eye. Let's check those out first. You've had plenty of K9 first aid classes, and you know the drill. As you move slowly and thoroughly over the entire surface of Max's body, you're going to palpate—I know it's tough for a dog dad to do. Lots of emotion. I want you to remove his collar and hold it between your chest and chin. As you move around his body, I'm going to use the camera feed to be a second set of eyes."

Max was happily chewing his ball, and Halo thought that was for the best. He pulled his headlamp from the ruck, tugged it over his head, and tightened down the elastic strap. He then unclasped Max's tracking collar, lengthened the strap, and wrapped that around his head. "Can you see?"

"Affirmative. Okay, he wouldn't be chewing the ball like that if he'd been bitten on the tongue. As you palpate, you're looking for anything red or swollen. Move the hair out of the way to see if you can find puncture marks from the fangs. Most likely, you would see blood, sometimes quite a lot of blood. You're looking for any signs of pain. These working dogs are stoic, so watch for him to stop chewing and look around at you."

Halo did as he was told, working methodically over Max's side, his tummy, the other side, head, and backside. Max seemed to delight in the extra long time he got with his ball.

"Max just walked up to the rattlesnake and bit just above its head?" Dani asked. "I'm trying to imagine a scenario that put the snake and dog into that position. I've seen enough. You can get his collar back on."

"I have no idea," Halo said, replacing the comms unit around Max's neck. "Maybe they took a tape of the camera feed?"

"I think you're good to get back on task," Dani said. "Watch Max. If you see any signs of vomiting or diarrhea, I need you to call it in. We'll go from there. Radio me if you have any concerns, anything that has Max acting out of the norm."

"Thank you, ma'am."

Halo was well aware that Mrs. Haze was out here in the woods with the same kinds of hazards as he'd face today—bears, venomous snakes, dangerous terrain, and an approaching storm. Add to that the confusion that put her up on this slope in the first place. But he took a moment to let his heart reseat. There was no room for mistakes that would pull eyes and resources away from Mrs. Haze should either Max or he need assistance.

Halo put his head down on Max's scruff and breathed the scent of dog fur. When he came up, he held his hand under Max's mouth. "Release." The slobber-covered ball dropped onto Halo's palm, and Halo shoved it into his pocket. "Good job, mate." Halo stood and pulled out the scent source to get Max back on task.

With a few chuffs into the bag, a few sniffs into the air, and a few circles over the ground, Max was back on the trail. And Halo was going to do whatever it took to stay close enough to keep an eagle eye on Max's safety. And, as the air rumbled with thunder, to press forward and find Grammie.

2

It wasn't five minutes after Halo had whipped the snake into the distance that Max, once again, stopped in his tracks.

A massive tangle of stems and leaves formed a lattice on which thick curtains of thorns turned the vegetation into a seemingly impenetrable mass. Max trotted to the left and right, looking over the vegetative structure.

Halo wasn't sure why Max had lifted his nose off the trail and into the wind. Normally, Max traced the scent around the impediment. Could it be something caught on his radar that needed identification—another snake that had been fun for him, or maybe that bear from earlier?

He was about to call Max over to offer him some water, a pet, and then another sniff of the scent source when Max let out a whine. Flattening himself into a pancake, Max used his back legs to scuff himself under the matted leaves and out of sight.

Pressing the button on his sat phone. "Halo for Bob."

"Go for Bob." The operations manager's voice crackled with static.

"Max disappeared into a hill of vegetation. I'm sending you a picture. Can you identify this plant for me?"

Today on the mountain, they'd clawed their way over the rocks, batted away swarms of gnats, blisters rubbed Halo's heels from the new uniform boots, and all of that was cake compared to the dense, seemingly impenetrable tangle that was in front of him. Halo waited for his low-res photo to transfer to Headquarters and for the AI assistive technology to help them decipher what was there. The static on the line was getting louder as the cloud cover thickened the sky above him.

This was the hour of desperation. He viscerally felt the seconds spinning toward chaos—the moment the sky would dump down on them, and their opportunity to save Mrs. Haze would vanish.

If Max crawled under this bush because he was tired or distracted, Halo could understand it; they'd pushed hard for hours now without a break. "But it would be bloody terrible timing, mate," Halo muttered under his breath.

"Bob to Halo. What you've got there, brother, is an unholy marriage of rhododendron bush and sweetbriar, the two banes of mountainside search and rescue here in Virginia. I've actually never seen it that big and dense. Max is in the middle of that?"

"Affirmative."

"You might be on top of our missing person. That kind of natural mantrap stops people with a dementia diagnosis in their tracks."

"How's that?" Halo crouched, inspecting the ground for signs that someone had passed this way. He found nothing. Of course, with the wind picking up, making the leaves skitter about, he didn't expect to find anything obvious.

"When people with dementia wander, they typically move in a straight line until they get stuck. For example, if they hit a hard surface, a tree trunk, or a rock, they'll ping pong off and keep going in the new direction. But if they don't encounter resistance, they continue forward. That's why you were told that every bush needs a thorough check. Especially briars. The thorns snag the clothes. That's where we end up finding our lost subjects —bound up in the bushes. See what Max says. But if he's interested in that area, that vegetation needs a thorough search. Over."

"Copy. Out." Halo now understood the thickness of the gloves and wraparound goggles. He was pulling his pruners from his pack when Max's tail emerged first, and then he wriggled his way out from under the vegetation.

Max had that intensity in his eyes that he got when he found his scent. Plopping onto his haunches in front of Halo, his tail swishing excitedly over the ground. This was it. Max found something significant. "What have you got, boy?" Halo held his breath.

What happened next was the crucial information.

Max was scent-trained as a live-find K9 and an HRD—human remains detection—dog. If Max found a human cadaver, he'd sit and drape a paw over his nose as if he were weeping.

Max rose up to take a step forward. He caught Halo's gaze, then touched his nose to the scent bag, sat, and lifted his paws in "prayer" to tell Halo he had a live human find. Interesting that he touched the scent source first. That was new.

Back in the day, when Halo and Ryder were working with Australian military dogs on assignments, these skills had been part of their units' survival. The dogs not only helped the team find insurgents, but if one of their band of brothers went missing, the dogs could work a scent source pulled from the guy's pack or tent. As miserable as it was to think of finding a brother had died, the dog's choice of signals meant the team knew what they were dealing with. If it was someone alive, it was go-go-go. If the person were deceased, the team had more time to plan and limit their risks.

Halo was pulling Max's reward ball from his pocket when Max caught Halo's gaze a second time, then draped a paw over his nose, and Halo's heart sank.

Max had never done that before, giving both signals—alive and dead.

Regardless, the find meant a reward and high-pitched praise. Halo tossed Max's ball into the air, "Good-boy!"

Halo said into the sat phone. "Max is indicating a find."

"Go ahead and radio your team," Bob said. "I'll send out a text with your GPS coordinates. Farthest team from your present location is twenty minutes. Team Alpha will rally to support you."

The fat drops of precipitation pattered on Halo's ruck. "The rain's started up. How is that radar looking?"

"You're light green for precipitation for another twenty - maybe thirty minutes, then your area turns maroon to black. On our forecasting color spectrum, that's as bad as we get. You can't stay put without shelter and the risk of mudslides. You need a plan to get down the slope despite the weather. The risk increases exponentially with time. This system will settle into the valley for about twelve hours. Then it'll be dark and the terrain slippery. Tonight's temperatures drop into the lower forties." He turned to Halo. "That's very unusual for end of August in Virginia." His gaze swept the terrain. "We're going to minimize the risk for the team and Mrs. Haze by moving you down to shelter. I'll convey that to Ridge. Over."

"Copy. Out."

As Max settled in to enjoy his ball, Halo pulled the leather gloves on. "Grammie? Grammie, can you hear me? I've come to take you to dinner. Are you hungry?"

After a moment of silence, Halo pressed his sternal button to put him on the team radio. "Clear the net. Clear the net. Clear the net. Team Halo and Max." In Iniquus' radio protocol, that phrase meant that he and the communications officer could speak, and no other radio traffic was allowed.

"Ridge. Go for Team Alpha."

"Max is indicating a find."

"Do you have eyes on?" Ridge asked.

"I'm standing at a ball of rhododendron and sweet briar, two meters high, must be three meters wide, dense vegetation, no visual. Over." Honestly, Halo wasn't sure about this. Yes, he always trusted his dog, but how in hades could a frail senior have gotten into this tangle without leaving a trace of broken vines, at least?

Then again, how could a bear take a dump in the woods and leave no trail? Halo just didn't know how to read this land yet.

Halo waited for a return communication, but the radio crackled and sputtered.

Thunder boomed close enough that Halo felt it in his chest.

Though, he wasn't sure anyone could hear him, he said, "Halo. Out." He hoped that the sat text from Bob with Halo's GPS location got through, or he'd be alone trying to get Mrs. Haze off this mountain.

Glancing down, Halo saw Max's muscles were tight with excitement.

As he lay on the ground, his ball trapped between his front paws, Max focused on Halo.

"In there, huh, Max? Both dead and alive?" Looking around at the bush, Halo asked, "Maxi, is this the best route to get to the lady?"

Max shifted his focus from Halo and stared into the foliage with an intense focus. Halo raised the blade of his hand toward Max's nose and swung it in a line forward. He adjusted his stance.

If Max went in and crawled out backward, that meant there was no place to turn around. This wasn't a façade with open space beneath. It was going to be dense going. And Halo wanted to get in and get eyes on the situation before the sky opened up.

Tightening his ruck on his shoulders, Halo lay on the ground, reaching in, feeling for thicker branches to cut and shove aside. He needed both a way in and a clear path for extraction, a clear way for his team to move in. Working as quickly as possible, cutting his way forward, Halo tried to reason out Max's signal. If Grammie had been bleeding, the blood would begin to decay the moment it left her body. Decaying blood was a cadaver scent. That was possible. Probable.

"Max. Stay," he called over his shoulder as he disappeared into the greenery.

He was feeling his way through this process, trying different strategies to get through the mass as efficiently as possible. It was a bloody miserable undertaking that he'd never faced before. The novelty of dealing with the briars catching at his clothes and tearing at his skin, the tangle at his feet made his movement frustratingly slow.

Halo was accumulating a list of skills he wanted to train if he was lucky enough to be offered an Iniquus contract. Skills that would make things safer for Max and for the subject they were tracking.

Alive and dead at the same time? What was Max trying to tell him? Was Grammie on the cusp? Could he get to her in time?

3

The Haze family, crying in the parking lot, filled Halo's memory, and he pushed their image aside to focus on the tickle that crawled across the back of his neck.

He was close to finding Mrs. Haze. He knew it.

"Hello? Grammie, I'm here to take you to dinner. If you can hear my voice, call out, please." *Please.*

He stilled.

"Grammie?"

When he slowed his breath to listen, all he could hear was his heart thumping in his ears and a rumble of thunder up above. Using the Commando bio-feedback training that allowed him to quickly calm his nerves and silence that thrum of blood, he tried again. "Grammie?"

This time, he heard mewling behind him to his left.

It sounded like a wounded animal.

Halo twisted to look in that direction. And there, inches from his boot, was a bare foot, cut and bloodied.

Now that he'd reached the epicenter of this section's tangle, Halo used the saw on his multitool to cut through the base, lifting a segment, then thrusting it up and over the top and clearing the space where the woman lay. "Grammie, hello," Halo said softly as he moved to her side.

Mrs. Haze had pulled off her pajama bottoms and hugged them to her like they were a stuffed bear, sobbing. "Grammie, I'm Halo. It's time for dinner." That phrase was the one that got Halo's gramps to cooperate on days when he was disoriented. Halo just hoped it had the same effect here.

Pressing his radio, he quietly said, "Halo to Team Alpha. I have Mrs. Haze. She's alive with injuries." He pulled the sat phone from his pocket and took her picture for Headquarters on the off chance it could get through.

He checked his watch—twenty minutes until things shifted from green toward Maroon. Halo's mind worked to set his priorities as muscle memory moved his hands and he got his equipment staged for action.

He pulled the tarp from his pack and draped it over the bush to form a make-do tent. He knew it wouldn't hold up to the impending deluge. But it kept the rain out of his eyes as he set about stabilizing Mrs. Haze.

His attempts at assessing her condition were met with screeches as she clawed and hit Halo with the kind of strength a brain conjures when it's fighting for its life.

He rocked back on his haunches to give her space. Having her combative amongst the briars was a bad idea. With a practiced eye, Halo let his gaze methodically search her from head to foot. He called his findings. "Halo to Team Alpha. Mrs. Haze is combative, and I am unable to apply field first aid without risk. My cursory assessment follows. Her breathing is ragged. Her lacerations seem superficial, and what blood I can see has coagulated. I don't see evidence of broken bones. Her skin is pale, dry, and cold to the touch."

"Ridge and Zeus, three minutes from your location."

"Tripwire, six minutes to your location."

"Ryder, if we can keep this pace, about ten minutes to your location."

The team continued the check-ins as they converged while Halo pulled out his hypothermia pack and a cup to offer her some water.

Once he had the team with him, they could devise a way to get Mrs. Haze down the slope. In the meantime, Halo didn't like that he didn't have eyes on his dog. Especially if the rain was going to limit his visual field. "Max to me," he called out.

Almost as soon as the command left his mouth, Max was there. He gave Halo a lick on his neck, then went over to sniff over Mrs. Haze. She seemed to like that. Maybe she would let Max lie down with her. At least that would keep her warm.

Max stepped past Halo as he unfolded the Mylar emergency blanket. His nose pushed into the leaves, then he turned back to Halo with a whine.

Halo squat-walked forward to ensure they weren't sharing this space with dangerous critters, and there he saw another foot. This one was slipper-clad and male. The exposed ankle was tinged bluish grey with the beginnings of algor mortis.

Halo pulled the clippers from his pocket, furiously snapping at the stems and vines that encapsulated the man until he could reach the guy's head.

Dead.

Obviously and thoroughly dead.

Bollocks.

And now Halo had his answer. Brilliant Max had told him, oh so clearly, the scent source was alive in the bushes, and there was also someone who had died. It was Halo that hadn't understood the communication.

"Good job, Maxi. Good find." Halo tried to make his voice high-pitched and happy, but this winded him.

Halo pulled his sat phone out and took a picture of the

deceased. Before he sent it on, he called Bob. Speaking through the haze of interference, he reported, "Halo here. I have a second find. Deceased gentleman in pajamas, robe, and slippers."

"Say again, Halo? You're breaking up with the cloud cover."

"Elderly male. Pajamas, robe, and slippers. Picture sent. Deceased."

"Breaking up. Confirm the word 'deceased.'"

"Affirmative. The man is dead. Guessing from his clothing and age, he came from the care facility. Since they are together in the bush, I think one of the residents followed the other out the door and up the hill. They are both tangled in the vines. I suggest the facility do another census and ensure they account for all of their residents. We need to know if any other people are wandering this slope."

"New resident census. Wilco. I'll—" Static crackled from the phone, and heavy drops thwacked the plastic cover above Mrs. Haze. The line went dead.

"Good job, man, just in time." Ridge appeared under the tarp. "She won't let you near?"

"Confused and combative," Halo said. "I don't want her to exhaust herself further or cause herself any more harm."

"She seems okay hugging Max. Let's see if she'll put up with Zeus at her back to get her temperature up." Ridge dropped his pack and pulled out a fleece that he tugged on as he called Zeus to him. Ridge used hand commands to silently get Zeus into place, disturbing Mrs. Haze as little as possible. They needed her calm for this next step.

Ridge turned his focus on the male.

"I have the body bag out," Halo said. "Since they treat civilian finds as crime scenes here, I wasn't sure about protocol." Halo lifted the bag.

Ridge accepted it from his hands and unzipped it the length. "We're going to be all hands on deck getting Mrs. Haze off this slope. We need to prioritize the living over the dead. We'll have to leave him here for a forensic team to evaluate and transport." Ridge explained as he and Halo maneuvered the man's body into the bag and zipped it shut. "At least we can preserve the body in as pristine condition as possible for the family. And the medical examiner."

Ridge used his handheld GPS unit to put a point onto the screen, marking the man's body for another team to extract once the mountain was stable. "When our team gets in place, we're moving down this mountain as fast as possible. In the heavy rain and dropping temperatures, Mrs. Haze's survival is going to depend on speed."

"Halo?" Ryder called out from outside of the tangle.

"Hold. We're coming out," Ridge replied.

Leaving the dogs in place, warming Mrs. Haze, the men crawled out from under the tarp. Rain flicking them with fat drops, they pulled on their ball caps and raincoats. They left their goggles in place for the moment to protect their eyes from the briers, but Halo knew that as temperatures went south, the lenses would fog very quickly, making them a hazard.

The team had gathered. Under the billowing clouds, the late morning sky grew ever darker. The men strapped their headlamps in place.

With the last man on site, they formed a huddle, heads together, yelling out their ideas as the wind whipped their words up and away.

"I spoke with Bob while we still had a satellite connection," Ridge said. "As conditions continue to deteriorate, the State rescue coordinator sent the equine team home. The mountain rescue team won't risk the slope until the storm's moved through. We're on our own."

"They can read radar as well as we can," Tripwire said. "They know the risks. I'm just as well with them staying put so the rescuers don't need to save the rescuers."

"Thoughts on sheltering in place?" Ridge asked the men.

Didit shook her head with a deep frown. "With the storm that's coming in, it's more than dropping temperatures and pelting rain. We could configure around that. Uncomfortably, sure. But we're facing mud slides, high winds toppling dead trees, and possible flash flooding when we cross the creek. Staying put is a bad decision."

"The amount of time I spent wrenching my ankles in the holes today needs to be a consideration, especially as the leaf litter gets slick," Tripwire said.

So it wasn't just me, Halo thought.

"We're going to lose visibility here in a minute. This is what I propose," Ridge said, pulling his all-weather field notebook from his chest pocket. "We're a team of five handlers and 5 K9. That makes this scenario work. We number off." He took a moment to sketch. "A two-person team rigs the length of our climbing lines from tree A to tree B. At the same time, we run lines between tree B to tree C. Tripwire, you're one, Didit two, I'm three, Ryder four, and Halo, you're five."

"Five," Halo said, watching the Ridge's pencil trace over the waterproof paper.

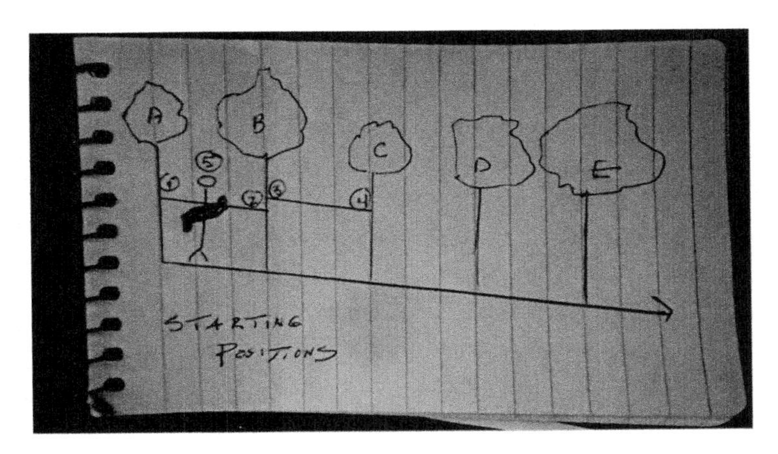

"NUMBER FIVE WILL ATTACH into the line and take the first length carrying Mrs. Haze. Once Number Two gets her line secured to Tree B, she attaches to the line and then climbs back up to Tree A. There, she will escort Number Five back down to Tree B. The escort's job is threefold. First, they will handle two K9s on lead. Second, they will be searching out any hazards—holes, roots, slick spots. These are to be communicated back to the carrier. Third, should the carrier lose their footing or need assistance, they are ready to render aid."

"Sir," Didit said. "Mrs. Haze is too frail for a fireman's carry over rough terrain, especially for the extended period of time it's going to take to get her down."

"Agreed. What do you propose?" Ridge asked.

"I say that we line a body bag with mylar and slip her in there," Didit said. "Leave room to breathe in the zippered enclosure. That set up should keep her warm and dry, especially if we can get the hand warmers in her armpits, groin, and down at her feet."

"The handles will help us with passing her from one carrier

to the next." Tripwire scuffed his boot into the ground and then turned his gaze toward the sky. Tripwire had spent a summer hiking the Appalachian trail. Halo would be paying close attention to what he said about conditions.

"She's being babysat and warmed by the dogs because she's combative," Halo said. "That could become a hazard on the slopes."

"Agreed," Ridge said. "I'd rather not medicate her. While we have permission to do so from her power of attorney, she's had her body challenged today. I'd like to get her down and assessed by a doctor. That being said, everyone's safety is paramount. Whoever is the escort will carry the syringe. You hand it on to the next escort, etc. It will be the escort's call if and when to deploy the sedative."

"Sir."

"Very well." Ridge put his pencil back on the paper, tapping the paper for clarification. "At the point where the carrier has reached the next tree—that's you, Halo as Number Five—you'll hand Mrs. Haze to Number Three, me, for carrying. Number Five becomes the escort. Number Two, Didit, you'll radio Number One, and the two of you will release your lines and move safely down the slope to run those lines between Trees C and D. And in that manner, with handoffs of responsibility, and times for those not in an active posture to rest, we will leapfrog our way down the slope." He looked over to Halo. "It was an hour and a half from start of mission until the subject was found. I estimate four to six on the way down. We'll speed up once we have our rhythm. We'll slow down when we hit obstacles. I'd very much like to get over the creek in the next hour, or things are going to get wild and hairy for us up here."

"Wilder and hairier." Tripwire let his hand rest on Valor's head. "At some point, we may end up carrying the K9s to avoid injuries to them as the integrity of the slope degrades."

"Agreed," Ridge said. "They'll be on leads. Leave their protective vests, helmets, and goggles in place. Turn on their location strobes. That'll help everyone keep a visual. I can't imagine losing radio contact in such close proximity but never say never. If that happens, we need to huddle up and make another plan."

"Sir."

And so they started the slow descent.

Every muscle in Halo's body strained and quivered, trying to stay balanced and upright with Mrs. Haze in his arms. Though, only a hundred pounds, her weight still tried to pitch Halo forward. At points, his escort had one hand on the rope and the other on his chest, pushing him upright. Max very quickly ended up lying across the top of Halo's ruck. And on Halo's turns being the carrier, Max's weight helped to keep Halo balanced on the slope.

This was tense business.

While the brim of his ball cap kept much of the sting of rain out of his eyes, his line of sight was the length of his arm. And in the torrent, it was impossible to check Mrs. Haze to make sure she was still alive. The terrible thing was that there was nothing more they could do for her than to get her down to the care center, where the doctors waited for their arrival. That and the love of her family. He believed strongly in that power. He'd learned that lesson from his brothers in the Commandos.

When the radio call went out saying that they'd hooked into the last tree, a stream of rescue workers swarmed forward to relieve Team Alpha and race Mrs. Haze inside. Halo had no concept of time and how long it had taken to get her down. Every part of his being had focused on moment to moment. Just like in the Commandos, he lived in a three-foot world, controlling what happened in the immediate space around him.

Concentration was energy. And Halo would admit to exhaustion.

Caked in clay, when the team moved through the doors, they were met with triumphant cheers, back slaps, and thankfully hot food.

Ridge asked if they could take it to go. The dogs needed to get a once-over by their vet.

Halo wholeheartedly concurred with that request.

While they waited for the servers to package up the meals, Halo was asked to sit off to the side while the team posted their reports. He knew it wasn't the hot wash and the mission reports that would follow today's events. That happened as a team.

What they were doing now took place on their individual tablets.

Halo suspected this was the assessment of his performance. Command would want to hear what they had to say while emotions were still fresh and before they talked themselves into or out of a perspective. Command would also want to know what the team members thought before they talked amongst themselves. That's the way it had been with Halo's Australian unit, anyway.

That task accomplished, the team was filled in on the subjects. "Mrs. Haze will recover with rest. The family sends their gratitude. The man that Halo found has been identified as Ernest Gregory. His identical twin had been counted twice by the staff, and Ernest Gregory had not been missed. A sad day for the family," Ridge said. "They offer their many thanks to the team for finding him and protecting his body."

The men quietly gathered their bags of grub, loaded into the vans, and were on their way back into the city.

Halo allowed himself to close his eyes, and when he opened them, they were back at Cerberus's headquarters.

Dani was waiting at the door and immediately took control

of Max, saying she would give him a thorough check, looking for any signs of rattlesnake poisoning or injury as they walked away.

When Halo tried to follow her to the washroom, Bob clapped a hand on his shoulder, stopping him in his tracks. "Halo, you're wanted in Command stat."

Halo looked down at his mud-covered body. "Would it be all right to have a five-minute cleanup and a fresh set of clobber? I don't want to drag into their offices and leave a trail of mountain debris."

"I'm sure they'd appreciate it. I'll call over and let them know you're on your way."

Moving into the shower, Halo leaned his head back and felt the luxury of hot water rinsing away the mud, if not the fatigue.

Yes, he was feeling his nerves. What happened next might well change the entire trajectory of his life.

Would Command offer him a contract?

Bear scat and rattle snakes aside, he and Max had got the job done.

Was it enough?

That depended a lot on what Team Alpha had said in their assessments.

And that Halo had no control over. *You click, or you don't.*

Last week, this job and the possibility of uprooting his life weren't even on his radar.

Things moved fast in the kind of life he led.

It was the way Halo liked it. He liked the challenge of a storm.

4

SEPTEMBER ONE

Norfolk, Virginia

MARY WILLIAMS ELBOWED her way through the kitchen door with a bag of groceries cradled in one arm. Just shy of a place to set her things down, the handle on the paper bag, dangling from the fingers of her other hand, snapped. Reflex was the only reason Mary was jostling and diving to grab the brown paper before the contents hit the floor.

She missed the bag but succeeded in catching the lip of the door frame with her flipflop. Stumbling forward, she came to rest draped across the kitchen bar stool.

Surprisingly, Mary managed to keep that one bag hugged to her, the ice cream cold against the side of her breast.

Oof.

As Mary pressed the surviving bag onto the counter, she mused that one of the benefits of living alone was there were no witnesses to her moments of klutz.

She didn't need to add insult to injury. Today had been one

of *those* days. Nothing really bad happened, but there were just enough hiccups that she was looking forward to a hot bath with a glass of wine and a book with enough drama to make her own life seem organized and uncomplicated.

Climbing back on her feet, Mary looked around at the fallen soldiers strewn over the floor. The egg carton was the first thing she grabbed up, thinking that with the price of the darned eggs, if they were all broken, she would be eating scrambled with cheese for dinner that night.

But it was all good. "All good," Mary said aloud to emphasize that mindset, reaching out to swing the door shut.

Limping from the whack she'd given her big toe, Mary kicked off her shoes and reached for the food on the floor. Blackberries in one hand, a jar of chocolate spread in the other, Mary stopped to stare vacantly out her kitchen window. A single yellow leaf had detached from the limb and floated down.

Mary sighed—not fatigue, not sentimentality, just a general release.

Autumn was here, her favorite season. Flannel and fleece. Pumpkin spice and bowls of hearty stew. Flames flickered in the outdoor firepit as she chatted with friends, the knees of her pants burning against her skin as the cold tiptoed its way down the back of her collar.

She loved it, all of it.

The kids going back to school was the most fun.

But that was no longer true in her life. Her twin boys graduated from university last May and moved to the West Coast to follow their careers in technological-something-she-didn't-quite-understand. Not a backward glance, no sentimental "We'll miss you, Mom!" Just gone.

Mary got it. It's what she'd done at eighteen. She eked out a few more years of having her twin boys around her than she'd given her own parents. They'd at least come home for summers and holidays while they were at the university. Mary figured she'd get the boys back in the new form they constructed for themselves when they got to be around thirty like she had with her own parents. Around thirty-one or so, she began to reach out a little more, going slowly with what she shared and how she shared it to see if they could be trusted to have an adult relationship with her instead of the parent-child one that she'd fled and shucked.

Yes, Mary got it. She wanted that space and freedom for her boys. It was survival biology, part of human DNA.

Still, it hurt like hell—a profound aching misery—how easily her boys slid from her life.

Mary got on her hands and knees to reach for the bottle of shampoo that had rolled under the kitchen table. This funk she was in might well be the anticipation of her birthday, knowing she was living through the last hours of her thirties.

Though, her best friend Diedre assured her that there was some turning-forties-magic that she could anticipate when she'd wake up with a new, better world view and life would transform.

Mary grabbed at her aching toe and squeezed it to stop the throb.

A little transformation wouldn't necessarily be a bad thing.

Mary found herself in a predicament that she hadn't anticipated as she crossed over the demarcation line between decades.

She was a woman who lived in no-man's land.

Twenty years ago, in the small town where she'd grown up, high school couples married after graduation. It was conventional and expected that she'd marry Dan Williams. They'd had their first date at the end of freshman year. They were two peas in a pod, finishing each other's sentences, ordering the same thing off the menu, and having the same familial lack of ambition in terms of seeing anything for their future selves beyond the mundane.

It honestly hadn't occurred to Mary to do anything else; her worldview had been as narrow as the strictly patriarchal edges of the county lines.

She was eighteen, and Dan was nineteen that May as they prepared to graduate from St. Ambrose High.

Married in June.

Dan left for Navy boot in July.

He was gone all of one week when Mary realized she was pregnant.

Surprise!

In their small-town Catholic school, seventy-year-old Sister Inez—who had been sequestered in a Spanish convent from the time she was ten until she was forty and came to America to teach languages—hadn't really taught much about sex in their state-mandated sex-ed curriculum. To say Mary was unprepared for her wedding night was exceedingly generous.

Mary kept the two-pink-lined pee test a secret until she could tell Dan in person that they were going to be parents when she saw him at his graduation, becoming a U.S. sailor. In turn, Dan didn't consult Mary in advance of signing on to submarine school, which would mean he'd deploy for six months' stints.

They both had surprises for that graduation day.

Mary couldn't imagine life under the sea with the escape hatch sealed tight.

Yet, that's where she found herself, too. For her, there was no way out; all she could do was power forward.

While Dan was at submarine school, she'd been on her own in their military housing.

Thin walls, her next-door neighbor, Deidre, heard her

vomiting at all hours of the day and night and banged on her door with electrolytes and saltines.

For weeks, Mary had been unable to open her eyes without retching up acidic bile. One day, Deidre knocked on her door. "Come on, I have an appointment for you to see my OB. This can't go on anymore."

When the ultrasound doctor sang out, "Congratulations! You're expecting twins!" Mary opened the black plastic yard bag she carried with her everywhere she went and puked.

At nineteen, with a husband sliding along the ocean floor near the Arabian Peninsula, Mary gave birth, squeezing Deidre's hand, becoming the mother of colicky newborns. And she, in turn, got out of her hospital bed to hold Deidre's hand when she gave birth to her own son the next day.

Yeah, life comes at you fast.

Twenty-one years on, Mary had fulfilled her adult duties of raising a family. The boys were grown and off learning how to adult. She and her now ex-husband divorced as soon as the kids left for college. She closed the cover on the story of who she had been from high school until the day of the "great good-bye" when the boys loaded their cars and drove in tandem across the United States, as far as they could get from her without diving into the Pacific. (Yeah, Mary knew that was self-pitying garbage, but that didn't mean she didn't think it.) All in all, it had been a pretty good book, taken as a whole. But it was finished and now sat on the shelf next to her baby book and school yearbooks, all gathering dust until Mary felt compelled to pull out moments of her past to reminisce.

Starting young meant Mary burst across the finish line just as many families her age were moving toward the starting gate for their own race.

She felt an odd disequilibrium now.

Untethered from a nuclear family sharing the same house,

Mary was flailing a bit as she tried to figure out this next chapter.

It would be helpful, she thought, if she could find some other women who were her kind of "Wow, you're so young to be so old!" as she was. Even Deidre, her best friend since the life-preserving saltine and electrolyte delivery, was twelve years her senior.

The fellow nurses her age working at the hospital all had to juggle daycare pickups and toddler dance tutus.

They came in with scouting peanut sales sign-ups and cookies, so many cookies.

Mary had done all that and was over it.

Now, listening to the other women talking about their families, Mary was exhausted in the remembering. How did she do it? How had she made it to this point? The point where her beloved sons were off finding out who they were going to be as adults and Mom—who had been their everything for oh-so-many years—was barely a passing, if not downright irritating, thought.

Divorced from Dan, ignored by her boys, and a square peg in the round hole of Norfolk society—not fitting comfortably into the demographics—and now, yeah, she was in a birthday funk.

She was chewing on the cud of her existence, again, Mary pointed out to herself. She'd get these thoughts and keep gnashing her teeth on them. The thoughts went nowhere, but there they were—repetitive and mood-crushing. Mary looked out the window at the sky painted a leaden gray, heavy and oppressive. Maybe that was adding to her mood.

Her phone jangled on the counter, and Mary leaned in to read the screen, Deidre.

Deidre was entirely too upbeat for Mary's present mood. She'd check the text later. Reaching into the grocery bag, Mary dragged out her yogurt and plastic box of strawberries, a package of salmon, and a couple avocados. She should have picked up a bottle of wine to go with her inner whine, she mused as she opened the fridge. Yeah, that needed a good cleaning, she thought as she looked over the glass shelves, and it wasn't happening today.

Her phone jangled again, signaling another text, Deidre.

Persistent. Mary leaned over and muttered at her unanswered phone, "Give me five minutes. Let me finish putting this stuff away. I'll grab a cup of tea and then be ready for a chat." She could have texted that, but then the conversation would be off and rolling. Mary tipped her head back and wiggled her shoulders. "Get it together."

The clatter at her window made her look up. The sky had opened up, and the rain pummeled the glass angrily. The sudden deluge was so heavy that she couldn't see anything beyond the water sliding down the pane. She was grateful she got home and into the house before the sky opened up and began dumping. Being out in that mess would be painful.

The phone rang, Deidre. Okay, that was out of character.

Mary snatched the phone up and swiped the screen. "Are you in an ambulance?"

"What?" Deidre asked. "No. What gave you that impression?"

"You usually wait for a go-ahead text before you call," Mary said. "Modern phone etiquette."

"I don't have time for that. You don't have time for that either. I am about to rock your world." Deidre sounded like she'd just won the lottery.

Pulling the coffee out of the grocery bag, Mary put her nose to the plastic and sniffed the slight scent of fall seasonings. Closing her eyes, she imagined how good it was going to taste in the morning. *Cinnamon Roll*, yum. "You can rock my world if I can do it in my pajamas," Mary said into the phone. "I'm about to curl up on the couch with a bowl of ice cream and listen to the rain on my roof."

"Why?" Deidre's voice turned momentarily concerned before it bounced back to excitement. "No, don't tell me. We haven't got time. I need your passport number."

"My, what now?" Mary tapped the speaker button.

"Your passport number for these plane tickets."

"Okay, I feel like I walked in in the middle of a conversation." Mary reached the coffee bag on to the shelf and shut the cabinet. "I have no idea what's going on here."

"Go get your passport while I explain. I don't want to lose these tickets. Go. Hurry!"

"For where?" Mary turned and found herself heading toward her bedroom.

"Amsterdam to Geneva, then a train to Haute Nendaz."

Mary stalled with her hand on the doorknob. "Why?" Switzerland, she could find on the map. Haute Nendaz not so much.

"Chocolate, of course." Deidre was laughing, her excitement palpable.

"Of course. Also, there's chocolate at the grocery store and that doesn't require my standing in line at the TSA. When is this that you want to go?" She pressed into the room.

"Tomorrow."

"Shit, Deidre," Mary stopped mid-stride. "Fly to Switzerland *tomorrow*? What are you even talking about? Did someone die? Can we send flowers instead?"

"Prescient. Yes, someone did die." Deidre coughed and gasped. "That went down the wrong tube. Sorry." She coughed again. "I told you about the woman I read about in a magazine, the horoscope lady."

"She does special charts to figure out where in the world

you're supposed to be on your birthday to change your life. Is that the one?"

"She's the one, Rushpa Viswan. I filled out a form to get on her wait list. I figured, why not hear what Mrs. V. had to say."

Mary regained her forward momentum toward her passport and couldn't figure out why she was still in motion. This was ridiculous. "Mrs. V. could send you to the middle of Borneo," Mary pointed out.

"Could," Deidre agreed. "But the website says you get three destinations: the best one to improve your romantic life, the best to change your career life, and the best to change the trajectory of your life. Well, she says, 'align with your life's purpose.'" Deidre drew in a deep breath. "Any change would probably be good, so I figured that I'd look at the places Mrs. V. tells me about and pick the one with the fewest poisonous snakes and cannibals."

Mary got on her knees, lifted the dust ruffle on her bed, and laid her fingers on the pad to open the safe with her prints. "That sounds like a solid plan. But your next birthday isn't until June, almost a year away."

"Right, well, she's got a two-year waiting list. I mean, this woman is really popular."

"Totally not following you here," Mary said, putting her cheek to the floor and using the flashlight on her phone to reach into the fire-proof safe she'd bolted into the floor.

"Mrs. V.'s client for day after tomorrow died."

"Died?" Mary grabbed her passport and sat up. "That's kind of an extreme way to get out of improving your life."

"I know, right? When the appointment became available, Mrs. V. looked over her list, chose me as the person she wanted to work with in that time slot, and said I had to come to take that appointment."

"The dead woman's spot." Mary's brow drew together. Did this sound legit?

"Yeah," Deidre dropped the cheerful from her voice, "that's kind of not the way I want to think about this. So she's in Haute Nendaz, Switzerland."

"Where there's chocolate."

"And lots of gooey melted cheese, I'm told. Do you have your passport number?" Deidre asked.

Mary opened the blue cover to the hideous photo of her with red clown lips. It was bad, worse even than her driver's license, and in that photo, the light reflected off Mary's glasses, making her look like an eyeless zombie. "Why am I giving this to you?"

"Because I'm not going by myself. Mrs. V. told me," Deidre affected a British accent, 'You're *not* to come alone.'"

"That sounds," Mary paused, looking for the right word, "ominous. Kind of Agatha Christie-esque."

"I already called my brother and told him he had to give me his travel points. With his wife on third-trimester bed rest, they aren't going anywhere, and the points'll just go to waste."

"Right, well," Mary said, "waste not want not."

"It says I can use the points for hotels, too," Deidre said. "And there's plenty for us to go together as long as we share a room."

"Tomorrow, though?"

"Stop. I can feel you digging your heels in. And I'll physically drag you if that's what it takes. You're going with me."

"I have my pole dancing class. I love that class. I—"

"Look, you don't start your new job until next week. And yes, you love your pole dancing class, but it's only an hour long. After that, you're not doing anything but moping. You were moping when I called, weren't you?"

"Little bit moping," Mary admitted. "Beginning of the school year used to be a big deal here. No boys. Just me."

"And your fortieth birthday," Deidre said. "That can't be overlooked. You're about to head over the hill."

"Yup, thanks." Mary closed her eyes and tipped her head back. "That, too."

"So why mope when you can eat yourself into a cheese coma?" Deidre asked, then plowed ahead. "The best tickets are for tomorrow at five a.m. We fly to Atlanta, then Geneva, then we have the train. It's only four blocks from the train to the hotel I've already booked. So pack into a wheely bag. The next day, we'll have the morning to do a little sightseeing and grab some lunch at a cute little outdoor café. I have my appointment in the afternoon, so you can do whatever you want. They have a pool and sauna at the hotel."

"Five a.m. *tomorrow* morning?" Mary shook her head.

"Now, I only signed up for two nights at the hotel. We can decide if we like it there and want to stay or—we're right there in the middle of Europe—we can go anywhere, you know? Grab a train. Be spontaneous. You're shaking your head. I can feel you shaking your head. Mary, isn't that what we both just pinky swore to? We'd work on being less organized and just get out there and experience?"

"I've never pinky sworn to anything in my life." Mary rolled her hips to plop her butt onto the carpet, allowing more blood flow to stop the pins and needles prickling in her feet.

"Huh, maybe I dreamed it. Okay, what's that passport number?"

As she read it out, all Mary could think of was the piles of dirty laundry with no clean clothes to pack. She didn't even know what kind of weather was in Haute Nendaz. And she'd just bought those perishables she still needed to get into her fridge.

5

SEPTEMBER SECOND
Washington, D.C.

THE DOOR STOOD OPEN. A brass plate labeled this the Panther Force War Room. He was in the right place.

As Halo paused in the hall, waiting for an invitation to enter, Max sat politely at his side, on his best behavior.

A man moved into his view.

Now, Halo was improbably big for special forces. As a rule, the men were about five foot ten in American measurements. Their wiry frames had musculature that was magnitudes stronger than one would suppose. They were the kind of men who liked to run ultramarathons for fun and could easily get into small spaces and out of tight situations. Honestly, moving the height and bulk of Halo's own six foot four, two-hundred-fifty-pound frame—using the Yank's measurements—had advantages and disadvantages. For one, he was an outlier among his team and the only one who dangled over the end of a standard-issue cot. Ryder and he stood eye to eye, but the others were a good six inches shorter. Even Halo's ex-wife, at six feet, was taller than the boys. They had hated it when she stood beside—towered over—them, looking down at their bald spots.

Normally, hulking over everyone, it felt nice when Halo met up with someone his own size. To be small in comparison? That was an unusual circumstance. But the man walking toward him had Halo tilting his chin up to catch his gaze, even if it was only a couple of inches. This guy was astonishingly large in the way Halo imagined that bear to be when he found the scat pile on his way to finding Mrs. Haze.

"Halo St. John?" the man asked.

"Sir."

The mountain of a man extended his hand. "Honey Honig, welcome aboard."

"Thank you, sir."

Honey turned toward the man at the desk, who lifted a hand. "I'm Nutsbe Crushed, Panther Force mission coordinator. You'll forgive me for not standing up," Nutsbe said. "I'm in my wheelchair today."

"Sir."

"We're going to tone down on the sirs when we're not in the field," Honey said.

"Yes, si— Okay," Halo said, glancing toward the table with a go-bag resting in the center.

"Yup, that's yours. As was explained to you during your assessments," Honey said, "Cerberus Tactical has a dual role to play here at Iniquus. They do search and rescue if any of our clients find themselves in dangerous circumstances. Typically, that's associated with mass disaster. Though, Team Bravo evacuated the entire corporation from a war zone last year."

"We stick around after our clients are safe and lend a hand as part of Iniquus's charitable outreach," Nutsbe added.

"Amazing work you all do. One of the many reasons I'm

glad to have signed on," Halo said.

Honey looked down at Max, who looked up at Halo for information.

Halo gave his dog the "all's well" brushing signal. And Max lay down, letting his tongue loll out as he panted. Yeah, Max knew that something was in the works, and he was excited for whatever came next.

"Since Max is tactically trained, you and Max will also deploy with the Iniquus force teams, like ours. On Panther Force, we meet diverse needs. It keeps things fresh on the job. Panther Force was over doing teambuilding with the Madagascar military for some months. And now, most of the team is in the Baltic region on a close protection assignment for Mr. and Mrs. Sutton. They own Pangolin."

"And it looks like our team will be over there longer than we'd expected," Nutsbe said, wheeling back from his desk.

"The Suttons have decided to move their board of directors retreat at the end of the month from Egypt to Estonia for safety reasons given our present global concerns." Honey moved to the other side of the conference table, pulled out a chair, and sat, gesturing for Halo to do the same.

Halo pulled out a seat and signaled Max under the table.

"Mrs. Sutton will be in Helsinki until the third, when she will take a ferry across the Baltic to meet up with her husband, and they will be flying home together," Honey explained. "Our team will now be staying on-site while we conduct our due diligence on Tallinn and their planned excursions. We want you to be part of the process so you have a good idea of procedure and policy."

"I like the challenge of working in new environments," Halo said.

"Good to hear since you'll spend the first few months rotating between the tactical teams, learning the ropes while

Command continues to build out Cerberus Team Charlie. With Iniquus, you'll find it's similar to your work as a Commando, but there are civilian rules, laws, and protocols that you'll need to have down pat."

"All right." Halo tipped his ear toward the go bag. "Looks like Max and I are heading out soon, then?"

"*You* are heading out in the next hour," Honey said. "Max is going to stay here to work with Reaper on two specific required skills needed before he'll be allowed to join a mission. The first is snake aversion training."

Nutsbe wheeled out from behind his desk and over toward them.

Halo glanced briefly down to see that Nutsbe had bilateral, below-knee amputations. Iniquus hiring veterans, recalibrated after sustaining permanent injuries, made them a shining beacon in a world that often chewed up its elite warriors—using and abusing their bodies for their countries' well-being, then failing to live up to the promises made in terms of physical and mental health. "We heard Max had a bit of a run-in with a rattle snake," Nutsbe said with a shake of his head. "That's a crazy story."

"I didn't even know there was such a thing on the East Coast." Halo glanced down at Max, and Max, in turn, put his paw on Halo's boot as if they were companionably holding hands. "Ryder warned me about copperheads in Virginia."

"There are others—water moccasins are also called cotton mouths," Honey said. "But the venomous snakes in this area pose the same dangers as snakes Max can run into worldwide. We want the dogs to stay away from all snakes no matter where your missions take you." His gaze caught Halo's and held. "You saw for yourself how the trajectory for Mrs. Haze's survival hinged *solely* on how Max got his mouth around that rattler. A few inches further down the snake's body, you would have been racing Max down to the vans and off to the nearest emergency vet to get the antivenom. A danger to Max. A danger to you. A serious danger to our lost subject, too. Max was minutes from finding Mrs. Haze. The rest of the team worked their search grids at a distance so their dogs wouldn't have picked up that scent cone. The survival time frame was so narrow—from the find until the onset of the storm—Mrs. Haze would have died but for the well-placed bite." Honey held Halo's gaze. "Close call, brother."

"Agreed. Snake aversion is a must for all those reasons." Halo dropped his hand to Max's head and scritched behind his ears. *Too, damned close a call.* "What's the other skill?"

"He needs to be toilet trained," Nutsbe said with a grin.

Halo stilled. "Come again?"

"Max has to be comfortable using all manner of toilets," Nutsbe said, "from the tiny cabinets on transportation to various kinds of sanitation found around the world—Japanese high-tech to holes in the floor to porta-potties."

"All right, this is a new one on me." Halo's lips pulled into a bemused smile. "Can I ask why?"

"If, for example, you're on an unplanned mode of transportation," Nutsbe said, "the client decides to go on a boat ride, take a last-minute plane, or jump on a train—trying to get away from some epicenter of destruction. Even when everyone's go-go-go, your K9 will need to relieve himself. Better to just go hit the head."

Halo crossed his arms over his chest, leaning back in the black captain's chair. He could quickly see the benefit of toilet training, though, it had never occurred to him before. Halo had always worked with combat K9; they relieved themselves wherever.

"Or let's say you're working a close protection assignment," Honey said. "You use the bathroom when your client uses the bathroom. Your K9 does, too, on command. You can't ask your client to go outside for a dog's bathroom breaks, especially in poor weather or dangerous surroundings. And you certainly can't leave your client's side to care for your dog."

"I get it." It was genius, actually.

"Max will stay here with Reaper," Honey repeated. "We're putting you on a plane to Helsinki. Once I give you this bag, you'll head to men's barracks, grab what you need—passport etcetera. Plan to be there for a week. A car will take you straight from here to the airport. Last minute, but our team member, Margot, tested positive for COVID-19 and is sequestered until she's clear and feeling a hundred percent capable of serving in her security role. She was one of a two-person team on Mrs. Sutton's Finland security team." Honey rapped his knuckle onto the surface of the table. "Now, a male guarding a civilian female takes some finesse. You have to keep her safe while navigating her environment. This often means she goes into women-only areas—again, bathrooms. Max will eventually be trained to accompany a female into the bathroom with a two-way radio collar, but that's not the situation now."

"I've been on security detail for various female elected officials," Halo said. "I'm comfortable with the assignment." What Halo wasn't comfortable with was leaving Max behind. From the time he and Max decided to be partners, Halo was never gone from him for more than a few hours.

Found by the side of the road and turned in to the authorities, Max had just arrived at the no-kill shelter where Halo was accompanying a friend, picking up the litter of kittens she was fostering.

When Halo walked by, Max uncurled from the back of his crate, stood, and locked eyes on him.

They'd stared at each other for a long moment, sizing each other up—Max, a four-month-old big-pawed, gangly-legged, flea-bitten, under-fed Malinois, and Halo an oversized Australian Commando in his last year of service to his government. "If we're doing this, mate. We're doing it. We're going all in, both of us, yeah? You up for the challenge?"

Max held eye contact without a waver—not aggression but a connection.

"Teammates?" Halo asked.

Max bowed low, his tail sweeping through the air, his gaze still locked on Halo's as if he thought that should he blink or look away, even for a moment, his opportunity would pass him by.

The attendant approached, and Halo pointed his finger at the cage. "That's my dog. Let's get the paperwork together so I can take him home."

The woman walked up and unlocked the door. "You don't want to spend some time with him first? Make sure it's a good match? This little guy is going to grow up to be a powerhouse."

"We've already got it figured out between us." Halo hadn't had thought one of getting a dog that day, but when the cage door swung open, Max leaped the four feet right into Halo's arms and bloody well straight into his heart.

It was going to feel odd to him. But both Max and HAlo would be focused on learning new things and on the job in front of them.

Honey pulled the go bag closer. "Reaper uses a dog-to-dog mentor program. He'll line all the K9s up to use the toilet and let Max watch. The hardest thing is teaching the dogs to balance on the slick surface and managing the different flushing toggles. If Max is catching on, I'll bring him over to Estonia with me so you can assess the use of K9s in Estonia. It's not part of our plan to use them next month for the meeting, but it's important that you can work through the planning stages with the tactical teams so everyone is working toward best outcomes."

"Agreed. Go back to the toggles. Because the dogs flush, too?"

"And put the seat down." Honey unzipped the bag and drew out a shirt and a handheld apparatus that was similar to a cell phone. "You'll arrive in Helsinki tonight and get yourself to the hotel. Thorn will get you up to speed. You'll get some sleep. In the morning, it will be your watch. You have a day in an office setting with meetings, and then you will escort Mrs. Sutton on the ferry from Helsinki across the Baltic to Tallinn, Estonia, to connect with her husband and take them to the airport."

"All right."

"It's about a two-hour ride. Very comfortable ride. No problems with seasickness. Thorn will drill down on the danger assessment with you once you arrive. Right now, we're watching the area closely. There was sabotage to a gas pipeline that ran between Finland and Estonia. And yesterday, there was an interruption to the communications cable."

"Was it in the news?" Halo asked. Somehow, he'd missed that.

"Maybe on page fourteen," Nutsbe said.

Halo swung his attention to Nutsbe. "Estonia boarders Russia near St. Petersburg. Do they think Russia is saber rattling with another neighbor?"

"Estonia is part of the EU. So we hope not. In this case, area investigators think this was a Chinese attack."

"I'm sorry?" Halo's brows drew together as he leaned forward. "The Chinese in the Baltic Sea?"

"The Finnish Navy retrieved a six-ton anchor from the area. There are indications on both the pipeline and the cable that there was contact. The gas line showed immediate signs of damage. The damage to the communication cable took longer to show the effects. It wasn't a total cable break. It was a tear."

"Purposeful?" Halo asked.

"Debatable," Honey answered. "The Finish Navy noticed that the Chinese vessel was moving in the area without a visible anchor, which is against regulations. When confronted, the Chinese said they were unaware of the missing anchor."

"Improbable," Halo's brows knitted.

"Agreed," Honey said. "And that the Chinese didn't think the found anchor was theirs."

"Easily proved," Halo said.

"And yet, a diplomatic nightmare," Nutsbe called over his shoulder as he wheeled back to his desk. "Especially as Finland is newly onboard with NATO."

"Since the picture is unclear," Honey said, "we need to ensure our client is safe and comfortable on her passage from Helsinki to Tallinn." He unfolded the shirt and lay it flat on the table. "A few months ago, Cerberus Bravo was in the Caribbean for a training mission at the Iniquus Southern Campus when Dominica lost communications just before the eye of the Cat 5 storm went over the island, complicating rescue. That was an anchor incident, too, but it was a wayward anchor from a yacht and not in any way nefarious. This is different. We know that as the Russian war against Ukraine continues, Russia has reached out to China for bolstering. That a Chinese vessel was operating in the Baltic Sea with mal intent while their navy is also acting provocatively near the Philippines is of global concern."

"Why Estonia, though? Or are they just being pissy over Finland?"

"Estonia is the Silicon Valley of Europe," Nutsbe said as he rocked his chair into position behind his desk. "Sorry to be over here, but I'm monitoring operators in the field."

Halo lifted a hand, "No worries, mate."

"So Estonia," Nutsbe continued. "They have more 'unicorns' there than anywhere else in Europe and, per capita, the most startups. Our clients want to have their foot in that door, accessing the creativity and technology that is available there at a reasonable price compared to other tech markets."

"It's a very safe city," Honey said. "However, with the Russian border only about a hundred miles from their capital city, a city where a third of the Estonian population lives, we have to keep an awareness of the geopolitical landscape and have exit strategies planned."

Honey tapped the gunmetal grey compression shirt with the tip of his finger. "This shirt is an important piece of your security and safety apparatus. DARPA—the United States' national defense research arm—often asks Iniquus to try out their prototypes and give feedback. Less red tape than going through our military."

Halo looked at the shirt and couldn't see anything outstanding about it.

"This doesn't get laundered. It's too high-tech. Just put it back in the bag and bring it home. Iniquus will replace it with clean versions when you need them for missions. While you float between the tactical teams, getting to know us and how we operate in the field, we want you to practice with the shirt. First, you should understand that they are wired for biofeedback." Honey turned to point to Nutsbe at his computer. "That data gets sent automatically from your shirt via satellite to Nutsbe."

Halo leaned forward and rubbed the fabric between his fingers. "This shirt communicates through a satellite feed?"

"While you're in the field, Nutsbe will be able to keep track of your heart rate, respiration, and body temperature and monitor your hydration levels. This means that as you drop below an optimal level of water consumption, you'll hear Nutsbe in your ear, encouraging you to drink." Honey stopped to grin. "We called him Mom before all this started. Now, we're thinking of getting him tattooed with the name."

"My hydration levels?" Halo pulled the shirt closer and

smoothed his hand over the surface. He felt nothing there until he reached the sleeves where he detected the slight quilting between layers of smooth fabric.

"So far," Nutsbe said, "This prototype works well in the field. This is a second generation. What you're feeling as you run your hand over that sleeve is a directional system. The researchers have added a GPS compression unit to provide real-time directions."

Halo looked up to catch Honey's eye, hoping for an explanation for what that could mean.

"There are compressors in the arm. You or Nutsbe will enter your destination information into the computer." He pushed the phone-like apparatus toward Halo. "Then, as you move along, when you are to turn right, you will feel your forearm squeezed on the right. Same on the left. You turn in the direction of the squeeze. A gentle squeeze means to veer in that direction to get on course. A hard squeeze means to take a ninety degree."

"Yeah?"

"We've been working with them, and it takes a bit of getting used to. If you're in line with your target destination, you will feel nothing. That, in itself, can feel disorienting because you aren't sure if it's stopped working."

"So far," Nutsbe said, "it hasn't suddenly stopped functioning on any of us. It's constructed for destructive environments if you will."

"So I'd never need to pull out a map or equipment?" Halo asked. "I can see that being really useful, especially when the lighting conditions are suboptimal, or my hands are full like they were the day we were coming down the mountain with Mrs. Haze."

"Exactly, the AI mapping could also have directed you down the easiest elevations. We've used them in some tight spots when having a minor distraction is dangerous. Night engagement with the enemy, or, in the case of close protection when things are feeling tense, and eyes are on a swivel." Honey slid the shirt to the side, then pulled the electronic unit in its shockproof case in front of them. "This is your portable unit. Your shirt, with the vitals and GPS, are best run through the TOC." He used the acronym for tactical operations center, pronounced "talk." "But let's say you were in an area without satellite coverage, be it weather or another interruption. The maps are all loaded into the computer in advance. The AI works on radio waves. It knows where you are and can continue to direct you. It'll also feed the information to your phone as long as your phone is close by, so you can pull up maps to look at them and make decisions."

"No visual on the handheld?"

"No. And that's by design for security," Honey explained. "If you and the handheld get separated."

"Copy that."

"But you're on your own to remember to hydrate if you go off satellite," Nutsbe said without looking away from his computer. "That won't be on me."

"Noted, thanks."

"Thorn will get you up to speed with this once you're on the ground. But since you'll be dressing out in it as you head to the airport, I thought I'd give you a heads up about why your arms are getting a hug."

"What happens if I don't want to be directed?"

"The shirt will always keep track of your vitals," Honey clarified. "So you wear the shirt while on duty. It will only direct you while a destination is programmed."

"I programmed your route from here to Helsinki," Nutsbe said. "So you can try it out. It will move you through the airports, and once on the ground, it will move you to Thorn. In the air, I have it turned off. That would get unnerving.

6

SEPTEMBER THIRD

Haute Nendaz, Switzerland

PUNCHING HER PILLOW, then faceplanting into the center, Mary hoped the fluff would stifle her grunts.

They did not.

"Can't sleep?" Deidre asked, her voice wide awake.

"Craziest thing. I couldn't sleep on the plane, couldn't sleep on the train."

"I could not sleep here nor there. I could not sleep anywhere." Deidre singsonged.

"Exactly. But when we finally got here, and I dragged my butt up to our room, I thought I'd pass out from the exhaustion."

"Did you sleep at all?"

"An hour, maybe. What time is it at home?" She reached for her phone, scrolled to her world clock, and sighed. Her brain didn't know if it was coming or going. "My skin is dry, my legs are cramping, I can't sleep. In my mind, I sound like my mom did when she was bitching her way through menopause. And, frankly, I don't wanna. I'm not ready to add insult to injury."

"So said every woman who ever lived. I'm menopausal. You're just dehydrated. That's one nurse to another."

"Yeah, that, and it's almost ten p.m. at home. Coming off of two months of night shifts, my body thinks I should have been at work for the last three hours. I'd say I'm sorry I woke you, but obviously, you were trying to be quiet for me, too."

Twelve years apart in age, Deidre and she had been fast friends since they'd supported each other through their pregnancies and beyond. Mary's twins—Kaleb and Kyle—had been raised as a litter of rambunctious puppies along with Deidre's son, Brady. Their husbands were on the same sub. So she and Deidre co-parented. It kept them sane. And, to Mary, it was better than having a sister. Both her sisters had childhood baggage they dragged into their adult relationships.

When Kaleb, Kyle, and Brady hit puberty the summer before freshman year of high school, overnight, it seemed, they were suddenly towering over their moms and already eyeing the door.

Their husbands came home from deployment and the writing was on the wall, the marriages weren't working. A plan was developed: Once the boys started high school, the wives should get college degrees, learning something that could put food on their own table and a roof over their heads. Since neither man wanted to go back to school for their own degrees, why didn't the women use the GI benefits? Then, things could come to a natural ending, and everyone could go on their way. The men would try on a different kind of life, and the women would have what they needed to enter the job market and support themselves.

That discussion had been a shock to Mary, who, up until that summer, had believed in her vows.

It also seemed exhaustingly inevitable.

In the end, Mary decided, why not go with a pragmatic plan that moved everyone into position for what happened next?

And that was what unfolded.

Deidre and Mary had decided to start nursing school so they could be study buddies, and then they signed on to work in the same Norfolk VA hospital.

When college graduation came around, and their husbands' twenty-year commitment was served, their husbands retired from the military and resigned from their marriages.

Amicable splits for both couples.

The kids graduated, and just like that, all five of the XY chromosomes were out the door and on to their futures, leaving the two XX chromosomes blinking at the sudden void.

They knew it was coming. It was still a kick in the gut that left Mary winded.

The "shift" happened years ago, and Mary still felt like she hadn't quite mastered standing on wobbly ground as an individual. Too much time building too much muscle memory. She still cooked five times more than she needed. She still woke up with lists of things to check off that no longer needed her attention. She still shoveled food in her face as quickly as she could at meals because surely something would interrupt—spilled milk, a temper tantrum over the spaghetti noodles. Mary had learned to suck up her meal like a vacuum, and now she had to make a conscious effort to breathe between bites.

Deidre seemed to settle into the new lifestyle with a lot more ease. Maybe it was their age difference that made this easier for her.

It was the children that were the loss. In her brain, Mary

knew this was all good. But every cell in her body told her to protect her offspring. Her ex? Meh. That wasn't the problem.

He was a ghost that glided through their halls at certain times of the year.

Dan wasn't there for the twin's birth. He was on the last thirty days of the ninety-day cruise, and the boys hadn't wanted to stay in for their due date. So she'd brought her neighbor, Deidre, to the hospital to feed her ice chips, mainly because Mary didn't fit behind her steering wheel no matter how far back she put the driver's seat. She didn't think the taxi would let her in with her plastic garbage bag and towel to sit on once her water broke.

Eighteen, mother of two. That, as it turned out, was the easy part.

It was all uphill from there.

But she'd had Deidre to lean on and vice versa. They were "in it to win it" together. It felt good to have someone like that in her life.

Deidre broke into Mary's thoughts. "Get yourself some water, take the first shower. My appointment isn't until three, and we have the rental car. Let me see if I can't find something fun to do for sunrise. Maybe there's a tram to the top of the mountain and a breakfast spot with to-die-for breakfast pastries."

"And coffee," Mary added as she clicked on the light and blinked at the sudden brightness.

"Coffee goes without saying." Deidre reached over to pull up her computer, a sure sign that she was heading straight into the rabbit hole of travel reviews.

Throwing off her sheets, Mary wore a pair of panties and a t-shirt. She grunted as she crawled into a bath instead of a shower. She'd left the door open so Deidre could talk to her.

With her head resting on the cool ceramic of the lip and the hot water massaging her toes as it came out of the faucet, Deidre showed up with her computer in hand and sat on the toilet lid. "Found it."

"Coffee?"

"Sort of. Listen to this. Just up the road, two hours is a ski resort."

"Nice. I bet there's a cute little restaurant and beautiful views. If we left now, we'd be up there to see the sunrise."

"Better. There's skiing."

"It's the second day of September at the end of the hottest summer on record."

"There's skiing. I kid you not." Deidre held back the curtain of hair on either side of her face as she leaned over the screen, reading. "You just have to get out on the hill by seven."

"Okay, you know how to ski. You do that. I'll sit very still and enjoy the view."

"You know how to ski. You took lessons last year."

"I was flailing around on the hill where the toddlers learn."

"Look." Deidre turned her computer screen. "Toddlers in shorts and little helmets. Aren't they adorable?"

"There are no parents in that picture."

"I'm sure they're just out of the lens. It says it's says there's a green slope. That's a step above the potato patch. Still a bunny slope, though."

"I don't have ski clothes."

She flipped to another picture to show Mary. A group of women in string bikinis that matched their ski boots, long flowing blond hair, and aviator glasses posed near the lodge. "Perfect tans. It says that skiing with the reflection of the sun on the surface means you get a full tan while exercising and having fun."

"Yeah, I don't know …"

"Listen to me. Usually, it's you who's doing the pushing. It's my adventure, so I feel not only entitled but also that it's compulsory for me to do the same for you."

"To me."

"*For* you. We are so darned used to being mothers, to thinking through every possible bad scenario so we are prepared to handle it, to corralling and cheerleading and cajoling."

"Cajoling, like you're doing now?"

"No, I'm pushing. We promised to help each other through this transition." She held up a finger to tick off her points. "We will try things that we think are for other people, not us. We will dare to fail and look stupid, so we have some personal grace to build new expertise. We will exercise our spontaneity muscle. See! See how great we did? I got the call, come and bring your friend. I knew exactly whom she meant. I knew my brother would hand me his points. And here we are, we embrace the possibilities!"

"Holy shit, do you hear yourself?"

"Sadly, I do. But I will remind you that I am paraphrasing you after you read that scientific study about word pairing."

It was true. Mary had gone on a whole rant while Deidre had listened patiently through all of it. Mary was in her final class before her final exam in nursing school when her professor wanted to explain why women made up ninety-eight percent of the class.

Where were the men?

In the darkened auditorium, the professor asked the students to do a simple task. On the screen, a word or a name would show up. If it was a man's name, they were to say left. If it was a woman's name, they were to say right. If it was a scientific word, they were to say left. If it was a word associated with the home, they were to say right.

The hypothesis was that there were word pairings, things that "just went together," without any thought, ketchup and mustard, cloak and dagger, king and queen. When we form a word pairing in our minds, it was hard to break free from putting those things together.

So, the words started flashing, too fast to think. It was a reflex that had Mary's mouth saying, Stan left, Lab left, Kevin left, computer left, Pam right, laundry right, algorithm left, along with the more than one hundred students.

Never a hitch. Never a mistake.

"Now," the professor had said, "we're going to do it again. This time, I want you to make one change. The category for things associated with the home will go on the left with the male names, and the scientific words will go on the right with the female names."

The words flashed. They all made mistakes, hesitated, whispered their answers where they had shouted them out with conviction in the last iteration. As the words kept coming, at first, Mary thought everyone, including her, was doing poorly on this task because they had just trained in the opposite way. The words kept coming. And once they'd been twice as long in this new configuration, they should be improving. They weren't. They were getting worse. It was almost impossible for Mary to say Bob left and diaper changes left while putting Claudia on the right was easy. Putting the test tube over there had her stuttering.

Mary walked away from that experiment enraged.

All of her life, boxes.

All of her choices seemed to be a result of society funneling her down to a predetermined place, and she had no freedom of choice.

Nursing suddenly lost its appeal when one of the times they had all successfully categorized: "Theresa right. Nursing right." The whole class was stunned. Three more words passed, and the professor had to roll her hand and say "left" to get the student body participating again.

It was at that moment that Mary knew that with her nursing exam complete, she would not follow the funnel. She was going to break free. She took a job in the Emergency Department to learn how to handle nursing under high pressure—high stakes. The mother of two (basically three, counting Deidre's son) wild gorilla boys who loved nothing better than to test out Darwin's survival theory, Mary found that she was good in that setting. But the next goal was to become a medical evacuation nurse, going to accidents to support the extractions and flying critical patients from small rural hospitals to larger trauma centers in the city.

Take that, society!

Not only that, but she wondered what other things she'd missed out on in her life because she thought they were only for "other people." What fun things might be for her, too?

She liked to sing. She sucked at it. But why couldn't she learn?

She liked to paint. She extra sucked at it. But why couldn't she learn?

She had always found pole dancing to be beautiful and athletic. In her word pairing paradigm, pole dancing was for strippers and loose women. But why couldn't someone who just liked the art form of pole dancing and wanted a more interesting way to build upper body strength than doing bicep curls? Yup that darned pairing crap was holding her back. She'd decided right then that she would look up local classes and swing from a pole.

She went. She sucked. It hurt like hell.

But when she figured out how to do a move, victory was so sweet.

And that's when Mary made up a new rule. If she thought something looked fun, no matter who it was "made for," the athletic girl, or the talented guy, or the math genius, whatever. Whatever pairing of words that tried to stop her from even trying, she'd try. Not once, but twenty times. As a matter of fact, Mary had yelled at Deidre, I will find twenty things to try twenty times.

Sipping a Margarita, Deidre had lounged back on the couch, watching Mary pace back and forth in her living room. "Why twenty?"

"I pulled that number out of my rear. Maybe because the boys are turning twenty. And," she held up a finger, "twenty times will make it a habit to look for things that might be fun. And," she thrust that finger toward Deidre, "twenty times will let me know if I really don't like something or that I just didn't want to go through the pain and humiliation of wobbly first giraffe steps."

"Hear, hear!" Deidre had raised her glass. "And don't get pissy when I hold you to that."

"I do think, actually, I'm tired of meeting people when the only stories I have to tell are me watching from the sidelines. And you're absolutely right that we were going to support each other out of that by generating a bunch of our own stories. It would be fun to say I was skiing in Switzerland over the summer. And there's no reason to tell them it was on the baby hill. Not many people can say that they skied the Alps in summer."

"That's the spirit. Next cute guy who wants to buy you a drink, you can impress the shit out of him with that."

"I'm not in this to impress guys. I'm in this to stretch myself and figure out who the heck I am when I'm not 'hey, honey,' or '*Mom*!' I need to be just me for a while until I get that figured out."

"I'm reserving our spots and boots. It says they only let so many people on the mountain."

"I can't imagine that it's going to be packed. Europeans are done with their summer vacations, and it's a Monday."

7

SEPTEMBER THIRD
Helsinki, Finland

"HALO?" Without moving from his position in front of the hotel room door, he extended his hand. "Welcome aboard. I'm Thorn Iverson."

"Halo St. John." If ever a man was properly named, it was this Thorn Iverson bloke. With a few furs thrown over his shoulder and perhaps long braided hair instead of his tight military cut, Thorn could easily fill the Viking role in any movie. His grasp as they shook hands was confident with none of the bone-crushing grips Halo often received from men who wanted to make some point about their strength. Halo always read that move like a rowdy dog—all bark, no bite. Here with Thorn, though, or really any of the blokes at Iniquus, Halo didn't pick up on any of the hazing, prove-yourself energy that tried to establish a pecking order. That might have something to do with the hiring process; each person was thoroughly assessed to ensure they deserved a place on the team.

And Halo was as proud of making that cut as he was of becoming a Commando.

"Command doesn't mind throwing people in the deep end, understanding they already know how to swim and prefer it that way." Thorn swept his gaze toward a door opening down the hall.

"That's me all right," Halo said with a smile.

"Cerberus is a tight team. You'll enjoy working with them." As an elderly couple left their room, heading toward the elevator, Thorn shifted his gaze back to Halo. "I bet you feel one limb shy without your dog by your side."

"It's an odd experience. But Max'll be back with me soon enough. Titus brought me up to speed on the Helsinki security overview. And my tasks with Mrs. Sutton this morning."

"He's on the ferry back to Tallinn now. He'll let us know if he learns of any concerns." Thorn spoke with the kind of special operator's timbre that was just loud enough to reach Halo's ear and no farther. No one behind their hotel room doors would be able to pick up this conversation. "In the meantime, after I introduce you to Mrs. Sutton, and you take over close protection duties, I'm going to grab some grub and then some shut-eye." He looked at his watch. "She'll be leaving in the next five minutes. The company sent a car. They've already pinged me that they're waiting out front. I'll forward the pictures of the driver and license plate to your phone. Did Titus go over the schedule with you?"

"Affirmative."

"Okay, well, Mrs. Sutton will be at the office building until lunch. I'll gather the luggage and meet you at the harbor. Our shirts will direct us to each other." He lifted his arm.

"It's been an interesting learning curve using the navigation shirts."

"Nutsbe's been on you to drink more water?"

"As soon as I got off the plane," Halo said with a grin.

"Operators try to be camels. The doctors say that affects cognition. Command hones every plane to give us the edge. Once Nutsbe's been in your ear, calling your attention to your hydration for a while, you'll start making drinking a better habit. While it might feel a bit intrusive, trust the process."

"Even with that said, mate, I do see the benefits of the technology. Nutsbe programmed my route through the maze of the airport and getting here. I was able to move with relative ease."

"It's a trust issue?" Thorn asked.

"Exactly. But Titus was in the middle of a crowd, and I was able to walk right over to him without a clue what he looked like. I'm sure it will get me and Mrs. Sutton to you at the dock. What about her lunch? Does that happen at the meeting?"

"There are restaurants on the ferry. She has reservations. She'll linger over her food. Once we're docked, we'll get her from Tallinn harbor to the airport. It's only a couple of miles. We'll take a cab for that."

"All right."

"We get her on the plane, and this afternoon, we'll be out in the Estonian bog. It'll be a first for me. But I hear you have bogs in your part of the world?" Thorn asked.

"There are bogs and fens on Snowy Mountain down in the southeastern part of New South Wales. I live—lived—close to Sydney. While I rock climb in the mountains, I've never explored that terrain. The bog will be new on me." Halo tucked his chin. "Is there a specific reason for the bogs?"

"The corporate planner hired a naturalist to take the group on a bog hike excursion during their retreat at the end of the month."

"Hike in a bog?" Halo scratched the side of his face. "These people are outdoor sports enthusiasts?"

"Corporate executives."

Halo lowered his voice to a mere whisper. “Maybe what I’m imagining and how things play out here are different. But, from what I know of the bogs, that sounds problematic. How do you walk on a bog?”

“That’s what we’re about to find out with our trial hike. If this works out, you and Max will be on the team that treks out with them.”

Halo grinned. “A dog on the bog?”

“Ha!” Thorn returned the smile. “From our initial research, we think it’ll be important to have a dog alert the team to concerning wildlife.”

“Such as?” Halo crossed his arms over his chest, angling his chin.

“Bears, wolves, moose.”

“Moose, that’s an animal I’ve never seen in real life.”

“I haven’t either. I’ve seen videos of them running, though, fast. And at six feet plus to the shoulders, nine hundred pounds, huge antlers, I wouldn’t want to upset one.” There was a flush of the toilet inside the hotel room. An interior door shut. “I understand your dog is getting his snake aversion training,” Thorn said as he stepped to the side of the door. “Good thing. You can add viper to that animals list. This afternoon’s trek out to the bog is part of our due diligence. Our task is to keep everyone safe and comfy. We plan and prep for any scenario.”

“We’ll be following along the same route as with the executives?” Halo asked. Even the recent search and rescue of Mrs. Haze was a reminder that different routes meant different outcomes.

“Same naturalist even, a seasoned guide named Marilin with over a decade of experience. I'm sure the executives won't be problematic if she can get whole classes of school kids in and out. Today, she’ll point out the dangers and talk through the strategies for keeping everyone safe and happy. It turns out that just yesterday, Marilin was hiking a travel blogger through the area for social media pictures, and the land he was standing on sank under his weight. She saved him by the straps on his backpack."

"Bigger question," Halo said, "why couldn't he save himself?"

"I guess that's something we need to ask Marilin. In the meantime, we've got Nutsbe ordering enough hiking packs that everyone shows up properly equipped and secured with both hip and sternal straps."

"Copy that," Halo said as the hotel room door swung open. He took a pace backward so that Mrs. Sutton didn't have two huge men looming over her as she came out into the hallway for their introduction.

Thorn reached for her suitcase handle. "Mrs. Sutton, with Margot ill, may I introduce your new security?"

MRS. SUTTON, dressed in a designer suit, balanced on pointy-toed stilettos that looked to Halo like torture devices. He was ready to lend an arm if she lost her balance or offer support if she started hobbling. Now, she was looking out of the office window, high above the famous Helsinki Senate Square, her gaze swept from left to right. "Lots of people out, enjoying the sunshine," she said to Edvin Koskinen, the company's vice president of finances, who was escorting her today.

From what Halo could gather, there was some kind of merger on the horizon. And reading from Mrs. Sutton's body language, she very much wanted it to go through.

"We are all taking advantage of the sunshine and the mild temperatures," Koskinen said. "In just a short few weeks, we will be in the dark and icy time of the year. It is very difficult on the psyche."

"Oh?" Mrs. Sutton blinked at him. "But Finland is listed as one of the happiest countries in the world. *The* happiest, am I right?"

"We have that distinction, yes." Koskinen smiled. "However, what an American hears when that phrase is offered is perhaps different than what is actually meant from that study."

"What do people in Helsinki do when it gets dark and cold?" she asked.

"Many things. Come to this window over here." He extended his arm to indicate the other side of the room. They moved toward it together. "You see there?" He pointed. "That building with the sinuous lines? This is our library. It is perhaps different from the ones you have. It is almost like a social center. There, you can check out not just books but tools for projects. There are sewing machine stations, 3D printers, sound recording booths, board games, video games, and many things to draw our people together. Otherwise, people stay at home and drink in their underwear."

She turned to Koskinen with a bemused smile. "In their underwear?"

"Yes, the word is in Finnish *kalsarikännit,* and this translates to 'pants-drunk.'" He moved to another bank of windows.

"Pants drunk?" Mrs. Sutton followed behind. "Huh. That sounds like something someone would do when they were depressed. Unless, of course, this is a party situation?" Mrs. Sutton frowned with her whole face but quickly smoothed out those lines, offering an interested smile instead, as Koskinen turned to her.

"Something we do alone," Koskinen continued matter-of-factly. "It is lovely to sit around and get drunk in one's underpants. It is quite done here."

"Interesting." By her tone, Halo surmised that Mrs. Sutton wasn't one to sit around in her panties by herself, getting drunk.

The sarcastic note of her reply seemed to have been lost on Koskinen. He pointed at the new section of the window. "Here, do you see this? The Ferris wheel?" He looked back to see that Mrs. Sutton was focused in the right direction. "It is interesting because—can you see that one brown car on the wheel?"

Mrs. Sutton squinted. "Yes. It's different from the others."

"It is a sauna." He pronounced it SOW-nah, and since it was a Finnish invention, Halo noted the proper pronunciation and would use it from then on.

She blinked.

"Yes, this is true," Koskinen said. "You get on, and as the wheel takes you around, you and your friends enjoy the sauna."

"But if you're in a sauna, and it's steamy, how do you see the view?"

Good question.

Koskinen skipped forward with his information. "Sauna is very important to the Finnish peoples. We have saunas everywhere. We have more saunas than we have cars. As a matter of fact, here in Helsinki, there is an American burger chain restaurant with a sauna. Many public saunas. It is a place to socialize. We do this because it is good for the physical and mental health especially in the dark months of the year. And, having shown you this," he checked his watch, "I have a lovely surprise." He focused back on Mrs. Sutton. "The executives of my department have arranged a welcoming sauna for you. This is a traditional greeting to a new business alignment, and we wish to extend this welcome to you."

Koskinen looked pleased.

Mrs. Sutton did not.

"How very kind." She put her hand to her chest. "Sadly, I will be on the ferry by lunch."

"This is fine." Koskinen lifted a hand toward the door, stepping forward. "We go right now."

"To the sauna? Now?" She turned to Halo, her eyelids blinking in a staccato pattern that made him think she was sending an SOS in Morse code.

Halo had received orders that he was there for Mrs. Sutton's protection and was in no way to inject himself into any situation. He stood stoically against the pleading in her eyes. It felt wrong. But he was honestly at a loss.

With a nervous laugh, Mrs. Sutton turned back to Koskinen. "What a delightful idea. I'm sorry, I don't have a bathing suit with me."

"This is a private sauna." Koskinen brushed his hand through the air, indicating that they should walk.

"For women?" Mrs. Sutton stepped forward. "I'm not sure I understand."

"Bathing suits are only worn for public saunas like at the burger restaurant." The two walked side by side, and Halo stayed a step behind at Mrs. Sutton's left elbow.

"In private, so at our office spaces," Koskinen continued. "Finnish people do not cover themselves. Neither do we segregate saunas male to female. This wouldn't be egalitarian, especially for work."

"I see." Mrs. Sutton's voice sounded tight in her throat. "Since saunas aren't part of the typical American culture, can I just check and see if I understand where we're going and what we're doing?" They'd stopped in front of the elevator. "Your team is honoring me with a department welcoming party in a sauna. We will be men and women together, and we will all—all of us—be unclothed."

"This is a wonderful way to get to know each other." Koskinen nodded to her, then turned to press the call button.

"Yes." Mrs. Sutton glanced over her shoulder at Halo. That look screamed, "Get me out of this."

Halo couldn't think of a single thing to say that would keep her out of this situation, barring some claim to a medical issue. But then, he didn't know if such a claim would bring her difficulties down the line.

She licked her lips. "My security." She vaguely gestured Halo's way.

"Is welcome, of course," Koskinen said as he tipped his head back at the sound of the elevator car descending to their floor.

Here, perhaps, was the way out. "Sir, my duty is to stay beside Mrs. Sutton for the duration of her trip to Helsinki. And I am required to remain in uniform. If I cannot enter the sauna, I'm afraid that I cannot allow Mrs. Sutton to enter the sauna."

Mrs. Sutton sent a look of profound gratitude his way.

"Well, it won't be very comfortable for you," Koskinen said as the elevator doors slid open, "but I can't imagine anyone objecting to your requirements." He blocked the door from shutting prematurely with an extended arm and gestured for them to enter, sending Halo a smile. "Of course, you can remain dressed in the sauna as you provide security for Mrs. Sutton."

8

SEPTEMBER THIRD

Haute Nendaz, Switzerland

TAPPING ON HER BLINKER, Deidre turned into the ski chalet's parking area. "What are you thinking about?"

"Deer." Mary looked into the tree line, where the slope was covered with snow. It was hard to fathom the change from two days ago when she'd gone shopping in shorts and flip-flops.

"Okay. Random." Deidre slowed to maneuver into a parking spot.

"These two juvenile deer were eating grass by the electrical lines the other day. On a whim, I called out to them in that kind of high-pitched voice I use for coaxing dogs."

"Yeah?" Deidre threw the gear into park and turned in Mary's direction.

"They took a few steps toward me, then looked at each other and stopped. So I kept doing it." Mary pitched her voice higher. "Hi, babies. Aren't you beautiful? Are you such sweet deer?"

"Yeah?"

Mary was back to her normal speaking voice. "And they kept coming toward me. Tentative. Unsure about what was going on, I thought, Mary, what the heck are you doing? You can't teach deer that humans are safe. So then I told them to go on about their day."

"Interesting. Why were you thinking about that?"

"Just that they acted like stray dogs. I want a dog in my life." Mary looked down to unbuckle. "I *need* a dog in my life." Mary looked up to catch Deidre's gaze. "Instead, I'm out there calling wild deer to my side. Ridiculous."

"What's stopping you? The shelters are full of needy pups. You're already fostering that terrible cat."

"My job." Mary sighed. "I can't figure out *how* to have a dog in my life since I'll be doing twenty-four-hour shifts when I start my job as a flight nurse."

"Maybe you could find someone who wanted to co-parent with you? You could share custody." Deidre put her hand to her chest. "Not me. I'm a goldfish person. That's about all the care I want to give outside of work. But someone. Maybe even a nice single guy kind of someone?"

"Yeah. Maybe." Mary opened her door and climbed out. The air was brisk. And while Mary had layered on the warmest clothes she'd packed. When she put her things in her suitcase, she hadn't contemplated being on a ski slope in summer.

Walking toward the cute little ski lodge on the other side of the lot, Mary thought wistfully that what she'd like to do this morning was sit in the window and quietly sip on a cup of hot cocoa. But she had already convinced herself that this ski trip would be different from her other attempts. And that if she wanted to break down the barriers that made her afraid to build new competencies, she would have to get used to that space of discomfort that came with trying new things.

She'd spent most of the drive up the mountain encouraging herself.

Deidre reached out, swatted Mary's arm, and pointed at a guy parachuting directly over the mountain's peak. As he descended, the women could make out the skis strapped to his feet.

"Wow," Deidre said. "Talk about extreme sports. Can you imagine jumping out of a plane in order to find a patch of virgin snow to ski?"

"Hardcore." Mary shielded her eyes with her hand.

"What happens if you crash and burn on the landing?" Deidre asked. "Who would go up there to save you? How long would it take?"

"Not the rescue crew I'll be working with. That's some high-tech, specialized shit. You'd have to be equally ready to just risk it all to effect a rescue like that." Crashing and burning wasn't really what Mary wanted to talk about right now.

Mary had been on skis twice in her life. Once, she'd gone cross-country skiing as a teen in West Virginia and, within view of the lodge, had moved over a patch of snow that hid a pit. She went straight down so the skis didn't release. The snow had filled over her, and she was effectively buried up to her neck. A group of scouts came over, laid on the ground, and used their mess kit skillets to dig her out. So that was a treat, Mary thought sarcastically. The second time she went skiing was a Christmas gift from Deidre. Deidre loved to ski and wanted Mary to be able to join her. So there she was, taking private lessons from a very patient ski instructor.

Mary hadn't been able to get her legs to cooperate even as the instructor called out instructions and encouragement. She hadn't mastered even the basics required to get on the ski lift—the uphill sidestep and pizza-wedge stop. Finally, Mary had told the guy there was something physically wrong with her, and she needed to head in from the "Potato Patch." The instructor seemed relieved.

Mary went to the clinic and discovered she had double pneumonia.

So, her experiences on the slopes didn't set her up for a delightful day.

This trip was about Deidre, though, so Mary was determined to suck it up and to try very hard not to be a killjoy.

Deidre was glowing with excitement.

In they went. They rented what they could, including (Thankfully!) parkas and goggles. And they bought the things that weren't available for rent—hats and gloves. The guy had looked down at Mary's yoga pants. "You don't have ski pants with you?"

"Sorry." There weren't any for rental or sale there, so it would have to do. She'd be on the baby slope anyway. "I'll be skiing with the toddlers. It should be fine." Mary noticed the guy hadn't said anything skeptical or paternalistic to Deidre. Of course, she looked and acted like the practiced hand she was.

"When you are on the baby slope. Please to keep yourself to the left. This is safer place."

"Left," Mary repeated with a nod. He probably wanted to keep her out of the path of the children who would be on the right. Right?

Deidre decided to skip the expert slope; she was still jet-lagged and had a restless, anxious sleep the previous night. "I'll go down the one marked 'advanced' a few times, then I'll meet you in the restaurant."

Mary moved past the blue slope for people who had a clue what they were doing, walking past the beginner green slope and all the way over to where Mary saw children clumping together. Mary would guess they were a kindergarten-aged group, maybe still preschoolers, who gathered around adults with whistles that they'd toot from time to time. Mary wondered if this was designated only for tots and if she'd be allowed.

In her bulky ski boots, Mary stomped up and looked over the area. "Very potato-patchy," Mary said as she laid the skis on the ground. "Basically flat." She poked her sticks into the ground to balance herself as she clipped her boots into the skis. "Nice and easy. It's okay to take baby steps next to the babies. It's okay to be a beginner," she coaxed herself as she moved forward. "Okay, bit more of a slope than it looked. Going a bit faster than I'm comfortable with." She was just talking to herself like she'd do with her boys when they were trying something new. "It's okay to suck. Just learn one takeaway today. One thing that will inform you the next time you try."

And that was when Mary—arms windmilling through the air for balance—slicked right past the trees on her left where she had tried to dutifully follow the shop person's counsel.

And then she was on her hip, desperately digging into the slick white surface, watching the three-year-olds with their teddy bear-eared hats swish joyfully past down the highest, longest slope that Mary had ever seen.

The toddlers were laughing at her.

Laughing.

Mary most certainly didn't belong on this slope. What was she thinking signing up for skiing on a glacier in summer? If Mary could get off this darned mountain with only a broken ego, she was going to take it as a win.

She'd gotten herself to a stop, braced against her poles that dug into the crust of glittering snow. Overheated from the exertion, Mary melted the ice beneath her, and she was sure that her thigh and butt cheek were at risk of frostbite. She couldn't feel her fingers.

How am I going to save myself here? Mary wondered as

she scanned for a solution. Looking backward, she focused on the last tree she'd passed. If she could somehow get up to it, she could move from tree to tree back off this mountain.

Just head to the restaurant.

Just get that pot of hot cocoa and nurse her wounded pride.

But with a shriek, she was slipping again, skidding toward the right side of the mountain. The side that the shopkeeper said was the dangerous side.

The babies were swishing and swooshing as they evaded her almost parallel path from one side of the ski trail to the other. She had no business being on this slope. No business being covered in ice and snow at the end of the freaking summer.

Wet and cold, bruised and cut, Mary hit stretches of sheer abandon where she just let herself hip slide without any measure of dignity. Into this, Mary peppered moments of terror that had her flailing her limbs with the attached skis. She was desperate for control as she panicked in the face of the inevitability of gravity when there was a dearth of anything, even vaguely resembling friction, to slow her descent.

All the while, there was happy laughter and calling back and forth between the toddlers—"Weee! Isn't this fun?" their giggles implied.

It seemed like taunting. "It feels cruel, to be honest," she grumbled. And now that the kiddos were out of sight, Mary raised a fist. "Screw you. Screw you all," she yelled, angry at her pain and the cold, wondering if maybe she had chipped the bone in her elbow and would need a cast. She felt like an old man yelling at the kids to get off his lawn. Only, in retrospect, maybe she was on theirs.

Well, cussing made her feel a little better.

Inappropriate, but better.

That and just giving up.

There was a certain peace to lying back—her legs spread eagle, her skis a tangle—letting herself body surf the damned mountain.

Tucking her chin, Mary could see that she was fast approaching the shed that was part of the ski lift system. Why things were set up catawampus like this with the lodge at the top and the lift taking the skiers from bottom at the end of a run instead of to the top at the beginning probably had to do with the geography and rock structures. Mary didn't care. She just wanted to hand in her equipment and find a corner to lick her wounds.

Using her abs to get her torso upright again, Mary mumbled, "All hail to whoever invented Pilates."

The last bit was sheer ice, and Mary was picking up speed and wasn't sure what to do about it other than to lift her poles in the air to get big and yell, "Incoming!" to protect the innocent bystanders.:

Some laughing guy stood wide-legged in front of her and stuck out his hands at the last moment, pressing back on her shoulders and bringing her to a stop.

Mary was panting. She did it. She was down the darned slope. "*Merci*," she mustered.

"American, right?" he asked in a nearly perfect U.S. accent.

He could tell that from my shitty ski performance? Mary nodded in stunned and exhausted defeat. "How did you know?"

"Bunch of clues. Your clothes. Your technique." He grinned. "Mostly the cuss words that were echoing down from the slope."

"Ah." She looked around at the children gathering in what looked like school groups with teachers counting heads. "Sorry, kids." Mary accepted the hand which was extended out to her. Wincing, she pressed into her heels and got herself upright. "Thank you." She looked toward the T-bar lift that was taking people up. Coffee was at the top of the mountain, and that contraption was going to take her there. She angled her skis in that direction.

"Ho, there. Wait just a moment. The dogs are coming."

Dogs ...

For the first time, Mary really looked at the guy and realized he was wearing a red rescue coat. He must be like a lifeguard for the kiddie pool. Here to help out if one of the toddlers took a tumble.

No kid took a tumble. Not a single child. Not anywhere along the trail.

Mary pulled the goggles onto her forehead to see the guy clearly, without all the scratches she'd put into the lenses. She realized she would have to pay for them and briefly wondered how much that would cost her. "Dogs?"

"The dog sled team is harnessed up. They'll be here in a minute to get you to the lodge. We have a first aid station with a nurse to look you over there."

"Sled." Mary was a nurse. So first, she could probably check herself over.

Second, since Mary had decided that she wanted a little less hospital in her nursing life and a little more challenge, so she'd been training for—and had just passed her test to become—a flight nurse on a medivac copter.

What she heard when Red Coat said "sled" was "basket."

Here was the thing about going into a basket: you lay on your back on the hard surface, and you're strapped in. Not a little strapped in, a lot strapped in. Blocks go around the head, a strap over the forehead, and spider webbing holds you down. This method of attaching a person to a basket that's being lifted from the ground up into the helicopter is life-saving. Mary had seen the rotor wash spin a basket around and around so fast that it lost form like a children's top. And, had that patient not been completely secured, they would have been ejected, catapulted out into the air, and fallen to their death.

Surely, the rescue team would perform the exact same protocol to get her up the mountain. If she came unattached, she'd slide with absolutely zero capacity to protect herself or stop. She could imagine gliding straight for the cliff's edge or into a crevasse and tipping in. The last thing that would be seen on those go-pros pointing her way was the bottom of the sled and the sound of her last long-held scream as she vanished into oblivion.

She imagined her son talking to a friend:

"How is your mom doing?"

"Ah, man! She died."

"Wait, what? She died? How did that happen?"

"She went to the dogs."

"I'm not waiting on dogs. That would be a no." Mary carefully sidestepped toward the lift. She wanted to unclip the skis, but the ice was pretty much caked and solidified. And then the babies were riding up with their skis on the ground. There was probably a reason. She'd just keep the skis on a bit longer.

"You sure? It looks like you got pretty banged up on the mountain. I watched you through the binoculars to track if we needed to send search and rescue when you headed in the wrong direction."

"The right side of the mountain."

"Is more dangerous, yeah. I was pretty worried when you disappeared, but you got yourself back on the slope."

"*You* were worried? You should have heard what was going on in my head," she muttered, then realized that he was being kind, and she stopped with the sarcasm, reaching out a hand as if to soothe. "I appreciate that you focused on me, hoping to keep me safe. I appreciate you. This whining and my stink face I'm making are because I'm wet. I'm cold. I'm a little bruised, body and spirit—ego. And I'm trying to make my way back to the top. Quickly. And so waiting for the dogs will take longer. You understand. Thanks, though."

"Stink face," he repeated as if tying it on for size or maybe to see if, by saying it aloud, the meaning might become understandable.

Mary kept side-stepping toward the lift. "Can you call off the dogs, please?"

The guy lifted his radio toward his mouth and then dropped his arm again. "How about we just keep them en route until I see you're up at the lodge." He touched the binoculars dangling from the cord around his neck.

Mary huffed out the oxygen and thought, yeah, she'd make that same call if it were her. But that didn't mean she liked it. She joined the line behind a class of six-year-olds rattling off their French. Sure, they spoke it as their first language here, but after struggling with it in high school, these kids sounded like geniuses to Mary.

And here was her turn.

She moved over to the T bar and balanced her skis. Turning, she gave Red Coat a thumbs up, then grasped the bar as a man came to the other side for balance. When the lift moved forward, Mary gratefully sat down. And it was with a split second's awareness that this wasn't like a bench lift. This was on an elastic, probably meant to adjust under the bum and push the skier up the hill.

All of that came fully formed into her head as she let out a scream, and she went down in a tumble of limbs and skis along with the man from the other side.

Down, down, down they fell.

Mary lay there wondering how she could get up the second slope with her skis still attached. When she examined them, she saw she had knocked the ice off the latches.

Tiny win.

She'd take it.

Off came the skis.

And up, up, she climbed. The only way she could get the skis up with her was to pile both of them and her ski poles into a mound and push them in front of her as she crawled up on her knees inch by crappy inch.

The man who fell with her was furiously yelling in a language that Mary, thankfully, didn't understand. Not yelling at the situation. Yelling at her. Spittle in the wind, yelling.

This wasn't fun.

Arriving at the top, the angry guy was already on his way up the lift. Mary figured he was probably one of the teachers, or he wouldn't have been on the baby hill. Surely, that was going to make things awkward for him in front of his class. But he'd only fallen half as far as Mary had and had crawled up super-fast, so he was probably within smelling distance of food by now.

Mary was trembling and knew that she was becoming hypothermic. She was wet and exhausted, with no breakfast calories to sustain her. Little in the way of oxygen up this high in the sky, and no sleep, yeah none of this was—Mary looked up.

"Are you injured?" Here came the ski savior with the radio and binoculars.

He came to a perfect swirling stop beside her. Now, Mary was just irritated. What a showoff.

"I have hand warmers and a mylar blanket. Let's get you stopped and wrapped up." He pointed at the sky. "You can hear them. The dogs are nearly here. Not a long wait at all."

She could indeed hear what sounded like a large team of very enthusiastic dogs off in the distance. And if Mary thought that a troop of scouts shoveling her out with their tin bowls was awful, this was the stuff of nightmares. Mary redoubled her efforts.

"Madame, I don't think you're aware of your situation. You're dressed for yoga. You've been wet for a long time, and you are—"

"Hypothermic, yeah, yeah. I know what's going on. I know I'm almost up to the shed and the lift."

"Madame, you need someone to go up on the other side of you on the lift, and I can't imagine anyone would be willing to partner with you."

That was fair. "Okay, well, we'll cross that bridge when we get to it."

Red Coat scowled and shook his head. "There are no bridges anywhere near here."

"It's a phrase. It's something people in America say. It means … never mind. Just. Whew! Look, I made it." She stood up, sinking the poles into the snow and shoving her boots back in the ski clips.

The helmet video cameras were still aimed her way, and Mary pulled the scratched-to-hell goggles over her face to obscure her identity. Mary called out, "Hey, which one of you wants to ride up the mountain on this T bar with me?"

There was general jostling and some elbow pokes.

By the sound of their barks, the dogs would be here in a few more strides.

She was going to *kill* Deidre. First, she'd wait to see where the star-reading woman was sending her. It was possible that Mary could just leave the task to the Borneo headhunters. Then Mary wouldn't need to deal with a body.

Today, Mary planned to be at her Norfolk home, getting her garden ready for winter. And instead, she was over here in Switzerland doing her darndest to push up the daisies.

Some kid about her sons' age slid forward, big grin on his

face, his chin-length curls a tangle under his beanie. "I'll go." He had the look in his eye like those dudes on YouTube got just before they ran and leaped into the air, strapped to a bungee cord.

Great, she was this kid's death-defying adrenaline rush.

9

PITCHING FORWARD AT HER HIPS, MARY GRIPPED THE CENTER OF the T bar with her right hand and jabbed her ski poles into the icy snow with the left. She propelled herself forward and away from the contraption that had (this second go-round) pushed her all the way to the top of the glacier.

When she focused on ski-boy to thank him for his kindness, he sent her a look that Mary read as disappointment.

With his helmet cam showing a green recording light, maybe he'd been hoping to post a video that went viral.

Was that ungenerous?

It wasn't like he'd tried to sabotage her or anything. The whole way up, he'd been coaching her. "Skis parallel. Focus on your breath. *Oui, Madame*. You're doing very nice job."

And as she listened and responded with appreciation, she was also thinking that this young man was a creature of the snow. There was no way this kid had gone down the children's slope because he hadn't graduated past that level of accomplishment. Mary remembered the number of adults and their phones trained on her when she crawled up from the first T-bar mistake; that group wasn't the same little school kid groups and their carers that she'd fallen beside as they moved happily down the Alp. Mary concluded that she was the subject of mountain-side gossip, and she'd pulled in a group of the curious. She'd been the accident on the side of the road that tugged attention and caused traffic congestion.

Great. Just great.

"What's your name?" The guy who had helped her through that balancing act stood there looking expectant as if the curtain were about to rise on the next scene in Mary's drama, but she was done. She just wanted a damned cup of coffee.

Bending to release her skis, then lifting them up to hug them to her side. Mary said, "Me? I'm Joan Crawford." She pulled up an actress's name too historical for a kid his age to know.

"Good to meet you. I'm Fabio. I'm from Ticino." He extended his arm as if he could point out his house.

Of course, *Fabio.* She had no idea where Ticino could possibly be. "Yeah? Well, thanks for being brave enough to help me to the top. Hope your day goes great." She turned toward the chalet and walked away.

Wrestling her skis through the door, Mary trudged to the rental guy to hand in her equipment.

"You enjoyed?" he asked, accepting the apparatus and looking it over for damage.

"Beautiful country," Mary said to the kid with the wide grin. Yeah, he knew. Wise ass. "I'll go ahead and buy the goggles."

He nodded and tapped the register. "You want to keep them as souvenir?" He held them up. "Or I just throw in trash?"

"Trash." Mary didn't want to remember this episode. "How do I get to the food?"

Mary followed the point of his finger, flinging a "*Merci*!" over her shoulder as she tried to walk into the restaurant with as much dignity as her abused body could muster.

Deidre sat in the warm glow of light at the window.

A pot of coffee with two mugs was on the table.

"There you are." Deidre pulled the napkin from the table and put it on her lap. "I ordered breakfast. You're going to like it." She lifted the mug to her lips for a sip. "Coffee's good."

Mary eased her way into the chair, blowing the pain out with her breath.

Deidre said, "I do black diamonds in West Virginia, and I thought, hey, I'm a little rusty." She poured coffee into Mary's mug, leaving enough room for cream, then pushed it over to her. "Since I haven't skied since last year, I decided to take the easier slope."

Mary wasn't sure she had the strength to lift the heavy-looking ceramic to her lips. Maybe she could just duck her head and slurp.

"Girl!" Deidre pushed the little pitcher of thick cream over to her, followed by the bowl of brown sugar crystals. "I thought I might not escape with my life." She shook her head. "I mean, up on the black diamond, I saw that the skiers wore ski pants and coats. So I figured I'd head to the slope where they weren't afraid of falling and breaking a nail, you know what I mean? So I went to the blue slope."

Mary stared vacantly at her. The day had been stunning. And her senses decided to take a nap.

"These chicklets in their Brazilian bikinis with the matching ski boots, working on their tans from the sun reflecting off the ice." She put her hands on her cheeks, pressing in to make a fish face, then reached out to wrap her hands around the warmth of her mug. "I kid you not. There were patches of ice, not even any bumps to slow me down. It was like they'd just brought out the machine on the hockey rink and polished it all up. The speeds I reached, Mary, the wind caught at my lips and flapped my cheeks like I was on a speed boat. I was so jealous that you were on the bunny slope having a gentle ride."

"Yeah."

Deidre tipped her head, trying to catch Mary's gaze. "You okay?"

She unwrapped her cutlery from the napkin to find a spoon for the sugar. "Turns out I know a bit of French."

"Ooh La La." Deidre lifted a shoulder to look coquettishly at her friend. "You found a hunk?"

"Mmmm. Crevasse."

"Crevasse?" Deidre pulled her brow together. "Like a tour of some kind?"

"Yeah, I took that tour. I took it right off the ski path, down a slickery ice patch, and stopped myself by grabbing hold of the post. As I dangled there, panting for breath, I had time to read the signage."

"What did it say?" Deidre asked.

"It said: This is what you get for being spontaneous and not doing due diligence."

"An actual crevasse, then. That would be a bad way to go."

"Yah think?" Mary leaned back so the server could put a plate laden with sausages, bread, fruit, and cheese in front of her. It smelled so good. Mary was ravenous.

"Glad you didn't die." Deidre picked up a wedge of cheese from Mary's plate, took a bite, and then pushed back in her chair while the server placed a steaming bowl down for her. "Merci," she told the server. "*L'addition, s'il vous plait,*" putting her credit card on the table to pay the bill before focusing back on Mary. "Listen, we need to eat and get back to the car. I put the address into the GPS, and if we eat and go, I have just enough time to get to Mrs. V.'s. We can change our clothes in the bathroom and just head on."

As Mary's muscles stiffened from today's survival exertion.

She wasn't so sure she'd be able to bend down enough to peel off her damp pants.

~

WHEELS CRUNCHING over the gravel drive, Deidre spun the wheel around the horseshoe, then slowed to park just beyond the sidewalk leading to the front door.

She hadn't said a word on the way. Very un-Deidre-like.

Climbing painfully out, Mary took in the typical chateau-designed home. The landscape had a stateliness that made Mary think this place was probably a hundred years old or so. It was on the large side of what Mary had seen on their drive from the ski debacle to here.

She drew a deep breath fragrant with lemon thyme, fresh and welcoming. A sweet garden, visible from where they parked, looked like a lovely place to gather with friends and enjoy laughter and ease. Yeah, Mary felt she might be able to relax in a place like this. She'd see if she couldn't replicate this feeling in the little garden of her Norfolk bungalow. Maybe Mrs. V. would allow her to take photographs later so she could figure out what plants created that herbal bouquet that made Mary want to close her eyes and dream.

As the two strolled up the sidewalk, the door opened to a woman in a long flowing top and leggings, both in the same sapphire raw silk, that managed to look both comfortable and professional. Her silver hair was scraped back into a bun at the nape of her neck. Smiling a welcome, she dipped her head and gestured toward the interior. "I will escort you back in just a moment," she told Deidre as the group walked into a large foyer and then off to the right to a receiving room. "Mrs. V. is finishing her meditation, centering herself in preparation for your appointment." The woman sent a glance toward Mary, held her eye for a long moment, and gave her a nod as if in recognition. That look was pregnant with … *something*.

Mary wasn't sure what to make of that silent exchange.

Deidre and Mary lowered themselves side by side onto the brown leather couch. Deidre reached out ice-cold fingers to grip Mary's hand in both of hers.

Nerves.

The room was set up, though, to assuage client anxiety. Rich in textures and subtle patterns, the colors gave the space depth and interest. It was lovely, Mary thought. She wouldn't mind sitting on the couch waiting for Deidre, thumbing through the art books stacked on the coffee table, or fiddling with one of the wooden puzzles that filled a pottery bowl.

Deidre jackhammered her heel, making the sofa shake.

Well, nerves were to be expected. Deidre *was* asking for the destination that would change her life. And life changes came with cost-benefit ratios. What if she had made the effort to come here, paid this—surely outlandish amount of money—and went to the required location, but nothing changed at all?

That would be its own kind of catastrophe, having hopes and wishes dashed.

It was one thing to wish for a unicorn and blow out the candles in one puff on an eight-year-old's birthday cake. Everyone knew that was for funzies.

In Mary's mind, this was the adult form of that very act. And this, whatever *this* was to Deidre, seemed like her friend had sucked in a lung full of air and was just looking for a direction to blow her wish.

Knowing that talking helped to allay her friend's anxieties, Mary asked, "You were telling me that at forty—my birthday tomorrow—I'd wake up with a new perspective on life. Now that you're newly fifty-three. Looking back, is there a big leap at that decade, too?"

Deidre turned unblinking eyes toward Mary. "Yeah, it's called menopause."

"Come on," Mary pressed. "Tell me something that's changed for you recently." Hopefully, Deidre could equate change with something besides magical destination-setting star charts.

"Teacups." Deidre sent a glance toward the door that the helper had gone through.

"All right."

Deidre pulled her glance back to Mary. "Sorry, I'm a little nervous. I don't want her to tell me to go to the South Pole on my birthday. I hear the penguins are cute but smell horrible." She skated a hand out. "Listen, at this point, I'm exhausted from trying to climb out of my rut. If a trip to chat with a polar bear will spring me forward, I'll do it. Just, if she could tell me that I need to be in Tahiti, that might be nicer, you know?"

Did Mary feel like she was in the same kind of rut as Deidre?

She held still to see how that fit.

No, Mary thought, she was a load of laundry, agitated then wrung out—that was how she'd describe the great uncoupling of herself from a nuclear family—her ex-husband by choice, her children by biological design. And now, through perseverance and effort, she'd moved herself to the dryer. Mary figured it was for a matter of time that she'd tumble around. Then, she'd come out of that stage, too. Hopefully, still warm and wrinkle-free.

That metaphor tickled the corners of Mary's lips.

"I'm listening. Tell me about your new-found teacup considerations." Mary extracted her fingers from the vice of Deidre's grip, flipping her hand to rub warmth into her friend's hands.

"It used to be that I could care less what I drank my hot

drinks out of unless it was styrene or paper cups. I hate how those ruin the flavor, and you get that weird lip feel." Deidre rolled her lips in.

"I'm with you on that one."

"But now," Deidre said, "I have certain mugs I want to drink my coffee from in the morning, others for tea. Coffee mugs are taller to hold more. Their circumference is large enough that I can wrap my hands all the way around them without overlapping my fingers, thick enough to feel substantial, thin enough that my lips fit correctly. Smooth enough that I don't think about the texture and can focus on the flavor of the coffee. I'm happiest when there's a picture of my son and his friends to keep me company."

"Wow." Mary held her brows high. "That's specific."

"Tea, I like my cups to be smaller, so the flavor is intense when I dunk a bag. I like a narrow bottom and a wide top. I want the sides to be thick enough and heavy enough not to topple if I brush it by accident. The wide top cools the drink, and I can tuck my face down and breathe in the herbal steam. That's pleasant." She ran her palms down her thighs and spoke to the highly-polished door as if it was part of their conversation. "I like muted colors—sages and earth browns. Colors that don't ask me to divide my attention with the things outside the window. In the stillness of taking a sip, I notice small things that change from day to day, in the color of the leaves or the shape of the clouds. I think in my fifties, I've learned to sit still and pay attention to the small things, the tiny pleasures."

"You're waxing poetic." Mary laughed, and it sounded a little nervous. Yeah, Deidre didn't normally talk like this. Mary wondered if there was something more to this visit than Deidre had told her, so she'd just take the direct approach. "Is there something you've been keeping from me?"

Deidre dragged her gaze back to meet her friends. "I've

been so busy living life that I have the strange feeling that I haven't been living life at all. My doctor says anxiety and depression are part of menopause. Maybe that's what I'm feeling. But I *need* this to work. I need a catalyst to get me headed in a better direction. You know?"

No, Mary didn't know. She was just trying to keep her own head up as she felt like she'd been in that washing machine caught in the whirlpool circling the drain. Mary thought she'd be fine. She just needed some time. But Mary got while she and Deidre were at the same points in their lives —divorced empty-nesters—Mary was still, for today anyway, in her thirties, and that had to make a difference in perspective.

The door opened to a woman wearing a traditional Indian outfit, a choli cropped top under a vibrant peacock green sari.

"You are Deidre," she said with a British accent.

"I am." Deidre stood.

"How do you do? I am Mrs. V." She turned her attention to Mary. "And this is the friend I told you to bring?"

Deidre also turned to Mary, her brows drawing in. "She is."

"I will work with Deidre first and with you after," she offered a regal nod.

"Oh, no, I don't have an appointment." How much had Deidre spent on this woman? Was she digging for another dupe?

The woman seemed to hear Mary's thoughts and, with a slow smile and gentle chuckle, said, "None of that is a concern. I will chart Deidre's path forward. Then you and I will speak."

Yeah, this woman didn't seem like someone looking for a sucker.

Mrs. V. turned and walked back through the door, leaving it wide.

Deidre sent Mary a look that said she had no idea what was

going on. With a downturned mouth and a lifted brow, she seemed to ask, "What should I do? Follow her?"

Mary made a shooing motion with her hands. Watching her friend disappear down the hallway, Mary tipped her head up, whispering her prayer. "Please make this good for her."

10

SEPTEMBER THIRD

An Estonian Bog

"DO NOT WALK in that little gutter," Marilin said with a smile that took the bite out of her words. "It is ant highway. You see?" With the Suttons on their plane, and the close protection stint complete, Panther Force was now learning about this new ecosystem they'd need to navigate with their client on their upcoming corporate trip to Tallinn.

The naturalist, taking the group on the same hike she'd been hired to provide for the executive retreat, was an affable woman with a no-nonsense presence that immediately put Halo at ease. She seemed completely comfortable with her surroundings as she made her way from the site where they had parked, through the woods, toward the bog. A series of vastly different ecosystems in an hour-long walk.

Average height for a woman, the team towered over her. And yet, she showed no signs of intimidation. As a matter of fact, she seemed amused by their group of four—Titus, Thorn, Gage, and him.

Last minute, Honey had switched directions, flying to some undisclosed location to negotiate the release of an Iniquus client being held hostage. Margot was fighting off Covid in Helsinki, and Nutsbe would be coming in tomorrow, bringing Max with him.

Apparently, Maxi had taken to using the dunny straight off. And he must have learned his lesson on the Virginia mountainside because he aced the snake aversion training.

Knowing Max would be getting in tomorrow morning, Halo had already talked to Titus about coming back on this trail and out into the bog on his own with his K9. With Titus's permission, Halo wanted to turn off his shirt's satellite connection to test how well he could rely on the data pack he carried. A truism that Halo lived by was the saying, "Never trust a gun you haven't fired yourself." And Halo applied that dictum to all equipment that went with him into life-and-limb-threatening circumstances. *All equipment*, he amended since he never knew what situations would present and how each and every item could help or hinder.

Equally as important, Halo needed to know how Max did in a bog. Out on a hike with the client was not the time to introduce his K9 to an untested landscape. The Virginia search had hammered that lesson home. Yes, Max was aces in the mountains in New South Wales. That didn't mean that all mountains had the same set of challenges.

Gage stepped to the side of the four-inch-wide channel as the team watched the parade of ants moving along. "Wow."

"Yes, very wow," Marilin agreed, swiping her fingers through her short blond hair. "This is a good place to stop and look around. First thing—and important thing—you see this tree? This is the tallest tree in the woods. We are about to step into an area where it is impossible to have a known and consistent path. The bog changes with the rains. So, if you get lost and need to return to the trail, look for this grandfather tree, which will be your signpost. This is especially important if there is lightning."

"Don't get near the tree," Gage said.

"This is true." Marilin put her hand on the craggy trunk, and it seemed to Halo that the gesture was meant as a hello to an old friend. "Don't stand under this tree in a lightning storm. But there is more to this. So, here we have two kinds of rain. One is mushroom rain."

"What is that?" Thorn asked.

She rubbed her thumb over the pads of her fingers and then lifted her palm. She must not have the word. Or maybe "mushroom rain" was the word. It just wasn't a term that Halo was familiar with. From the gesture, he read it to be a misting kind of rain.

"This kind of rain is safe," she said. "The time that you need to move and move fast is if there is lightning when you are on the bog. It is important to get to the tree line as quickly as possible. Aim for this grandfather tree so you can find the trail." She patted the trunk.

"Why?" Titus asked. "Is it a question of exposure?"

"When lightning strikes, the rain that follows is very heavy," Marilin explained. "You will lose sight of grandfather. You will even lose sight of the woods."

Having just been through a torrential rain with three-foot visibility, Halo imagined his time getting Mrs. Haze down that mountain in the make-do rain sack would be about a hundred times easier than getting a group of executives back to the safety of their vans from a bog.

"And most dangerous," Marilin continued, "the bog will fill not only with the rain but the water that runs down the hills into that low-lying area. You will—how they say in English—get bogged down. You will not be able to get out or even know which direction to take, trying for safety."

"Oh," Gage said.

"Not only this, but more. There are the winds. The winds become aggressive. There are many trees in the woods that stand but are not alive. The strength of the wind will make them fall. With the sound of roaring in your ears, you will not hear them coming down until they are on top of you. The wind is very strong. Very dangerous. Very intense."

"The client will be out here in three weeks," Titus said, "at the end of September. Our research says that September and October aren't in your rainy season."

"Yes, historically, this is true." Marilin started forward again. "I say this is a very good time to be here for the weather. Our rain season—the time when we expect the lightning rain—has been for most of my lifetime in June and July. Our heaviest rains come in November. But as things change with our climate, we no longer depend on this. Last year, in September, we had several lightning storms. Very bad. Trees in the road. Emergency vehicles cannot pass. Bad."

"What about in the city? How do they do in the rain?"

"Tallinn?" Marilin shook her head. "Is not good in the rain. It is an ancient city not built for today. The roads become impassable. When it rains, stay in your chair with book, relax. It will pass. But when we are out here on bog, I will watch the sky and give warning to go back. When I say this, we act. We don't argue."

"Yes, ma'am," Titus said.

"Go back to ants." Marilin pointed. "See this pile of dirt that comes to my waist just below us on the hill?" She didn't stop for an answer. "This is anthill."

"Anthill?" Thorn asked. "It's over three feet—a meter tall."

"Yes, millions of ants." They stopped. "Bears love to eat the larva. Sometimes, I come into woods and find anthill toppled over from bears having a feast. You see beside your foot?" she asked Titus.

Halo followed her gaze. "Bear scat," he said. They didn't hand out pepper spray at the beginning of this hike like they had done on the Mrs. Haze rescue. Once home from that mission, Halo had done some research into bears. And though, the Virginia black bears were less fierce than grizzlies, they could still be ferocious and deadly. And the bears he'd seen in the movies were still the visual that came up for him. "So the bears, if we see them out here, we just get big and make a lot of noise?" Those were the instructions listed on the many state and national park websites he'd read through.

Marilin blinked at him for a moment, obviously trying to put his words into context. "Make noise? No." She shook her head. "We are in bears' home. We are guests. If we see bear, we slowly and respectfully back away while it goes on about its business." Her brow creased. "You yell at bears where you come from?"

"There are no bears where I come from." He pointed toward the scat. "I just … I've seen their piles before in America."

"Okay. Well good that we stop here. I show you." She leaned down with a sharp knife in her hand. When she stood, she had a large mushroom in her fingers. "These are chanterelle mushrooms." Deftly, she sliced off a portion of the stem, saying, "Yes, this one is good. You should taste it." She handed a piece first to Titus, then worked her way around to the other team members. "People come from all over to go into the Estonian bogs at this time of year for hunting mushrooms. Russians come. You see their cars parked along the road of the forests."

"Russians?" Titus bladed his hands onto his hips. "Do they

ever create issues in the bogs? Anything my team needs to be aware of?"

"No." She pointed beside him. "Right now, your team needs to be aware of this mushroom."

There, beside a bush, was a little cluster of red mushrooms with white spots that Halo had seen in almost every child's fairytale illustration. His gran would call the outcropping charming and turn them into a watercolor.

As the men turned and formed a semi-circle, Marilin said, "This is called 'fly agaric mushrooms' or 'Amanita muscaria.' These are how they say, 'magic mushrooms.' They contain psilocybin and psilocin that works as a hallucinogenic."

"Is it illegal here?" Thorn asked.

"To have it in your pocket, yes. To try to sell, yes. If someone picked it up and ate it in bog?" She shrugged. Then added emphatically. "Don't pick it up and eat it in bog."

"Why? What would happen?" Halo asked.

"Depends. Each mushroom has a different, how you say? Different toxicity. So dangers depend on how specific mushroom grew. Depends on person's body and mind. Depends on quantity." She adjusted the straps of her pack. "I don't touch them. I don't want to rub my eyes or pick a berry with those fingers and accidentally ingest it. Any of it. So why? Many things. It makes you feel like you are in a dream. Maybe like you leave your body. Sometimes, people think they can see clearly for the first time in their lives. Sometimes, the five senses are jumbled up. People smell music. They hear colors. Sometimes, their vision gets blurry to be effectively blind for a time. Watery nose. Dripping eyes. Wet, you know? Lots of sweat and too much saliva in the mouth. Some Estonians use this for medicine. But you have to be knowledgeable, learning how to do it right way from your grandmother. You don't wish to make mistake." Her blue eyes twinkled with amusement.

"You know, they think this is where Santa Claus story comes from. The people eats the mushroom and sees the flying reindeer." She bent again to cut the stems on the other chanterelle mushrooms at her feet and put them in the basket, dangling from her left elbow. She stopped and closed her eyes, breathing in deeply. "You smell that? A little bit lemony?"

The team stopped and sniffed.

"Yes, this is Labrador tea smell. It is a plant that is all over. It is hallucinogenic also. It is the reason many come out to the bog. It makes you feel good, relaxed. You lose sense of time. So make sure you have a watch. Maybe set an alarm. Time drifts when you smell this plant."

"Is it dangerous, too?" Thorn asked.

"Sure, it's like most things, right? For one person is fine. If you have an allergy, this is not fine." She pointed. "See there? More fly agaric. Little bit different coloring."

"Huh." Thorn put his hands on his hips. "Let's say one of our group read up on the possibility of finding the fly agaric mushroom out here in the bog and sampled it, how long would it be effective in their system? Would they need medical care?"

"It could be very bad, you know?" Marilin said. "The person would have to be very sure that they are eating the right mushroom. If they make a mistake?" She shrugged. "They could die. There is deadliest of mushrooms out here. All over." She turned and pointed at a mushroom that Halo couldn't tell was any different from the mushroom he'd just tasted.

"The nightshade. You hear this in the news?" Marilin asked. "There was a woman in Australia yesterday convicted of three counts of murder and two counts of attempted murder. She made a beef Wellington that she served to her guests, and it was made with the nightshade mushroom."

"In Australia?" Halo asked. "Yeah, we have nightshade mushrooms in the wet areas. We have to watch that our dogs don't get into them," Halo said, thinking with nightshade and fly agaric, he'd need to keep Max on a tight lead. The rattlesnake was scary enough. But then there was antivenom. Halo could do nothing to protect Max from poisonous mushrooms other than keep control of his nose.

Titus caught Marilin's gaze. "And we just ate …"

"Chanterelle. I am very good at identifying them. I collect them for my friend who has a restaurant. Nobody gets sick. No police knock on my door."

"When we have the tour go out, perhaps point out the mushrooms and label them, but let's not have them taste-testing them," Titus said.

"Are you sure?" Marilin asked as she started down a path not readily visible. "I will only hand out safe mushrooms."

"Most Americans get their mushrooms from the store," Titus explained. "They won't necessarily be aware of the subtle differences that you see. If you handed them one and another looked similar, I could see someone from my culture picking it up and putting it in their mouth."

Marilin looked bemused. "We just tell them to leave the red mushrooms alone."

"All of the mushrooms," Titus said.

"Okay. Well, over there, you see? Those are wild raspberries. Will you allow the people to eat those?

11

September Third
Haute Nendaz, Switzerland

While she sat waiting for Deidre, Mary had been musing over the puzzle that asked the player to remove the ring from the whole. She had no clue how one would go about solving this enigma short of taking a blow torch to the game. When the door swung open, Mary quickly dumped the puzzle back in the bowl and pulled her hands back like a child who had broken a don't touch rule.

It was a strange reaction, but this had been a strange forty-eight hours. Mary was bruised, achy, sore, and jet-lagged. And this hocus-pocus stuff—even though nothing so far seemed made for tourists and crystal-clutchers—had Mary out of her element.

The helper lady who had answered the door when Mary and Deidre first arrived moved into the sitting area. The woman had the feel of someone who had done yoga all their life—centered and balanced, unfazed by someone else's thoughts or prejudices about how she chose to spend her time.

It was a cultural difference, Mary reminded herself. She'd seen it firsthand. There were a number of nursing students and nurses from India that Mary met along the way who thought having one's charts done was banal. Just part of a decision-making process. Granted, they usually sent the inquiry via a website and got the answer back. Mary had never heard of someone having to travel halfway around the world. Okay, not halfway; that was an exaggeration, but still.

The helper smiled at Mary as if she could hear Mary's inner monologue and found it amusing. She scooped her hand in a follow me, and said, "If you would please come with me, your friend is just concluding."

Mary glanced at the clock and was surprised to find that nearly two hours had gone by. It had felt like ten, maybe fifteen minutes. "Oh," she said. "You know that I don't have an appointment, right?"

"Yes, your friend Deidre was asked to bring you."

"Bring me? Me specifically?"

Helper lady smiled and turned to walk down the hall.

Mary scrambled around the table to follow.

Emerging from an ornately carved door, Deidre clicked it gently shut behind her.

As they came toward each other, they grasped hands. Mary leaned in, "Weird?"

"Interesting." Deidre frowned. "A decision to be made."

"Borneo?"

"Career came up Fairbanks, Alaska." Deidre's eyes looked troubled.

"That's the traveling nurse's program." Mary squeezed her friend's hands harder. "That's exactly where they wanted to send you in the summer if you took the fall rotation to Mississippi."

"Yeah, I know. Uncanny, right?"

"I don't know," Mary whispered. "Did you mention it to anyone? Did you post about it on social media?"

"And have our bosses know I'm looking for another job? Heck no. You and my cat, but Socks promised not to meow it to anyone."

"Okay." Mary released their grip to brush a hand down her arm. "Goosebumps."

"Please." The helper lady looked at Mary and gestured into the room, indicating Mary should go in.

Deidre leaned in to whisper. "We'll talk about it later." Then, back in normal conversational tone, she added. "I'm going to walk in the garden and think. If I'm not back in the sitting room, that's where you'll find me."

Mary nodded and then moved into the office. Could be a therapist's office or a lawyer's. It was professional, with a large desk that Mrs. V. sat behind. There were scrolls of charts in front of her.

"I'm not sure why I'm in here," Mary said as the door clicked closed behind her. She stood wary and uncomfortable on the oriental carpeting. "I'm between jobs and not getting a paycheck, so funds are tight. I can't afford," Mary looked around the sedate luxury of the room, "this."

Mrs. V. scratched her nose. "Yes, well." She extended her hand toward a chair. "Please sit."

Mary perched on the edge, lacing her fingers in her lap.

"It's in the stars." Mrs. V. smiled a stress-free smile, and Mary wondered what it felt like to be like that, like a brook babbling along, swerving out of the way of rock and obstruction, easy. Mary hadn't felt easy in her skin since she peed on her at-home pregnancy test back in her teens.

"I was looking at my own chart a few days ago," she swept her hand over her desk where the rolls of parchment formed a pyramid. "And it was so curious. I saw that a client who was to come this week had died." She leaned back, folding her hands beneath her bosom. "Within moments of reading that, the phone rang. It was a client's daughter saying that her mother passed away unexpectedly. She was asking if I would reimburse her mother's payment as they needed that money for the funeral."

Mary blinked. This cost Deidre some amount of money sufficiently large enough to pay for—or make a significant contribution to a *funeral*? What was she thinking?

"I have found that everything is aligned," Mrs. V. said. "A space was open, the last in my day. So I searched the charts, asking who needed an intervention?" She stopped. "You do know the time of your birth, correct?"

Did she? Why yes, yes, she did. It was a lifelong insult to her older sister that Mary had had the audacity to be born on her birthday.

"Twelve-oh-one on September fourth. I know this because my mom tried super hard to push me out before midnight so my sister Diane—also born September fourth but three years earlier —would have her own birthday. But no." Mary felt her shoulders rising protectively toward her ears, and she put some effort into lowering them down again. "I sucked in my first breath at twelve-oh-one."

Mrs. V. put her pen to paper, and blue ink looped over the white surface.

"Throughout our entire lives, Diane, my older sister, complained that." Mary changed her voice to mimic Diane's. "'Everything that's mine, Mary wants, and she just reaches out and takes it.'" Too much information and yet, Mary couldn't seem to stop herself. If she kept talking, she'd push away whatever it was that Mrs. V. wanted from her.

It honestly didn't feel like this was some kind of trick to pry Mary's non-existent funds from her hand. But something was going on here, and weirdly, Mary could feel in her bones that this was *it*. Her life was about to change in a dramatic and drastic way. "Now granted, what Diane thought was hers wasn't always. The last piece of pizza. The last scoop of ice cream. The opportunity to lick the bowl after Dad made a cake. Yeah, it was usually food-related." Mary felt the corners of her lips wiggling nervously as she forced a smile. "Other than food, our tastes weren't very much alike, and I wouldn't want her things. She liked playing board games and doll babies. I liked books and more books." Her mind sent her pictures of her younger self under the covers in her childhood bed with a flashlight and a book that gave her more than goosebumps. They required her to keep reading until the heroine got to safety, which could take all night.

Those books pushed Mary to read faster and faster, hoping to get to the end where the hero and heroine were safe in each other's arms.

That was how Mary had framed life as a child. A series of disasters that, when surmounted, brought the hero and heroine to their reward, a happily ever after.

Just a silly worldview that her own life trajectory had tried very hard to debunk.

Mrs. V. tipped her head, clearly reading Mary's discomfort.

Mary swallowed hard. "Yes, ma'am, I was born a minute after midnight."

This scene seemed like it could come straight out of one of her beloved novels. Even Mrs. V.'s response was perfect for the pages of a thriller. "One minute after midnight. And to so many lives, that minute means everything."

What?

"You're lonely." Mrs. V. put her pen back on the pad.

Mary felt tears press behind her eyes. "No, I'm here with my best friend, Deidre. We've been inseparable for over twenty years."

"You're lonely." She repeated with a heavy emphasis on the lonely.

This felt like a trap, like she was being coerced into an emotion. "No. I'm an introvert. People exhaust me. I'm a nurse like Deidre. I spend twelve hour shifts in the hospital. Lots of people. Good colleagues. We all get along well. And when I had days off that job, I was training for my certification to become a flight nurse. You know, I transport patients in a helicopter either from one hospital to another or a medical emergency to the hospital. Lots of people. Too many people, really." And as Mary tossed out her words like ineffectual buckets of water on a raging fire, Mrs. V. nodded along.

Mary's emotions became a pressure in her sinus cavity, reaching toward her ears and down her neck. She took a deep breath and sensed the inside of her chest as hollow and dark.

And lonely.

Mrs. V. laced her fingers as her elbows perched on the armrests. "I'm sorry for your loneliness. We shall see if there is something in your chart." She leaned forward to pick up her pen and poised it to write. "And the place of your birth?"

"Cranberry Falls, Rhode Island. It's just outside of Providence."

After writing that down, Mrs. V. searched a phone app and wrote out a string of numbers and circles to indicate longitude and latitude degrees.

"Uhm, I don't live there now. I live in Norfolk, Virginia."

"The place of your birth helps me to calculate your astrological sign and houses."

"No, I wasn't born in a house. I was born at St. Catherine's Hospital in Cranberry Falls."

"Yes." Mrs. V. nodded, a smile in her eyes. "There are different influences on human life on Earth. These include the movement of heavenly bodies. We are interested in learning today how you interact with the celestial movement. Let's discuss Deidre for a moment."

Was that ethical? HIPAA really didn't apply here like it did at work. Still, it felt like gossip.

"Why did your friend wish to know the GPS coordinates of the places she is supposed to be on her birthday?" That question sounded rhetorical, so Mary sat still. "There are three things that people usually ask." Mrs. V. tapped her thumb to her pinky. "Tell me about my career, prosperity, and wealth." Her thumb moved to the ring finger. "Tell me about how to fill my heart with love." Then, her thumb came to her middle finger. "Tell me what the heck I'm supposed to be doing with my life." It was funny to hear Mrs. V. say heck. "I try to help my clients progress in one of these areas by giving them three coordinates for a place where they can shift their life trajectory. It's up to them which they pick and if they follow through. I have given three destinations to Deidre, for example, and now she has a specific date and her options. She must grapple with and decide which to take or to leave all three unexamined."

Mary felt odd. Her stomach was churning. Today had been weird.

Mrs. V. continued. "I look at the different influences and find the place on the globe that best facilitates a choice. Your friend will tell you on her birthday that it is far better for her career to be in Fairbanks, Alaska. But that is a choice. I found in her charts that if she goes there, she will lose the opportunity to experience great love. If she goes to the great love, she will have difficulty throughout her life with her money."

"Love or money. She should pick love. Unless—don't you give a third choice?"

"What will advance her in this lifetime? Yes, this is a third choice."

"And couldn't you see how that will impact her? Like, if she's in that spot on that day and this thing happens, her finances would look like this, and her love life would look like that?"

"I can tell her how the Heavens align, but there are still hard choices for her to make. What does she want most?"

"What would you say?"

"I am a spiritual being moving through a human experience. This is a phrase repeated throughout the millennium in myriad ways. I do not seek out love, fame, or fortune. I try to learn and grow. That is how I spend each birthday, in a state of growth, in a place that will best facilitate my evolution. But this is my path in this lifetime. Others need to learn other lessons. Bringing the opportunities to someone's attention is all I can do. And, too, once presented an opportunity, not everyone can open themselves to grasping it."

"Because it requires spontaneity?" Mary was beginning to sense a theme over these last couple of days. And then she suddenly remembered that she'd left her wet clothes in her washing machine back home where they were rotting.

"Typically, this is so. And you," Mrs. V. held up a finger, "seem to be someone who might struggle with spontaneity."

Mary pressed her lips together. *Wow, that felt too personal coming from a stranger. Deidre, sure. But this lady?*

Mrs. V. smiled with that tiny exhale of amusement as if she heard Mary say that aloud. "So, I was explaining to you, that as I looked at my personal charts and as I went into deep meditation to speak to my soul, I discovered that I was being called to intervene in a series of events that were unfolding. I discovered that your friend Deidre had the birthdate I was looking for among those who had reached out to me for future appointments. I saw in my meditation about her role in this process that she was not the person I sought, but she had a friend—you, I am hopeful," Mrs. V. turned her palm up to indicate Mary, "to go to the right place and be there at the right time." She patted the scrolls in front of her. "But I will look. Your birthday is tomorrow, Deidre told me."

"Tomorrow. Yes. Forty." Mary held up jazz hands. She wasn't sure she was following this. Was Mrs. V. saying that—? *Nah.* "Why do people have to come see you in person?"

"Simple. I read the charts, but I also read the person." She laced her fingers. "These two things inform me and the approach I take."

Mary put her hand on her chest, spread her eyelids wide, and shook her head. She didn't have money for any of this.

"Yes, I know you are not a paying client. Put yourself at ease. No one will follow up with a bill. I will ask only one thing from you: when I discover why you are here, you will heed the call."

Mary gave an unblinking shake of her head. "Look, you already know my birthday is tomorrow, and I have no travel money. So unless this place is close by—" Mary shrugged.

Mrs. V. extended a languid hand toward a table. "My assistant has set out tea for you. The view out the window is lovely. If you would give me some time, I will work on this question."

Mary was awkward as she got up from her chair to move to the other side of the room. She didn't seem to be able to coordinate her movements. Mary wondered briefly if she had hit her head going down the mountain and, in her terror, hadn't realized it. After pulling a napkin across her lap, Mary glanced over at Mrs. V. Her glasses now rested on the tip of her nose as she focused on her desk. With her fingertips under her hair, Mary started at the base of her scalp and moved her way over her head with slow, concentric circles, looking for tender spots. She was a little disappointed to find none. So, not a head injury.

The tea was fragrant. The finger sandwiches and pastries yummy. The view out the window peaceful. And Mary let herself rest in the wingback chair, head supported in the little corner.

Mary was surprised when she heard Mrs. V.'s voice rouse her from the half-doze. When she turned her head, the look on Mrs. V's face gave Mary pause. The yoga had slipped a bit, and there was stress there. Probably not like the lotion of stress that Mary rubbed into her skin on a daily basis, but yeah, there was stress there.

"It's quite extraordinary." Mrs. V. leaned back in her chair, sliding the glasses from her face and dangling them from her fingers as she assessed Mary.

Mary moved the teacup from her lap where she had rested it back to the table, then gripped the sides of her thighs, clenching her stomach, ready to take a blow.

"Three questions: love life, career and material life, internal life."

"Yes?" Oh, this seemed bad.

"All are informed by your going to the exact same geographical location on your birthday tomorrow." Mrs. V. leaned her head at an extreme angle as if trying to see Mary from a different point of view. "Well, I knew from my meditation that this was a special case." She laid her reading glasses on her desk. "I've never had a client reading where two locations coincided, let alone three." She breathed in and squared her shoulders. "Yes, quite extraordinary."

Mary clenched her teeth. Shit! She was being sent to Borneo.

"Tallinn, Estonia."

Mary pulled her chin back and considered that name. *Esto-*

nia, she knew she'd heard of that country. Place it on a map? Not so much.

"It's across the Baltic Sea from Helsinki."

Nope, if it wasn't a place a submarine might go, Mary didn't pay it much attention. Geography wasn't a big part of her education or her interest. She only had a passport because she and Deidre had gone to the Canadian Expo last year. "Okay." She'd do an Internet search back at the hotel.

"I highly suggest you leave in the morning on the first flight. The *very* first flight available in the morning." She emphasized. "You need to be there without any hitches as early as you can on your birthday."

"No hitches." Mary's takeaway was that in her meeting with Mrs. V., Deidre had been handed the quandary of deciding her priority shift next year. But Mary was handed an ultimatum.

"If I understand this situation right, Mrs. V.," Mary stammered, "you looked at your charts, and now you're telling me that if I, Mary Alice Williams, get on a plane and fly to—where was it? Tallinn, Estonia? That everything will change—my love life, my career, even my life's trajectory?" A nervous giggle peppered her words. "That's a lot to ask of a single geographical spot on a single day in one's life."

The giggle was replaced by a chest-crushing wave of anxiety and a dawning sense that there was some truth to what she was being told.

Whew. This was not part of her normal reality.

At. All.

If fate was calling, should she pick up and say hi?

Or had she already tumbled down a mountain today, and that was enough spontaneity and adventure for one trip?

12

SEPTEMBER FOURTH
Tallinn, Estonia

HALO MET up with the team in the lobby. They were doing a ruck run to the airport since it was only six miles away. They'd connect with Nutsbe and Max, then take cabs back to the hotel for breakfast. Halo adjusted his straps so they wouldn't rub blisters into his shoulders. Doing their morning runs with a light pack, say thirty or forty pounds, was one of the ways his special forces team stayed primed and ready to jump and go when a mission went hot. Seemed Iniquus trained like the Commandos.

Halo would admit to himself as the team fell into line—him respectfully at the back of the pack—that he was anxious to get to Max. He didn't like that he wasn't the one caring for his dog. However, part of his Iniquus contract stipulated that there would be times that—for training or other reasons—they might be working apart with Max kenneling under vet supervision at Cerberus.

The care Max would receive there was world-class. But that didn't make this easier on Halo.

Max was a phenomenal dog and the first dog that Halo owned outside of his childhood family life. He'd never had a dog that he got to train himself from the beginning, shaping and supporting, deeply bonding with the K9 so that they were in sync, reading each other's minds.

When you handle K9s for the special forces, the kennel masters match the K9's skills with the needs of the unit and the personality of the handler. Halo had gotten along with most of the doggos. With some, they begrudgingly put up with each other. But they were brothers on the battlefield, and those K9 brothers belonged to the military. Halo always knew he'd be saying goodbye when the needs of his Commando team changed. It hurt like hell every bleeding time. It was one of the major downsides to Halo's chosen profession.

So when he came upon Max at the shelter in Halo's last days as a special operator for the Australian military, Halo finally had a working dog partner that was his. And the pencil-pushing numbers-crunchers, without an iota of understanding of what reassignments did to both man and beast, would have no say.

Since then, Max and he had bonded tightly. They were two parts of a whole, Halo thought as he jogged through the airport parking lot.

That run had gone fast.

The wait at baggage claim went slow.

Finally, a stream of people moved through the doors, and one of them, standing head and shoulders above the others, was Nutsbe.

As he approached with his pack slung over one shoulder, Halo was glad to see that Nutsbe maintained the proper handler position with Max on a loose lead.

Max looked none the worse for wear. He had slept through the long leg of the flight from D.C. to Amsterdam after the Cerberus vet, Dani, prescribed a sleeping pill for him. But he'd not been medicated for the shorter flight to Tallinn.

The passengers ambled by the first baggage conveyor, where another plane gathered their belongings. One of the women tucked her long auburn hair behind her ear and squatted down to the side of Max. She didn't call or entice. She didn't hold out a hand for Max to sniff her. She did nothing that would attract Max's attention. Just got down and looked.

Max danced to the end of his leash toward her. He flipped his head to catch Halo's gaze and then back to the woman, whining his desire to go meet her.

That's when the woman stood and looked Halo's way, mouthing "sorry." Offering a contrite smile and a little finger wave, then turning and quickly walking away.

While Max continued to walk along with Nutsbe, his attention was on that woman until she moved through the doors.

Halo was proud that Max hadn't missed a step, even with the distraction.

With tactical K9s—just like with any other deadly weapon—there were rules, including a safe and proper handoff. So Halo swallowed his impatience, waiting for Nutsbe to put Max in a sit, then hand over the lead and step away.

Halo lowered to one knee, getting low to receive copious Max kisses. Max circled in Halo's arms, whimpering, whole body quivering, and tail wagging furiously. "I missed you, too. Hey, what was up with that women? Huh? They have treats in their pockets? Did she smell like she had a girl dog that you'd like to meet?"

Max spun around and positioned himself between Halo's knees to get a good rub while Halo looked up at Nutsbe. "You two do okay on the flight?"

"On the leg to Amsterdam, Max snored and passed gas, so I was buying drinks for everyone around me. It seemed to smooth things over. The snores were kind of cute, the gas not so much."

Halo grinned down at Max. "Sounds like you were good and relaxed."

Titus pulled an Iniquus suitcase for Nutsbe and one for Max off the belt. "We just need the crate, and we'll get a cab."

"Did you all get out to the bog yesterday?" Nutsbe asked as Halo stood, signaling Max to a down-stay.

"We did," Thorn said. "Our guide was knowledgeable and professional. She went through a laundry list of things that could go wrong on the bog. Everything from flying reindeer to wolves. We're going to need to get plans together in advance, ones that comply with Estonian laws."

"All right." Nutsbe shoved his hands in his pockets. "I'll be glad to hear about them."

"I think some of the situations need to be tested out," Halo said. "Titus gave me permission to go out with Max tomorrow and play around with some scenarios. I want to try some of the survival techniques Marilin mentioned. See how we do without the expert there to talk us through."

"She'd be there with the executives on their tour, right?" Nutsbe asked, his gaze on the conveyor belt and the rotating garden of colorful luggage.

"Do we want to depend on her as the sole expert?" Gage asked. "What if someone were to fall behind to look at something interesting?"

"Want to come with me?" Halo asked Nutsbe. "Or are you going to be busy with your own list?"

"I usually don't turn down opportunities," Nutsbe turned to Halo, "but there are certain things I'll take a pass on. I'm thinking that strapping the bog shoes to my prosthetic legs might not be the best choice."

"Yeah, sorry, mate, I wasn't thinking that one through."

"And you shouldn't." Nutsbe focused back on the carousel, watching for the dog crate. "I want every opportunity presented to me so I can make the decision. No need to exclude me on the off chance that I might be offended. I'm not."

"Well enough. Will do. Seriously, though, thank you for taking good care of Maxi on the way over."

"All's good."

Once the passengers had their bags and the carousel came to a stop, Nutsbe's phone pinged. Turning to Titus, he said. "I just got an alert that the crate didn't make it onto this flight. It's on the incoming. The staff will deliver it to our hotel in the next three hours."

"We're good then?" Titus asked. "Let's roll."

SPLIT BETWEEN TWO TAXIS, both vehicles were at a standstill as a construction crew maneuvered heavy machinery toward a gaping hole in the road.

The driver in Halo's car opened his palms. "It is sometimes like this. They are trying to fix the roads, but when they dig down, there are ancient ruins. The ruins must be protected, and then the roads must go back over. It is a long process. It will be years like this. But not for us." He sent a smile toward Titus. "For us, the inconvenience is another ten minutes."

Titus handed over a credit card. "We're going to walk the last couple of blocks. Thank you." Card swiped, the driver got out to pull their rucks from the trunk.

Seeing that, the other half of the team got out of their taxi, as well.

"We're walking?" Nutsbe called forward.

"That's the plan," Titus said, reaching for his pack and pulling it over his shoulders.

As the team moved to the sidewalk, Max had his nose in the air, chuffing in some ambient scent. That wasn't a typical Max move. Halo sniffed too to see if there was something obvious, but Halo had that sad human nose, while Max was a sniffing machine.

Titus looked down at Max's posture. "Something's up."

"Yeah." What, though, Halo hadn't a clue. "Dunno, mate. This is his 'mission ready' stance."

Suddenly, Max stopped and caught Halo's gaze, his whole body rigid with concentration.

"He's locked onto something," Halo said. "What's up, Maxi? Something you want to show me?" Halo turned to Titus. "I'm curious what this is. I'd like to check it out."

A scream wrenched their attention up the street.

"Go. Go. Go," Titus said, his hand over his head, blading toward the woman's shriek.

The team was in motion.

"Show me, Max." Halo took point, the team falling in behind him.

As they pounded down the pavement, the people flowed out of their way, clearing the route.

Up ahead, men's voices raised, yelling in the frantic way that happens as a catastrophe unfolds.

The team rounded an enormous wall into the old district. Many of the buildings had been there since the 13th century. On this road, it looked like they had additional modern stories on top of the ancient buildings.

Oily smoke billowed black clouds from one of the top windows.

"On the enclosed balcony, one female and two pre-school-aged children," Nutsbe called out. With his binoculars raised, he scanned across the floor and into the four corners so no one was overlooked. "No pets."

Appraising the architecture and the space between the windows, it was going to be a tough go. An extraction would have to happen from the exterior. Without firefighter equipment, no one was getting through the interior blaze. Halo tipped his head and focused on the traffic sounds. No sirens sliced the air, letting them know a ladder was on its way. And there was no time to waste.

Those around them saw the Iniquus uniforms, their packs, and possibly even their size and assumed the team had the ability to make the rescue.

The crowd of faces, all painted with horror, looked upward where the trapped woman was swinging a café chair like a hatchet, chopping at the glass.

The roof above the victims opened with a volcano of sparks. Flames licked skyward. Halo watched as the glass enclosure filled with smoke, clouding the family behind the density.

That mother was desperate for air.

She needed it. Her children needed it.

But the same air that would preserve their lives, even for a short time more, would also feed that fire. It would roar stronger and hotter with the increased oxygen.

It was one of those terrible no-choice moments when you had to do the wrong thing to have any hope of survival. There was no way to breathe or be rescued until that glass broke.

"Get everyone clear," Titus yelled. "When the glass gives, the shards will rain down on everyone below."

The team spread their arms and pressed the people back. The citizens quickly got the idea and complied. With the people well out of the way, Panther Force positioned under the balcony. Max was in a down-stay up against the wall, Halo curving his body protectively over his dog.

With a massive crash, the glass gave way.

The chair flew through the air, hitting the cobbled street and bouncing high again from the sheer velocity.

The glass twinkled down like an ice storm.

Coming out from under the protection of the overhang, Halo locked eyes on the little kids as they clung to the bars, pressing their faces through, gasping. Halo would guess the boys were three, maybe four years old.

"I'm going to take the pole up." Titus curved toward the flagpole. "And see if I can't throw her a line to feed through the bars and have the woman throw it back to me. Then I can swing my way over." He reached for Nutsbe's binoculars and scanned the situation. "That ledge outside of the bars looks like it's wide enough to get my feet squarely in place. I'll use the bolt cutters to open the bars enough to get them out. Kids are coming first. I'll need more rope."

They each reached into their pack and grabbed their climb kit.

Titus popped magnetic comms buds into his ear canals and slid the pressure mic over his head and under his shirt. The team did the same.

Titus pointed at Nutsbe.

Nutsbe reached for his radio. "Nutsbe. Comms check: One. Two. Three."

Pressing his sternal button, he responded, "Titus. Loud and clear."

Nutsbe gave him a thumbs up, and Titus was moving.

Shoving two extra coils of webbing into the net pockets on the sides of his rucksack, tightening the pack on his back, Titus stepped forward, dragging on the tactical gloves with the grip material on the palm and thumbs that helped operators stick when they fast roped into a situation. Pinching the pole between his boots, he dragged himself upward, hand over hand. He'd made it past the second window, shimmying toward the family when Nutsbe used the radio to call him back down. The farther up the pole Titus scrambled, the more his weight made the base tip out of the ground. Titus looked up and down then over to the window frame on the building, assessed, then slid to the ground.

There was nothing for him to do but abandon that route.

Halo could see the woman. She was pushing and pulling at the safety bars, trying to bend them to the side. Even with adrenaline, she wasn't going to succeed.

The historic high ceilings made the distance between the windows taller than the men could reach. The one benefit that Halo could see from this architecture was that the windows were recessed about ten inches into the wall. It gave a pretty good ledge to stand on and wall space on either side for bracing.

Up Titus went to the first ledge. Bending his knee into a lunge, he signaled to Thorn. Thorn moved up beside their leader, placing his foot on Titus's thigh. As Thorn reached for the next sill, Titus gripped Thorn's leg and shoved upward.

Thorn had to do a muscle up—a pull-up that moves past the chin to get the hips on the bar, or in this case, the sill. He threw his leg up and, pressing his hands into the wall, gained his equilibrium and signaled to Gage.

That was going to work. With Nutsbe managing from the road, they would have enough men to get to the window below the balcony.

Hell of a rescue, though. A circus act with no net below.

Gage was up, pressing his boot onto Titus's thigh. Thorn squeezed to the side to give his brother as much room to maneuver as possible.

Halo gave Max a reminder sit-stay signal, then caught Nutsbe's gaze. Nutsbe's nod conveyed he'd watch out for Max. And now, Halo was moving up beside Titus, pressing his weight into his hands on either side of the window, balancing his foot on Titus's knee.

As Halo dragged himself up to the second ledge, he also had to push away any distracting thoughts that wriggled around in the back of his brain.

He was going to act as if they were superhuman and the team could make this save.

But Halo knew that because of that overhang, barring a miracle, there was no way they could get to this family in time to save them.

13

September Fourth
Tallinn, Estonia

The first flight to Tallinn that morning had departed at six o'clock, and Mary was still uber-jetlagged.

Having wrestled her way through another sleepless, restless night, she was a might cranky today.

Sure, she'd gone along with Mrs. V.'s directives to get here on the very first flight. Mary figured this was still Deidre's adventure. She was paying for all of it. Why put up a fight? "Yeah, fine, I'll spend my birthday in Tallinn." It was either that or a lifetime of Deidre speculating "what if." This was easier.

And why the heck not? Mary hadn't even planned on any kind of travel this week. She hadn't planned anything for her birthday except maybe her boys might send her a text: **Happy Birthday** with maybe a cake emoji.

Probably not.

Mary was going to try very hard not to feel punished. They were young. They hadn't a clue how their behavior impacted her. Heck, they thought of her as "Mom," and somehow that made her sub-human. Mary had been through those days. Days when anything parental felt burdensome and forced. She'd grown past that stage just in time for her to tell her parents how much she appreciated them before their unexpectedly early deaths, one, then a few months later, the other.

Still, she'd never understand how she went from sitting on the floor in their room every single night, holding their hands until her fingers were bloodless and numb, providing a sense of safety, stability, and love only to become a nuisance in their lives, a burden, perhaps a source of mild guilt if they didn't do some perfunctory special occasion contact.

Yup. It hurt like nothing else in her life had ever hurt before.

It hurt like a bruised sole that she had no choice but to keep walking on, reinjuring with every step that she tried to take forward.

Bruised sole—bruised soul. Yeah, I see what you did there. Yup, that's about right.

"You are lonely," Mrs. V. had said. She wasn't, not on the surface. On the surface, she felt fine. But peeking just under that top layer, yeah, it was kind of spongy. Damn Mrs. V. for saying that out loud and forcing Mary to look at it. There were some holes. Some more tender than others. Some outright ached.

Maybe a dog?

A warm cuddle buddy.

Another being who would meet her at the door and be happy instead of making her feel like an inconvenience. Like she was something to be managed and sometimes placated, but basically unwelcome.

I need to get off this loop. It stings.

But that was how her brain had spent the entire flight from Geneva to Tallinn.

At the airport that morning, Mary had seen the most precious Malinois in his little working dog vest. They'd locked eyes, and Mary had thought, Oh! I want to pet you. And give you treats. And cuddle up with you.

As she'd thought her love thoughts, he'd pulled on his lead, trying to get to her.

Instantly, Mary thought about the deer she'd called to her with her high-pitched voice. And immediately, she knew that even sending out those *You're gorgeous; I want to snuggle you* thoughts must have shown up in her posture, and he was down with it.

She was distracting him from his work.

Mary had sent a mouthed apology to the guy who looked like he might be the handler, waiting for his dog to get to him. She'd given him a little wave, then turned her back. But she'd taken a mental picture. *Wow*. Mary reached out and squeezed Deidre's arm, widened her eyes, and tipped her head back to give her friend a direction to look so she could see him, too.

Deidre stopped in her tracks with her mouth hanging open.

"Are you freaking kidding me right now?" Deidre asked. "A whole team of them?"

"I know. Right?" Mary set off, dragging her case. "Now stop drooling. And stop staring. Come on. Wrench your eyes away."

Deidre came up beside her. "Okay, so that was a treat. I hope they make all Estonian men like that. If that's the case, I completely understand why Mrs. V. sent you here."

"Onward," Mary said. "Taxi to the hotel."

"It's only a few miles away. A ten-minute drive through morning traffic."

And Deidre had been right. Except for the delay from the street repair, they'd made it right to their hotel. It was a nice place. Everyone spoke easy English. While Deidre had gone in search of coffee, Mary got their luggage stored in the closet behind the desk until they could check in later that afternoon. Then, she went outside to sit on the bench under a tree, waiting for Deidre. They needed to figure out what they were going to do with themselves until three when they could check into their room.

Deidre moved into Mary's view. Her hands wrapped around to-go cups of coffee. "I know why you're here," Deidre said, plopping down next to her friend, handing the cup with a B penned in black marker.

Black, high test—that was how Mary liked her morning brew.

"Yeah?" Mary pried the cap off to let the steam out and cool it to a drinkable temperature. "Why's that?"

"Mrs. V. sent you here to change everything. Career, life trajectory, and love. And I know how it's going to happen."

"K." Mary blew across the surface, then breathed in the rich aroma.

"I walked by the hotel a block up. They're having an open mic tonight. I went in and signed us both up. I'll sing, and you'll do your standup act. Someone's going to be in the audience, think you're funny as hell, and put you on tour. Then, you'll be the comedian who gets laid by some fabulous guy that you hit it off with, and you fall in love and have the kind of supportive, amazing life partner you deserve."

"I wouldn't mind getting laid. It's been a dry spell. I don't even need a tour contract."

"I hear you," Deidre said. "It's been a bit of a dry spell for me, too. We're talking Sahara dry spell. And frankly, I'm over it. I wouldn't mind enjoying someone's company while I'm here in Tallinn."

"K. If someone's in the room having fun, let's make sure to

hang the Do Not Disturb sign on the door and send a text. No all-nighters."

"Right. In and out. Get it done. Buh-bye."

Mary laughed. She knew neither of them was going to sleep with a damned stranger in Tallinn, Estonia. "Well, at any rate, I'm down for all that. From your mouth to god's ear."

"Yeah? So you're game?" Deidre asked. "It's your birthday day. And it was your chart reading. I don't want to step on anything here."

"We can *always* change our minds, right?" Mary shrugged, then touched her lips to the cup to test the coffee.

"Not always," Deidre said. "But yeah, sure, in this case, we could bail."

"Speaking of bailing." Mary set her cup down. "My muscles aren't great after the ski adventure yesterday. If I'm going to have my life changed on a dime, I'm going to need some muscle cream or something. The desk guy said there's a pharmacy up the street in the old city. I'm going to leave you here with my coffee while it cools. I'll be five, maybe ten minutes."

"Yup." Deidre leaned her head back, resting it on the trunk behind her. "I'm just going to enjoy the morning sun on my face and relax. Take your time."

Rounding the corner, the walk was exactly as the front desk guy had described. She spotted the pharmacy sign up ahead.

Mary's whole body braced when she suddenly saw a chair go flying through the air and bounce on the cobblestones. A crowd of people gasped and cried out.

She was running toward the billowing smoke.

She sprinted past people lining sidewalks, glass shards twinkling thickly from the street.

A massive man in that same uniform as she'd seen in the airport minutes earlier was on the flagpole. He was too huge.

From her distance, Mary could see that as he went up, the flag-pole slowly leaned under his weight.

He slid back down again.

Now, the team was trying to get up the side of the building, scaling from window to window. They were right. Without equipment, if they were making a rescue, it would have to happen from the exterior.

Leaning her head back to find the victim, Mary's gaze caught on the balcony.

Two boys.

Two baby boys.

Mary's mind did some kind of crazy jujutsu move, and those babies' faces were her boys'. That was Kyle and Kaleb. *Her* kids. *Hers.* She had to save them.

Her head swiveled frantically for a way to fly to their side, and her gaze landed on the pole. She didn't weigh as much as that man did. And she had been taking classes; she knew how to climb a pole. She could get to her boys.

There was a sensation in her chest of immense power. Of strength. Of capability. Her whole being seemed to swell and shift, morphing into something she didn't recognize.

Powerful.

She was *powerful.*

The next thing she knew, she was next to the flagpole, toeing off her tennis shoes, flopping to the ground, yanking her belt open, and scrambling out of her pants and shirt. To climb the pole meant her flesh had to make as much contact as possi-ble. The cloth would make her slide.

And there she was, wrapping her legs, reaching her arms, gripping at the brushed metal surface.

She was climbing toward the inferno. "Hang on, babies. Hang on. I'm coming," she screeched up to them.

14

In her dance class, three, sometimes four, was the number of times that Mary had been able to grab and pull her body up the studio pole. *This* was five stories. She knew these things in the back of her head. She also knew that unless someone with a big assed ladder showed up, the babies would die.

They'll die. They'll die. The babies will die.

When she leaned her head back, she still saw Kyle and Kaleb's faces staring down at her—the same black curls and rosy mouths, but these were held wide and tight with fear.

The pain of their anguish ground behind Mary's sternum with excruciating force.

Hitch breathing, she reached and pulled.

Mary peripherally knew that the men in gray were working hard to get in place. She was aware of how one man climbed onto the teammate for added height, then reached for the sill and did a pull-up with inhuman strength. It was heroic. But ineffectual.

Even if the guy who made it to the fourth floor had some

Peter pan-like, "I can fly!" move up his sleeve, once up, what could that man possibly do to get the children down?

What way did *she* have to get the children down, for that matter?

Mary's brain wanted to process, to form a plan. But there was something deep and primal driving her. She had no choice but to act. Maybe there was a strategy somewhere hiding in the thick folds of her gray matter, and it just hadn't presented itself yet.

She made it to the top. She was just under the flag now. Parallel to the balcony.

There was a woman near the boys that Mary hadn't seen before. Hope and despair etched her face as she wrapped her arms—streaked with black—around the boys.

The heat was intense. The smoke filled Mary's lungs as she squinted past the sting in her eyes.

"Hey!" The man's voice broke into Mary's awareness. "Hey!"

She was afraid that if she looked down, she'd understand that she clung to a flagpole five stories over a cement sidewalk. Mary kept her eyes on the boys. "What?" she called back.

"I have bolt cutters and rope."

K. Those were important. Mary did a quick calculation. Should she slide down and try to reach them? Her stomach flopped, churning green bile that splashed into her throat. *Yeah, that would be a no.* "I need to get over on the balcony first." And with those words, she realized just how far away she was from the ledge.

And scarily, the only way to get from the pole to the balcony would be to reach as far as she could with her hands and lean as far as she could from the pole.

She could do this. It was a basic pole sit. It was one of the first things she learned to do in her classes.

"English?" Mary yelled to the woman.

"Yes!" she yelled back, then coughed hard.

"I'm going to reach my hand toward you. Listen to me. When my hand comes near you, grab my hand and guide it to the bar. I need to get a good hold of the bar. Tell me what I said."

"Yes. I do this. Grab your hand, help you hold to bar."

"Good." Not *good.* Just yeah, the woman understood. Mary turned herself on the pole and kicked her legs up until they stuck out long in front of her, crossing her feet at the ankles, shifting to the side so the friction of her skin tearing against the metal would hold her weight. "Yikes." She exhaled. Her chest tightened down. "Scary," she muttered. How many times had she said that in class mere feet off the ground? Mary looked over her shoulder and locked in on the littlest boy. Kyle's eyes looked pleadingly back at her.

"I'm coming! I'm coming, baby. I'm going to get you!"

Mary gripped the pole with one hand, pressing her hips up, pressing her toes down, creating a taut arc with her body. Her other hand extended long as she leaned backward into a pole plank. "Help me!" she yelled.

Suddenly, her hand was grasped and gently pulled, her fingers forced over to wrap the bar.

And now Mary was good and stuck.

Literally stretched between the pole and the balcony, she had no other choice than to keep going.

Her thighs screamed.

Her survival brain screamed.

The people beneath her screamed.

And Mary wanted the silence and conviction of looking into her son's eyes. There was *nothing* she wouldn't do for her boys.

Even this.

Gripping tightly with her right hand, Mary tried to force her left from the pole. But her brain bucked at the command. She'd been scared in pole class, too. So, she used that technique to motivate her body into action. "Don't think, do. Don't think, trust." And as she said this, Mary heard two little voices screaming in terror, possibly in pain. That was all Mary needed to spur her into terrified action. With the first hand secure, Mary pointed her toes harder, arched her hips up higher, created as much friction as she could, then released her second hand from the pole, reaching with rigid fingers held wide toward the solidity of the security bars.

Again, she was guided into place.

The move was punctuated with a swell of gasps coming up from the street.

Ignore them. Ignore everything. Get the babies.

"Hold my wrists," she called, and the woman complied with an iron grip. With a deep breath, Mary released her legs, swinging them hard to the right, using the sudden momentum to get her heel onto the wide lip of the balcony.

Four little hands reached through the safety bars and clung onto her ankle.

Using all her strength, Mary pulled and twisted to get her other leg there, too.

The heat radiating out of the apartment door was searing. She pulled her elbow over her mouth and nose as scant protection from the acrid smoke.

The little ones pressed into the bars, trying to get away from the heat.

She was here. Now, what?

"Tool Guy below me!" Mary called without looking.

"How can I help?"

"I need the bolt cutters."

"Ideas?"

No good ones. "I'm going to hook into these bars and do a

back bend. You're going to find a way to get the cutters into my hands."

"Wilco."

Military. Okay, that made all the sense in the world.

Mary had to scoot over as close to the wall as possible. And honestly, that was the scariest thing she'd done yet. She wiped her hands across her cotton sports bra. There, she threaded her legs through the bars and crossed her ankles. "Hold my legs down," she told the woman, who then crawled up and sat on her feet, wrapping her arms around Mary's calves to counterbalance Mary with her own weight.

Mary couldn't make herself lean back. The best she could do was squeeze her eyes shut and walk her hands down her body until she felt her hair fall straight down like it had when she was a child playing on the monkey bars.

I'm here because I was sent here. I'm doing this because this is mine to do.

Mary didn't flail for the cutters. She merely hung there, arms doing the bidding of gravity. Hopefully, she was in proximity to the supply guy.

"I'm okay. I'm okay." She breathed the words out with each exhalation and pulled them in on each inhale.

She was surprised when she felt rope tapping the back of her hand.

"Put that between your teeth and curl up."

That was the most rational thing that had happened since her brain snapped, and she went full mother mode. Her bite clamped down on the roping; Mary put her hands behind her thighs and crunched herself up.

The woman on the balcony reached and dragged Mary until she was sitting on the foot-wide ledge.

The babies. It was too hot to survive near that fire. Their little faces pressed through the metal bars as they screamed and reached for the cool air outside. Mary pulled the rope and up came the lifesaving bolt cutters.

So far, the metal wasn't scalding her. She couldn't imagine that would last for much longer.

Between the two women and the ratcheting design, they were able to get two of the posts off, making a space wide enough for the boys to fit through.

"How long is this rope?" Mary called down without looking.

"What are you thinking?" the man shouted back.

"I wind my end through a few of the posts for friction. The first kid gets a hasty." She used the term for a way to secure a climber with a rope technique that wrapped the legs like a diaper. "You secure your end of the rope to something as a backup. Then I go backward, again to lower him to you. I can release the rope from the bars. You tether him in again. Then, you can lower him to the next guy and so on to the ground."

"How are you going to get the second kid down? That balcony is at risk. We don't have time for that."

"Okay—" Mary had no plan B. "Ideas?"

"One, untie the bolt cutters. Two, tie the rope onto the post for security. Three, lower the rope back to me, and I'll send up three more lengths. That will be one for each of you."

"Okay!" Okay. He was rational and solid. Those were important things in this high-stakes crisis. Mary's shaky fingers didn't want to comply, but if she pushed her breath out in short bursts through rigid lips, she could get the job done.

As she lowered the end of the first rope to the tool guy, Mary realized this breathing cycle was a Lamaze technique. Who knew that skill would come in handy two decades on?

"Pull it up!" he hollered.

Mary was grateful for the instructions. Clear, concise, no wobble. Actionable. Good.

The promised ropes came up to her as she pulled. And there were carabiners that would make the process of attaching the children's harnesses that much easier—that much more secure.

Mary used one of the ropes around her waist to tie herself in. If she should slip, it would be bad, but she wouldn't splatter her brains over the sidewalk.

The mother held her smallest child still while Mary wrapped the rope around and around. She tugged and tested. "Good," she told the mom.

Straddling the newly opened space, Mary slid her legs between the next bars over. She positioned herself so that her knees would bend over the edge when she leaned back again. Even with her safety belt in place, the idea of going upside down again stopped her heart. Mary pounded a fist into her chest.

In her pole classes, Mary had just advanced to the point where she was learning how to do inversions. Yes, she was new to these sensations. But if she could hang six feet off the ground upside down from a class pole with only the friction of her skin to keep her from falling on her head, then hanging like a kid on the monkey bars—no matter the height—should be no problem, right?

"Rope secured?" Mary yelled.

"Affirmative. Rope secured."

"Get ready," she called down, but really, that directive was for herself.

"Ready!"

The kid with the rope tied around him must have just figured out what would happen because he freaked. While he clung to his mother, fighting and screaming, the mother forced one of his feet into Mary's hand and then the other.

The mother trusted Mary with this child's life.

Could she do this?

Honestly? They had no choice.

Very shortly, they were all going to die. So even if Mary dangled the child and dropped him, there were men below who might grab hold of a flailing limb as he fell.

Doing anything now gave the child a better chance of surviving the next few minutes.

And as if mirroring Mary's thoughts, the woman said, "He's going to die if you don't go, the boys will die. Just go! Just *do* it!"

Oh, man. This was the part of nursing that Mary hated most. It was the point when a mother stood over her child and looked her in the eye: this is my everything. My world is in your hands. I'm giving you my life when I hand you this child. I'm *trusting* you. *Depending* on you.

When Mary had jumped on top of the gurneys, straddling an unconscious child so that she could bag while her fellow nurses ran them down the hall, moving the bed toward the critical care resources needed for survival, she'd been part of a team. The team was trained. They knew—or had a darned good idea—what came next. There was no team up here with her.

There was just the desperation of the mother's utter flat calm.

15

As the mother held her squirming, terrified kid, Mary gripped that child's ankles with her full adrenaline-fueled strength.

"Now!" Mary screamed and went over backward, jerking the kid through the bars.

Dropping backward, Mary slid the child along her body.

As soon as the boy left the woman's grasp, she grabbed back at Mary's ankles, giving Mary a counterweight that would keep her from slipping off the balcony.

The weight of the child pulled Mary's arms long. Her hands had become vices, trapping the child's ankles as he swung—upside down and screeching—five stories above the glass-sparkled ground.

Mary hung there, feeling her body stretched by his weight, feeling the tug of the sinews in her shoulders and the begging scream for relief from the nerves behind her knees.

There was no oxygen upside down. There was snot and saliva.

"I have him. Release."

Mary's fingers froze in the grip. And though she shouted at her hands to cooperate, she couldn't make them comply.

"I have him," the man hollered. "Release his feet and get the next child."

In her mind, Mary was back at pole class when the teacher would say, "Let go with your right hand. Trust that your body will hold in place. Let go and reach."

Let go and reach.

Mary closed her eyes, remembering that feeling the first time she was upside down with the pole trapped between her thigh and calf when she was able to force her hands open so she would hang. And she had been fine.

Remember that. You were fine, Mary cajoled herself.

Her nerves ablaze with terror, she forced her joints to extend. The weight slipped from her fingers.

Squeezing her eyes tightly, she kept herself from looking. The child survived, or the child didn't. She no longer had any control over his outcome.

There was still a little boy above her at risk of burning. Mary thought that falling to one's death was a far preferred way of dying than broiling in a flame.

The tool guy on the windowsill below hollered. "Good job. Perfect! You're doing perfect. Get the other baby."

The blood rushing to Mary's head made it feel like it had swollen in size. The heat burned the pads of her feet.

Get the other baby.

She folded up again.

This time, the child wasn't fighting. He lay in his mother's arms, oxygen-deprived and shocky. This was cutting things much too close. His little head lolled back, and Mary saw Kaleb's face. "I'm here. I won't let anything bad happen to you. I'm here, baby."

Any fatigue, any fear, any hesitancy left her.

She reached for the boy. As she wound the hasty into place, Mary's gaze slid over to assess the mom. The woman was slight, small for an adult. Lightweight didn't mean easy. Even the weight and size of the first little boy had been hard.

The mom smoothed a hand down her child's face and kissed him.

Mary had seen that in the hospital, too. This woman thought she was saying good-bye. She didn't think she was going to survive. As Mary positioned the boy against her chest, the mom came up on all fours, hacking and gasping.

There was the billowing, noxious smoke stinging and clouding Mary's eyes. There was the heat of the flame torching her skin. The metal posts grew ever hotter. Even through her hazy, watery sight, Mary could see the child's face was black with soot, and his lips were turning blue.

"In coming." This time, there was no ready, set, go. This child needed fresh air. Now.

Mary grabbed his ankles, thinking absurdly, *I have the talons of an eagle. I can hold a flailing fish tight in my grasp and get it back to my nest.* She flipped over backward, draping the child along her body until gravity dropped his hands within reach of the guy below.

No one grabbed at her ankles, and Mary slid until her feet caught on the bars. This, too, she'd done on the pole, holding her feet rigidly back to support her weight. It was familiar enough that she had done it automatically. But still, the tug of the rope around Mary's waist was a welcomed reminder that she wasn't going to plunge to her death. Not unless she chose to. Not unless there were no other options for escaping the flames.

"Got him! Release."

Releasing was easier the second time.

The screams and gasps from below were less of an upswell.

But now, mucus flowed into her mouth and clogged her nose. Her system was trying to clean its airways, and instead, it was suffocating her. Her stomach muscles clenched as she coughed and sputtered and choked.

There was no counterbalance sitting on her feet and holding her legs this time. Mary was on her own to tighten her abdominal muscles and curl herself up. She writhed this way and that as she clasped her legs, trying to use her arm strength to hand over hand walk herself up her thighs, grab the heated bar, and drag herself up.

Up there was less air, more smoke, and her system worked overtime, dragging in the needed oxygen only to cough it back out.

Mary scooped her arm toward where the mother had been.

Where was the mother?

With her head down, through squinty eyes, Mary could make out the curl of the woman's hand, and she reached for it to no avail. The cutters lay to her right. Mary cut the third bar and then a fourth as if it were butter—the effects of the adrenaline pumping through her system like a geyser that made her lips buzz, and possibly the help of the fire's heat.

The opening was now adult-sized. Leaning through, the woman lay just out of Mary's reach.

Using the handle on the tool, Mary scraped at the woman's skirt. She was able to drag the fabric close enough that she could pull the weight of the mother.

Was she already dead?

Mary leaned over her shoulder and yelled, "Mother." Then hacked up a lung.

"Ready!" he called.

Yeah, well, Mary realized that the woman's deadweight was beyond her capacity. Unless this woman was actively clinging to Mary, there was no way this was going to work.

But what were the options?

The sirens wailed below, but they were too far away. By the time the trucks pulled up and the ladders raised, it would be over for this woman and maybe for Mary, too.

Mary climbed through the open bars. Then, lying on her stomach, Mary inched her way to the edge and peered over at the Tool Guy below her, seeing him for the first time.

It was the guy from the airport. The man waiting for his beautiful dog.

It felt right that she had a moment of non-urgency to see this man before they were tossed together into life-or-death circumstances.

It felt like some kind of hand had moved them into place. He was at the airport, too. Had the universe also brought him in for this specific task?

Pre-ordained.

Written in the stars.

Mary cupped her hands around her mouth to project her hoarse voice down to the guy below her. "I can't hold the woman's weight and hang upside down, and you can't hold her weight perched on that window like that."

She saw that he'd cut the shutters open and kicked the window clear. Smoke billowed from that apartment, too. The fire had moved down to his story of the building.

"I've already figured this out. I'm coming up. My teammate is moving up to take my place. We lower the woman. Then I lower you. And I'll follow."

He was already roped up in a hasty made of lime-yellow webbing, the color for emergency equipment. Something about that color calmed Mary's system.

In her job in the emergency department, there was adrenaline—lots of it. Everything was life or limb. She'd learned to maneuver around the adrenaline with muscle memory. She didn't have much in the way of repetitive practice to apply at this stage of the rescue, but a man with lime green would. He *did.* His team did. They knew what they were doing. Trust.

"Lace one of those ropes through three rods, then send both ends down to me."

She knelt on the ceramic tiles, complying with the directives. Her knees burned. Mary conjured cool nights in the woods with the fire blazing up, heating the knees of her jeans to scalding temperatures while the rest of her froze, though, everything here at this moment was painfully hot.

After she followed the directives, Mary pushed the mother over next to the bars, angling her face outward. She had no idea what was inside that apartment, what toxic fumes were billowing out, and no idea why this woman was unconscious. Was it smoke inhalation or something more?

The man moved with practiced ease up the side of the building.

But in the end, how brave was he?

How determined?

Would he stay to get both the other woman and Mary down? Or would he assess his own chances of survival and bail?

Lying under the blanket of smoke, Mary got herself as far out of the way as she could so Tool Guy had space to maneuver.

Smoke mushroomed through more of the building's windows as the fire spread through the interior.

Soon, Tool Guy might receive his orders to abandon his position.

When he saved himself, Mary would lose her own shot at survival.

Had she flown to Tallinn to die?

The woman with the star charts had sent her to this place on this day to do *the* thing.

Not the three choices offered to Deidre. Not the career, life trajectory, romance opportunities.

Just be here.

Be *here*, where Mary's exercise hobby allowed her to save those babies.

There must be something huge in those children's futures—something Mrs. V. saw aligned in the stars that needed safe-guarding by the universe.

And to save them, Mary would be the sacrificial lamb.

16

HALO HELD THE MIC BUTTON BETWEEN HIS FRONT TEETH. HE bit down to open the communication channel and spoke with exaggerated lips and tongue to make himself understood. “Subject descending.” Halo edged the unconscious woman down toward Gage, who had taken up the position in the fourth-floor window.

Feeding the line through his grip as smoothly as possible, Halo worked to keep the subject from beating into the side of the building.

Halo didn’t take the time to assess the mother’s condition as he'd packaged her up for this descent. With face and clothes black with soot, Halo couldn’t tell if she was breathing. But flames were quickly engulfing the wall that attached to the balcony. If required, CPR would need to be rendered on the ground.

Nutsbe was in his ear, giving directives. “Nutsbe for Halo, hold, hold, hold. Gage, get out of there. Move down to Thorn’s window.”

“Halo. Holding.”

“Gage. Moving.”

Feet braced against the bars, Halo pressed into his legs, leaning back to keep the subject in place.

The warrior goddess didn't hear any of that. She'd have no idea what was happening.

Right now, her focus had locked onto the flagpole she'd climbed up and was probably calculating the possibility of jumping for it.

The bravery of that woman. Just like his team, she had moved in for the rescue with no sure exit strategy.

But what else could they have done?

The children were alive. Possibly, the mother could survive, too, if they got her medical help right away.

They still had some time before they hit the kind of desperate straits territory that would necessitate the leap from burning platform to flagpole.

"Nutsbe for Halo, the fourth-floor window is engulfed. I need you to get your subject up three feet to keep her away from the flame while Gage gets into his new position."

"Halo. Wilco. Tell me when the subject is in a safer place." Hand over hand, Halo pulled the mother back up the side of the building.

"Nutsbe for Halo. Good. There. Hold. Be apprised, Gage is with Thorn on the third floor. You'll need to lower the subject down to them. The lines are fire resistant, not fire retardant. Make it a speedy descent."

"Halo. Not enough rope to get her two floors farther down," Halo responded with a saliva-filled mouth. With the mic between his teeth, it was hard to swallow. "Working the problem."

He turned to the warrior goddess off to the side in a little pocket of clearer air. Raising his voice over the roar of the fire, he called, "I need that rope you have around your waist."

She looked down, put her hand on the line, and then looked over to where she'd tied in.

"I'm wearing webbing. Connecting two like ropes is better," Halo said.

She focused on him, unblinking. There it was again, that crazy sensation. A connection like he'd never experienced before, though, he had been in many a life-threatening circumstance with his Commando brothers. This was something new for him. It had a strength to it. A conviction.

And as those thoughts formed, the woman rolled her lips in and nodded. Then, she turned to untie the hasty from around her waist and then the subject's line from the bar.

While she worked to release the knot, she had to be doing survival calculations. With the rope around her waist, she'd most likely make it to the flagpole. Without it, her chances of leaping, grabbing, and sticking were about zero.

Halo was very aware that he was asking her to take a risk that he wasn't taking himself. "Only for a minute. I swear to you, I *will* get you down." He desperately hoped that he could live up to that promise.

Sticking her hand under her sports bra, she ducked her face down to rub the fabric across her eyes. Then she looked down to where the woman hung from the harness, framed by smoke. "Figure eight?" She didn't wait for an answer; she just flipped her hand, joined the two lines, dressed the knot, pulled it tight, and then added a stopper knot to each line. She knew what she was doing.

"Excellent," he told her, then bit the mic. "Halo. I have enough line rigged to get the mother to the third story."

"Nutsbe for Halo. Let her down." Nutsbe stayed in his ear.

"Subject descending."

"Keep coming. Keep coming. Three feet. Good. Halo, hold. Gage, get that rope released before it catches on fire."

"Gage. Wilco."

And after another moment. "Nutsbe for Halo, spool up the line stat."

The much-awaited fire trucks slowed in front of the neighboring buildings. The emergency workers jumped from the still-moving vehicles as they assessed and got into place at the same time.

No ladder truck, Halo noticed.

"Hey!" Halo asked as he brought up the last of the line, "You hanging in there?"

The warrior goddess tried to speak but was barking a cough. She extended a thumbs up.

"Nutsbe for Halo. Be aware, Thorn and Gage have to abandon their window," Nutsbe said. "You need to get the two of you down to the second story."

Suddenly, the balcony lurched to an angle. "The fire must be eating away at the connective structure," he yelled past the roar of flames. If that happened, there was nothing else to tie into. For a moment, he considered holding the woman's wrist and swinging her back to the pole she'd climbed up. Considered making a jump for it himself.

He tucked those thoughts away as a last resort.

If they could get to the second story, even dropping from the end of a rope was a matter of broken bones. And shouldn't kill them.

There was no time to lower her by herself.

They were going to have to go over together.

17

THE MAN HAD HOLLERED AT HER TO WRAP HERSELF AROUND him. And as soon as she complied, they went over the lip.

That was—whew! This was—yeah.

Clinging to him, her system was freaking out.

When training to be a flight nurse, learning how to care for patients in the back of a helicopter, she had seen rescue-types working with ropes.

It looked pretty easy.

But then again, when people knew what they were doing, pole dancing looked effortless. And it was anything but.

At her pole dancing school, they also offered aerial silk classes that Mary wasn't brave enough to try yet. The women would knot themselves into long drapes of fabric and perform graceful gymnastic flows. Seeing them perform didn't translate into the body coordination needed for achieving the move.

But the silks class provided a better, more proximal image for her to hold. Unlike the jacked-up rescuers, the silks class was comprised of women of all ages, shapes, and levels of physical ability. Heck, there was even a class for kids that taught "fairy school" and how to "fly" on the apparatus.

Granted, they were doing it three feet off the floor, and there were mats and spotters.

Feeling them come to a stop, Mary batted her lids open to find the Tool Guy looking directly at her. His eyes were warm, intelligent, and full of concern.

"What's happening?" Her legs wrapped around his waist, and her thighs rested on his as he crouched against the wall. Her arms wrapped over his shoulders, his wrapped around her, holding the rope behind her back. Their limbs knotted them into a single whole. With dawning awareness, Mary understood how a man and a woman could partner to reach their goals, each contributing their skills. Equals. It was a powerful moment—a zing of electricity.

"No more line," he said. "Don't panic." He smiled when he said it like it was a joke. Like he knew he could trust her the way she was trusting him.

He had a great smile.

"No." She wasn't panicked. She wondered how much it hurt him to have her weight adding to his own. She'd been trying to think "light as a feather" thoughts. But how much could that have possibly helped? "Sorry," she said without offering any context.

"Patience. We're almost down. I promised you I'd get you down. You trust me?"

"Completely." Mary didn't have to think about it, didn't need to consider it. Her conviction came from the very marrow of her bones. She knew that with this man, she was safe. "Absolutely. A hundred percent."

And as he smiled his response, the mic still caught between his front teeth, Mary thought, *Please, don't let the ropes catch on fire.*

She didn't want to look down to see how far they still were from the ground.

Tool Guy bit down on the metal necklace. "Wilco."

There had been someone in his ear directing him.

"You're going to feel my teammate reach for you," he said.

A hand snaked around her waist and detached the carabiner that had held her and the man together. She wanted to fight against the release. Mary was afraid that they might save her and leave him. And that was unconscionable. Her eyes were frantic as she looked into the man's. She should know his name. She should have asked.

"He's got you." Tool Guy reassured her. "You're okay."

Mary believed him, but still, she didn't want to let go.

"Lean back into my arms. Release your legs," the man behind her said.

After unknotting her ankles, her body hung long. Strong hands reached for one of her wrists, then the other, and Mary knew enough to turn her hands and grasp his wrists, as well.

Mary realized this guy was balanced on a teammate's shoulders as she was passed down. It was something out of a circus act how they got her feet positioned on the sill.

"Hold onto my leg for balance," the next man said. "Keep moving down. There's help below."

She didn't know what that meant, but Mary walked her hands down the man's leg to a crouch, then setting her butt on the ledge, she rolled herself over until the sill bit into the front of her hips, like a gymnast on the uneven bars. From there, she lowered herself until another set of hands wrapped her waist, scooped under her knees, and cradled her to his chest as he carried her over the sidewalk to the street where she was set down, away from the glass.

She looked up as her Tool Guy climbed down the stack of buddies.

Glancing around, she didn't see the babies or the mother. A rescue worker approached her, and she just wanted to be alone.

Wanted to get away from the smells and roar of fire that muffled words that she couldn't understand. She waved her hand to tell him she was all right and he should go away.

And before anyone could press and insist, Mary turned and walked down the street in search of cooler, cleaner air.

She was surprised as hell to be alive.

That was going to take an adjustment. She realized that she had come to the conclusion up there that her birthday was also going to be her death day. She hadn't expected to survive.

As people approached her with open hands and worried eyes, Mary shrugged them off. She was claustrophobic and didn't want anyone or anything near her. The water that filled the gutters felt so soothing on her feet. Blissful and cool.

Walking down the block and another and finally, free of the crowd, Mary walked behind a delivery trailer and sat on the curb, where she hugged herself tight and let the tears flow. There were no sobs to go with it. No sounds. Just the cleansing release of tears.

Did the family even survive?

Mary felt the rough cement through her thin polyester panties, the ones with sparkly fireworks she'd found in the sale bin after the Fourth of July.

She'd have to go back and try to find her clothes eventually. Her phone was in her pocket.

Then she remembered Deidre. Her friend was probably done with her coffee and wondering what had happened to Mary. But Mary didn't have the energy to care.

Right now, she just wanted to sit still until she could accept that she was okay.

And in her okay-ness, Mary was both horrified by what Mrs. V. sent her to do and immensely grateful.

Mary could feel Deidre being frantic. But she tucked her chin and rested her forehead on her knees. Deidre was going to have to wait. Mary needed another minute to still her limbs from their quivering. And test to see that her legs would hold her up.

The last time she had been this rubbery and exhausted, she had just pushed her second twin, Kaleb, out into the world and listened while he let out his first hearty yell.

She rested there with her arms wrapping her knees until she was startled out of her stupor by the poke of a cool, wet Malinois nose. The dog dropped her pants next to her; her shirt was shoved into one of her shoes. He circled around to sit behind her, looking in the direction he'd come from. Inch by inch, he shuffled over until her back was against him.

Mary felt like he was telling her to rest, that he was there to support her. She wrapped her arms around him and tucked in, rounding her forehead against his neck, and this time, she was able to cry out loud. It was a cathartic blubbery, sobbing kind of release.

As the stress left her system, she petted the Malinois, her fingers dancing over the work vest. He was the dog she'd wanted to love on at the airport. And now she was getting her wish.

While the Malinois she knew from the Norfolk military base were all war dogs—eat the bad guy dogs, dangerous dogs—this one was gallant. "Look, you brought me my pants and both my shoes. And one sock." Somehow, he'd picked them up, followed her all the way out here, and then gave her a place to rest and a feeling of safety in a strange city.

He was a protector dog. And if Mary was right, he belonged to Tool Guy.

"There you are, Max."

She knew that voice.

Mary turned her head and watched Tool Guy striding up the sidewalk toward them.

It made complete sense that this dog was *his* dog. The one that had sent the bolt cutters up to her, the thing that had potentially saved those lives. The man who had called instructions to her. The one who had caught the tiny hands of the dangling babies and looked her in the eyes with such intensity as she climbed down the rope tethered to him, praying that it didn't melt, or fray, or burn, and drop them to the cement below. It was magic rope, and he had been a magic helper with his warm brown eyes focused hard on her. Ready, she knew, to do whatever was necessary to help her while his own situation was just as life-threatening.

He was the very essence of valor.

"Max, you found her, good job, mate." He circled into the street, crouching in front of Mary. "You had me worried. I'm glad Max found you."

Mary was caught up in a whirlwind of sensation. Something she couldn't label or define. The best she could do was give it a phrase: *Thank goodness you're here*.

"Holy shit, woman, I have never seen anything that crazy brave in all my life. And my life is chock filled with crazy events."

When Tool Guy called her 'woman,' Mary felt it in every cell of her body. It made her tingle as she morphed into an Amazonian warrior, a woman full of strength and potential.

He gestured toward her feet resting in the flow of the rain gutter. "Can I look?" The kindness and warmth in his eyes dumbfounded Mary. No one had ever looked at her that way before.

Suddenly, Mary wasn't sure that she wasn't hallucinating this demi-god. Shoulders. Mmm, thighs. The size of his boots. Yeah. It was a lot for one man. This glory should be distributed between two, maybe three guys, even out the improbable a bit and make the vision less overwhelming. Add in an Australian accent—what red-blooded American girl didn't get a little nutso over an Australian accent?

Back at the hotel, when Mary described this hallucination, Deidre wouldn't believe a word of it. Mary thought about pulling out her phone and taking a surreptitious photo as proof, but then, her phone was in her pants, and her pants were under the dog. And the dog was kind of holding her up. So this might just go down in their shared friendship as "Do you remember when you told me about the archangel that tried to get you to put your pants on?" And they'd laugh and laugh.

Mary lifted her leg and placed her ankle in his hand. Oh, boy. This was the kind of thing that she had nightmares about, showing up in class naked. Only in this case, she was in her panties in the city, feeling tingly while this drool-worthy man was gently looking at the bottom of her foot.

Was this whole thing a weird dream seeded when Mrs. V. had looked deeply into her eyes and said, "You're lonely."?

Mary might have sucked in some noxious, hallucinatory chemicals up there. She reached down and pinched the side of her thigh hard enough to wince.

And that drew his attention. "Does it hurt there?"

His hand soothed over the spot.

Hurt? She shook her head. No, that actually felt really nice.

The dog was still behind her, providing a backrest, but he'd angled his head to drape over her shoulder, and his tongue hung long as he sent out a soulful whine.

"I know, Max. I know. I've got her," he told his pup, then looked at her. The look of hard focus he'd had as she inched down the wall was gone, replaced by warm concern. "My doggo is worried about you." He put his hand to his chest. "My name is Halo."

Of course, it was.

Some kind of angel that dropped down from Heaven.

This *had* to be some weird dream. Any minute now, the morning alarm was going to go off, and she would tell Deidre this story over coffee.

"Halo," he repeated, then pointed to his dog. "Max," he said.

"So I shouldn't call you Tool Guy?" As she said it aloud, she thought he would have no clue what that meant, but he responded with a grin and said, "I'm assuming your name isn't warrior goddess."

That actually drew a chuckle from deep in the pit of her abdomen.

That was how he'd labeled her?

"What's your actual name?" he asked.

In a dream, she could be anyone; she could be Belle or Sophia—no, those would be hard to pull off. She blinked up at Halo, and just in the off chance this wasn't a dream, she said, "I'm Mary." And then she coughed long and hard. Such a graceful flower.

Someone from the café across the street came with a bottle of water and handed it to Halo. "*Aiytah*," he said. "Thanks."

"Mary, was that an American accent I heard?"

She nodded vigorously as she covered her mouth with the back of her hand and coughed again.

"More scrapes and bruises than I would have thought," he said gently. "These look like they might be a few days old?" There was a question in his comment and a deeper concern.

If Mary saw these kinds of bruises in the emergency department, she'd ask if the person felt safe at home. "Yes," she managed. "Long story. I'm traveling with a friend. We were up on an Alp skiing. And my story goes downhill from there." Hey, that one wasn't bad. She'd have to work that into her comedy routine somewhere along the line.

Shoot, Deidre had signed them up for the open mic tonight.

This morning's events, though, would be a good enough reason to call it off.

"The kids?" Mary asked anxiously. "The woman?" Their safety was what was important at this moment.

"No idea. I'm sorry. They are off in the ambulance. I'm sure they'll mention it in the paper tomorrow. The news tonight. We can keep an eye out. Speaking of ambulances, do you feel like you'd like to get checked out? You breathed in a lot of smoke."

"Yeah, I'm good. I just need to cough up the soot. A little saline up the nose. A throat lozenge, I'm good to go."

"You're quite the monkey. I've never seen anything like that."

"Ah, well, it was good that you guys put your weight on that pole first. It would have been an easier climb had it been at a ninety-degree angle, but I would never have been able to reach the balcony if it was upright."

Halo lifted her arm, turned it, and searched along its length with the practiced eye of a medic. He replaced it in her lap, then reached for her other arm. "Were you a gymnast? A circus acrobat?"

"Pole dancer."

His brow drew together in confusion. Apparently not in his paradigms. Having turned forty at one minute after midnight, maybe he thought women had an expiration date. Well, lucky her, she didn't much care what he thought.

She was down. This was solid ground. There was fresh air. Life was good.

A stiff drink, though, might make life great.

Did they drink at nine in the morning in Tallinn?

He laid her hand gently on her lap. "The burns look like they're first-degree. Painful, but I don't think they need medical intervention." He reached out for her pants. "Max."

Max shifted off just long enough for Halo to pull her clothes free. Then Max budged closer to Mary, and she'd never felt safer. More supported.

Why didn't she have a dog?

She wanted a dog.

Halo handed the pants over. "I don't know if you want to put them on or if that would be painful."

Mary snapped the pants out so they laid in front of her. Avoiding the water, she grasped the waist band to tug them over her feet.

"Pole dancer. You know of all the things you could have said to me, that was not one I would have conjured."

"I don't look athletic enough?"

"No, you look like a lady." His eyes grew wide, and she saw that he was scrambling around in his mind. "I …" His face flamed red; it was endearing.

There she was with no shirt, her legs spread, her pants around her thighs, and her glitter panties. "I pole dance for exercise and because I get to hang out with an amazing group of women and have some fun. And *they* don't judge."

"I deeply apologize. That's not something I … So, I don't know … movies and such."

"You're okay." She stood up and jumped herself the rest of the way into her pants, feeling the back pocket to pull out her phone to quickly peck out: **I'm alive. I'll meet you at the hotel in a few minutes.** She sent the message to Deidre.

"Your rescue of that family was probably one of the bravest things I've ever witnessed. I'm in awe. How about this—" His phone rang. He listened for a minute. "Yes, Max is here with the angel who went up the building. Max was checking to make sure she was okay." He paused. "I think so." He turned to her. "I'll flag down a taxi and get her back to where she's staying."

He called her the angel that went up the side of the building, and his name was Halo.

Did that mean anything?

Nah. Mary didn't live that kind of charmed life.

Halo raised his hand, and the guy in the taxi pulled smoothly to the side of the road. He jumped out of the car, leaving his door wide, speaking with his hands around his face.

"You are hurt!" the man called to her. "The fire?" He pointed, and Mary turned to see the clouds of black billowing up behind the ancient rooftops.

"I'm okay, just … Can I get a ride home? Not home," she corrected. "My hotel. It's walking distance. I'm sorry. I know you guys hate that. Just … tired."

The man stepped forward with his hand extended. "Of course. Of course, this way."

Mary lifted her face to thank Halo. He stood there with unspoken words twitching at his lips, a conversation raging in his eyes. Stricken, he looked stricken all of a sudden. Mary blinked at him; wasn't that an odd word to think?

Halo quickly leaned over, gathered her shoes and shirt, and handed them to her.

"Thank you for saving my life." Mary raised up on her toes and pressed a kiss onto his cheek.

She shouldn't have done that. Something in her system exploded into sensations she couldn't name. Big. Jolting.

This had to have something to do with the shock of being alive, Mary surmised as she tucked into the cab. When Max scrambled to get in with her, Mary curved her fingers into his collar. "No, baby. As much as I would love for you to come with me, you need to stay with Halo."

"Mary, how can I check on you later?" Halo stepped forward, putting his own fingers into Max's collar. As their hands brushed, that sensation whooshed through her system from the tips of her toes to the top of her head. It unbalanced her. It snatched her breath. It was surreal.

As Halo pulled Max from the cab. Max stretched his tongue long, giving her kisses.

"Back it up, mate."

The accent. The shoulders. The worry and confusion in his eyes.

Mary had never experienced being disembodied before, but surely, this was what her patients had described to her.

He was expectantly waiting for an answer. Had she heard a question?

The taxi driver shut her door, slid under the wheel, and shut his own. "Ma'am. If not the hospital, where?"

Mary couldn't remember anything. She pulled her room card from the back of her phone and handed it to the man. He handed it back. "That's just around the corner."

As he drove away, Mary turned and put her hand on the back window.

Halo stood in the middle of the street, gripping Max's collar, staring her right in the eyes.

18

After retreating to their hotel and getting themselves and their equipment cleaned up, Titus called for the team to join him in the hotel conference room to do their hotwash over lunch, going over the rescue while the details were still fresh in their minds. What were the successes? How could they train to do a better job the next time?

Just like on the Commandos, Iniquus was always burnishing their skills.

All in all, Halo thought they'd moved through that scenario as successfully as their equipment and the circumstances would permit.

Everyone agreed that without Mary going up the pole and performing her death-defying aerial feats, the team would have had a difficult time coming up with a winning strategy.

She was the lynch pin.

That look in her eyes as he made the hasty, running the ropes around her waist and legs, making double, triple sure that they were secure. "I've got you." She'd licked her lips and nodded.

She believed that.

Believed *in* him with her life.

It was crazy what she did to him in the moment that he reached for her and pulled her into his arms, tight against his body, as he clasped them together. He'd felt her trust as he tied off the line—her escape from the inferno and his.

Focused as he was on keeping her ride slow and steady as he walked them down the wall, he was still aware of what was happening in his body.

Up in their room, as Halo was getting himself cleaned up and changed before the team meeting, he talked things over with Max. The best way Halo could describe the experience to his dog was that Halo was like a baby chick hatching. The shell cracked, and he'd been bewildered and confused as he stretched out in the new sensations he felt when he was near Mary.

Max had smiled at him as Halo said that. But he got it. Max had fallen in love with Mary, too.

Only problem was that Halo had no idea how to find her again.

Halo was hoping that as he sat with his team—spooning up the rich cream of mushroom soup and chomping on his sausage sandwich—that someone along the way knew who she was and would post her name and a social media link.

But so far, none of the social media posts that Nutsbe had been playing through this hotwash gave them any more information about her identity.

"I'm sure it felt like you were on the side of that building forever," Nutsbe said. "But you were up and down pretty fast." Nutsbe pressed a button on his computer, bringing up a timeline. "I have information about the delay in the rescue vehicles getting in." Nutsbe used a laser pointer to underline the arrival times of the various rescue teams. "The ambulance was there pretty fast. It was the firetruck with the ladders that was problematic. I called to find out. The fire house is blocks away and should have been there with a three-to-five-minute response time. Unfortunately, the crew was already in the field dealing with an industrial spill. Dispatch brought in a crew from further away. It's important to remember that while this is the capital of Estonia and a third of its citizens live here, it's still a relatively small city. About the size of Richmond, Virginia." He named the capital city of the state just south of Washington, D.C.

"Nutsbe, I'd like you to map out various issues that might come into play when the Sutton board goes out for their bog walk," Titus said. "We know from your arrival this morning that there's ongoing street repair."

"Wilco," Nutsbe said. "Now, I've culled through social media posts, and I have some bystander videos of the incident."

Reel by reel, they assessed technique, opportunities that were used to their best advantage, mistakes, and near misses. Every time Mary was in the frame, Halo was impressed by her sheer determination. And a sense that she was both winging it and that she had real training under her belt.

Pole dancing, though. It confounded him. There had to be a story there, and it had to extend beyond his personal framing of that sport. Past-framing—he'd evolved.

"Ready for the next one?" Nutsbe asked as he queued up another bystander video that had been posted on social media. Different angles meant different opportunities to assess. "I'm calling this one, *All Hail Queen Mary*."

Here, someone had focused on the first moments when the team decided to scale from window to window.

Mary sprinted onto the scene, plopped onto the pavement, wrestled out of her pants and shoes, and was inch worming up the pole.

Halo wondered why she'd taken her clothes off.

As she climbed, Max stretched as far out as he could

without breaking his sit-stay and dragged her clothes back piece by piece. Then, he'd laid across them, protecting Mary's things.

Halo hadn't taught Max that trick.

"And this one I'm calling, *Hey, You Forgot Something.*" Nutsbe moved to the next video. "Before I play this, I'm going to say that I was focused on the team getting off the wall. But at this point, Mary was part of the team. She is clearly shaken, maybe in shock. I should have had my eyes on her. I should have tried to corral her—something. She shouldn't have been left to wander half-naked and possibly injured down the street like that. I'll work on protocols for future events and run them by the team. All I can say is that I'm very grateful that Max did what he did." Nutsbe tapped the play button, and there was Titus pulling Mary from the last windowsill into his arms. He carried her over the broken shards of glass and set her down on the road in front of a paramedic.

"Hold there," Titus said, and Nutsbe hit stop. "I agree with your assessment, Nutsbe. She was a team member at this point, and it was up to us to make sure that the whole team was safe. I will say that there might have been a language barrier that the rescue worker couldn't understand her. She might have declined aid, as she has the right to do. But shock is shock. Someone should have been supporting Mary at this point. Go ahead and press play again."

Mary was waving off help, turning, and staggering down the street. People reached out to her, spoke to her, and she brushed them off as she walked in the cool rainwater that filled the gutters.

The video moved away from Mary and toward Halo and the others as they were still getting off the wall. The lens panned to the right, where Max was gathering Mary's things into his mouth, dropping them, processing them, then wrapping the clothing items together, biting into the bundle, and trotting off after Mary. Granted, he'd dragged the pants under him, and a sock was left behind, but he was still able to get his snoot to the ground and trail along after her.

Halo hadn't taught Max to do that series of tricks, either.

As soon as Halo put his feet on the ground, he'd looked over to check on Max only to find his dog was gone. Even though Max had been put in a down-stay, he was highly intelligent. Halo figured that Max had moved to a place that was close but safe. He needed to find Max, then he needed to find the warrior goddess and assure himself that she hadn't been injured while performing the wildest lifesaving mission he'd ever experienced.

When Halo sent out a "Here to me" whistle, a woman leaned around a shop door frame, pointing down the road. "Dog go that way with woman's clothes."

It was at that moment that Halo placed the woman. Max and she had already bonded. She was the woman at the airport who had crouched down, looking at Max. And Max had wanted to be with her, tugging at his lead. That was the first time Halo had seen that happen.

In the airport, Max's nose had been chuffing the air as he tried to get over to her.

Yea, Halo was sure that Max had recognized her scent.

Pulling up the tracking app, Halo saw that the red dot representing Max was three blocks away and wasn't moving. Halo's heart had gripped, wondering if a car had hit Max.

He raced up the street until he saw the two of them together. Her in her panties and sports bra, feet in the cool gutter water, draping over Max, her head on his neck.

As Halo approached, without moving his body, Max turned to Halo, and Halo clearly read in his dog's eyes that he had decided that Mary was his to guard.

Yours and mine both, mate.

Bloody hell, that feeling of her getting in the taxi without him, Max wanting to jump in beside her. He knew her name as Mary. He knew she was American. Nothing else.

Calling out, "Can I have your number," or "Where are you staying?" or any of the other things that sprang to mind made him sound like a creep. Like someone who wanted to take advantage of the situation. All he wanted for her at that moment was that she get safely back to her hotel where she could rest.

When the taxi drove away, Max was *pissed.*

And Halo stood there feeling like his soul had been snatched away.

"Gentlemen," Titus said. "The agenda for the rest of the day. I'd like you to spend some time individually walking around Old City, Tallinn, getting a feel for the area and the people. This evening, I've made reservations for the team downstairs in the restaurant. There is an open mic tonight, so if anyone wants to sign up, go ahead and do that on your way out." He turned to Nutsbe. "I'd like you to eat early so you're ready for your meeting with Honey. Max's crate has arrived, and the staff set it up in Halo's room. I'd like Max to stay crated this evening while you supervise him, Nutsbe." He turned to catch Halo's gaze. "I'd like you downstairs with us, get some grub, and get to know the Panther Force team."

It was wisely against Iniquus' policy to leave one of the Iniquus-affiliated K9s unsupervised. And since Nutsbe had brought Max all the way over from the states, Halo was cool with that. "Yes, sir."

~

THAT EVENING, right on time, Nutsbe arrived at Halo's room to find sleeping Max lying on his back, legs sprawled wide, snoring.

"Enjoy yourself. I'll text if I have anything come up," Nutsbe said as Halo patted over his pockets to make sure he had everything and headed out the door.

Dinner with an open mic might be distracting. And Halo desperately wanted a distraction.

He was still hoping that Nutsbe would come up with a name and contact information so he could reach out to Mary.

Until then, yeah, distraction was the best he could do.

He walked down the hall and decided to take the stairs to pound away some of this odd sensation that had bubbled through his system ever since Mary kissed him goodbye.

He was thinking about Max's desperation to get in the taxi with Mary and his last determined lunge to lick her cheek.

As they'd walked around Tallinn earlier, Halo had been going over the how and why of Max's connection to Mary that had started in the airport.

Dogs were alert to even the smallest changes in a person's posture or environment. They knew what a human would do even before the human had recognized that a decision had been made. That's why a dog would run over and sit by their lead, waiting for a walk, before their human realized that they would go out.

That scenario was a very domestic application of a dog's keen sense. In his job, that ability to see micromovements was about minute-to-minute survival.

The dogs Halo handled were taught to focus on a weapon.

A weapon in the hand of a bad guy might be alright; there might still be time to talk the guy down, and everyone could leave whole and healthy. This was particularly important when they were on foreign lands negotiating through difficult situations.

But if a finger were to slide into the guard and rest on a trigger, then all bets were off.

From helmet cameras that the team used to analyze the various situations they'd found themselves in, they watched time and time again as the dogs launched into the air as the bad guy's finger still laid along the guard. As their mouths opened wide to wrap the wrist, they'd be chomping just as the finger moved into a lethal position on the trigger.

Their jaws locked down on the tendon, making it impossible for the finger to pull back and fire their weapon. The excruciating pain of having the arm bones crushed between the pressure of those jaws preempted any thoughts outside of survival.

Through these tapes, Halo learned to always trust his dog.

Halo also learned that as a K9 handler, he couldn't act like his teammates, who often walked around seemingly armor-plated when it came to emotions. Even keel, unperturbed, that's how operators managed. They bypassed emotions like anger, anxiety, and sadness. But, Halo observed that if his brothers were unwilling to face negative emotions, eventually, they lost their emotional range on the other side of the spectrum. If his brothers stood at the fulcrum, not letting things tip the scale where feelings might outweigh training and calculation—which could prove lethal in the field—it also prevented them from the other end of the spectrum where joy lived.

A human's closed-off emotions, though, shut a dog down. It was as if they didn't trust that person and wouldn't bond.

In Halo's early days learning to work with military K9s, he and a handful of others were sent to special classes on emotional intelligence. They attended therapy as part of a research initiative to find out if being a full-spectrum human with healthy mental health habits made for a better dog handler.

The scientists never presented the findings to Halo, and he didn't much care about the researchers' conclusions. Halo's gut told him that the research hypothesis had been tight.

When Halo had expressed emotions, talking to his dogs like they were the intimate partners that they were, he felt certain that his authenticity and candor built trust between them as working partners.

To gain a dog's trust was the ultimate reward. It was something that Halo was glad to work toward. And he felt like that translated into better relationships outside of the job as well. Friends, family, yeah, that was all going to plan.

But now that he was turning forty, Halo was getting a new perspective. He could see over the hill down into the length of fertile soil that stretched out to the horizon. And for the last little bit, he'd come to realize that he no longer wanted to walk that trail alone.

He just didn't.

Pulling all those thoughts together with one big, red, shiny bow, Halo came to this conclusion: When they were at the airport, and Max saw Mary, he bloody well knew something about her that Halo had not yet perceived.

And in that airport, Halo made a terrible mistake.

He should have trusted his dog.

19

Mary had dragged her shirt over her head in the cab on her way to her hotel. By the time they pulled up, she was lacing up her second shoe.

Pulling her credit card from the sleave on the back of her phone, she extended it over the seat. The man shook his hands in the air. "You need to go in and take care of yourself."

Kind. "Thank you so much."

Deidre was still sitting on the bench outside under the tree, scrolling her phone. She turned to Mary. "What in the actual heck?"

Waggling an exhausted hand in the air, Mary turned toward the automatic doors.

The front desk staff followed her progress with wide, unblinking eyes.

Mary approached the guy who had given her the directions earlier. "I was on the way to the pharmacy." She turned to look toward the door. "There was a fire."

"Do you need a doctor?" he asked.

"I could really use a room. I know it's early, but a shower and a nap would be nice right now."

"Of course!" He unlocked the closet and wheeled their bags out. Deidre was kind enough to shut the hell up as they went up the elevator, down the hall, and into their room.

"Shower," Deidre said as she pointed to the bathroom.

Standing under the water, letting it sluice over her back, Mary lifted her hair and sniffed it. It stank of chemicals and ash.

As she closed her eyes and just appreciated the feel of clean water, Mary pictured Halo looking at her through the back window of the cab as she drove away.

He hadn't moved other than to put his hands on his hips and furrow his brow as if this whole scene was beyond him. Shards of fractured glass that were supposed to fit together. Mary couldn't fathom what might be going on in his head, standing there like an action hero on a movie screen.

Shit, he's a hero on a movie screen.

She laid her forehead on the tile.

Tallinn, Mary had read in the book she'd snatched up in the Geneva airport, was known for the number of movies that took advantage of the gorgeous settings.

That *must* be why that group of massive, handsome men and their dog were in the street with matching uniform-like outfits, speaking English.

Mary felt herself blanche in horror.

She had defined the group as special operators, men who had trained to do crazy-dangerous acts of great athleticism. Yeah, they had to be athletes, or they wouldn't have bodies like that.

Maybe they were trained stunt men?

She had put her life in what she'd convinced herself was their capable hands.

That was a lie.

Retrospective fear was an icy wash. And her whole body jolted.

When the sensation passed, Mary asked herself, did it matter?

She was alive, whole, mostly unscathed. The family was down.

Still, Mary was shaking her head at the idea of the Halo that she'd conjured.

She unwrapped the mistake, reformed her thoughts, and tried to get herself realigned.

The door opened, and Deidre came in. "Okay, you've been in here long enough. You should be ready to talk by now. Are you hurt?"

"Nope." Mary reached for the soap.

"I was looking this up on social media and almost vomited when I saw what you did. That was terrifying!" Deidre said.

"Videos? Shit. I was in my underpants."

"Full coverage ones, not string thongs." Deidre pointed out. "So that was good. And you didn't have your period, so no maxi pads were strapped to your crotch."

"Small favors. Can you imagine?"

"Imagine? I'm watching the video and can't wrap my brain around it. You risked your life. You are a hero. I know you're in there playing this over in your head. You can't keep today on a loop in your mind. You'll make yourself crazy."

"I thought it was my boys," Mary whispered.

"What?"

"My brain," Mary poured shampoo onto her head, "did a wackadoodle thing. When I looked up at the burning building, the two boys were side by side. I thought they were my sons."

"You're a mama bear."

Mary breathed through the anxiety attack that bloomed across her chest.

"Pole dancing for the win?" Deidre asked.

"Who'd a thunk it?" The foam sliding down her body was like a black lava flow.

"Next question. Who was that guy up there with you?"

"His name is Halo. It's got to be a last name or a call sign or something. No mother in her right mind would name her kid Halo."

"I don't know, I had a patient once whose name was Truest."

"That's not that bad," Mary said.

"Her last name was Ho. Now, granted, the parents were new to America and translating from their own language."

"Still." Mary turned to rinse before moving on to the repeat.

"Hey, I'm handing you in my makeup removers. They'll work better on that greasy soot." Deidre's hand shot past the curtain with the packet of wipes. "Halo and Mary," Deidre tried on. "If you two were a couple, you can have one of those celebrity names. You know how they mash things together like Brangelina. People could call you Hail Mary."

"Sounds like you're jinxing us. Nope. There is no *us*—I have no idea who the guy is. Some actor, probably."

"Actor? He didn't act like an actor," Deidre said. "Listen, you just pulled two kids and a mom off the fifth floor of a burning building. And I will remind you that you were sent here specifically to this single spot. That's career, love life, and purpose. One spot on one single day. This is written in the stars, Mary. There's no jinx about this at all."

It took a while to feel fresh and clean, for the heat of the water to ease her muscles.

Mary dragged herself from the bathroom and flopped onto the bed. Deidre only allowed her a thirty-minute nap.

She forced Mary to get up and go to a restaurant for lunch, saying that she wouldn't sleep that night if she slept now.

Then she made Mary walk along the Baltic Sea, in case fate wanted to jump out and say boo!

Nothing more had happened.

"Dinner," Mary said, checking her watch. "And then, I'm done. I'm not sure I'm up to an open mic thing you have us signed up for. I want to go back to our room."

Deidre wrapped her arm through Mary's. "You'll lay down, try to fall asleep, toss, and turn all night because it's too early. You're still jet lagged. Let's pull on our dresses, we'll go have a drink. I'll sing, and if you feel like getting on stage, fine. If not, no pressure."

"Pass." Mary tried to sound unmovable.

"That's not how we deal with the horrors of life," Deidre said. "When shit goes down at the hospital, when we're on the team dealing with tragic things, we don't go home and wallow. We change the energy. What if we didn't go anywhere tonight? What would you do?"

"Get drunk in our room."

"You can do that around people who are laughing and enjoying themselves so you can see that no matter what, life goes on," Deidre countered.

"I'd soak in a hot bath."

"We have a shower. No bath."

"Don't get technical with me," Mary grumped. "I want to wallow. I was in my kitchen unpacking my groceries, then forced against my will onto a plane, I fell down a mountain, then fell down a second one, then I was forced on to a second plane."

"No one forced you." Deidre came to a stop to let a car pass, then they started across the road. "You were encouraged and maybe a little pushed. But pushing isn't forcing. And I will remind you that you made me go to your pole dancing studio, and I hung from a pole held in place by the friction of my skin. Did I love that experience? I did not. Am I glad I did it? Yes, I am, if for no other reason than you continued to go and learned how to do those tricks. And in the videos of today's events, those tricks saved lives."

When Mary didn't respond, Deidre reached out and squeezed her hand. "Try this on: we go downstairs and have a nice meal. I read the offerings in the restaurant, and there are lots of carbs and fat to help settle your nerves. I told them you were coming, and they have cake," she singsonged.

Mary looked up. "Chocolate cake?"

"Absolutely."

"Okay, to dinner."

"Once you're full of potatoes, you'll feel better. And then, if you do feel better, we'll go down the street. Look, I'm reminding you again you are here because three things are supposed to happen. Something that affects your career. Something that affects your life trajectory. And something that is about love."

"Yeah, I thought about that as I was dangling above the sidewalk. Maybe the other two didn't matter if my life trajectory had mere seconds to go."

Then she remembered what Mrs. V. had said about the one minute past midnight meant everything to others, and a shiver raked up her spine.

Deidre stopped and looked at her friend with worried eyes. "You okay?"

"Yeah. Yeah."

"Mary, you're supposed to get all three things here. As far as we know, none of that has happened. You have six more hours. You can't be in the hotel room wasting your opportunity. You have to be out there." Deidre whooshed her arms toward the door.

"Okay, just so we agree that on the stroke of midnight, my duty to this whole scenario is done."

"Agreed." Deidre reached to pull Mary's arm. "At midnight, it is *finis*. Over. Done."

20

Deidre was singing her little heart out. She was going for it, and it was spectacular as she cupped the mic and curled over, squeezing every last bubble of oxygen from her lungs to hold that note long and strong.

Something had gotten into her that night, Mary mused. Usually, she wasn't quite so … dramatic. Or good. This was a quality performance. Mary was glad she'd propped up the camera on Deidre's phone to record just how well things had gone.

As Deidre came up with a radiant smile, the audience whooped, whistled, and clapped in appreciation. And in a very un-Deidre-like way, she did a little curtsy. "Ladies and gentlemen, thank you. If you would indulge me for a moment, I wonder if you would help me celebrate my best friend's fortieth birthday. She's here with us tonight." Deidre stretched her arm out, palm up, to focus everyone's attention to where Mary sat.

Offering the room a flat-lipped smile, Mary gave them a finger wave.

Deidre started them off on "Happy birthday to you—"

Mary was surprised they knew the words and had joined in,

raising their glasses in her direction and swaying to the tune. It was sweet, Mary thought. Yeah, it was nice. She didn't mind turning forty. She didn't mind everyone knowing that she'd hit that milestone. She just *hated* it when she went out for a birthday dinner; it was mentioned to the waiter, and the wait-staff came pouring out of the kitchen to sing to her when she knew darn well that it was probably the most miserable part of their night. This didn't feel that way. She was fine with this, Mary decided.

What she wasn't fine with was the second part of Deidre's ask.

Once the clapping stopped and the audience turned back to Deidre, she winked toward Mary. "So my birthday friend is quite the burgeoning comedian."

Mary shook her head.

"She was signed up to try out her new schtick tonight."

Yeah, Deidre had signed her up in her new-found "Grab the bull by the horns" life philosophy that she had adopted. Just like Mary's own twenty-new-things goal, Deidre seemed to put her head down and plow ahead as a way to cope with her own child-off-in-the-world, her own divorce, and her hot-flashing, menopausal brain warp.

"But tonight, she was feeling a little shy."

Bruised. Burned. Exhausted. A bit in shock. *Not* shy.

"I think if we give her a little encouragement, though, we could get her up on the stage. What do you all think? Should we invite the birthday girl up to entertain us?"

The audience did as asked. The clapping extended on and on until Mary was able to get up from her table and move to the stage stairs.

The look Mary sent Deidre as they passed each other would make any normal mortal wither into a pile of remorse on the stage. But as Deidre handed the mic over to Mary, she smiled her wicked smile and popped her brows, leaning into the privilege of a lifetime of mutual support and sisterly love.

Mary wasn't feeling that love so much. But she was feeling genuine warmth coming from the people who had gathered. She decided to try on her new material, do her best, bomb if she must, then slam a glass of something strong, and go to bed to pass out.

"My friend Deidre, ladies and gentlemen." Mary extended the mic in Deidre's direction as her friend took the two steps down from the platform and wended her way, gratitude arm in the air, back to their seats.

"So here I am. Kinda of spur of the moment. A lot spur of the moment. So I'm afraid that you're going to get what you get. And I'm going to tell you right here and now that if you don't enjoy yourselves, it's your own darned fault that I'm up here." She pointed toward the back of the room. "I was minding my own business, and you all insisted."

The crowd laughed.

Laughter was good, actually. After a day of terror, yeah, laughter was good. Maybe she should trust that Deidre had her best interest at heart.

"The great thing about having a standup mic night here at the comedy club in Tallinn, Estonia, is that almost everyone here listening to me is an English-as-a-second-language person. Don't get me wrong, most of the men and women I've spoken with in my short time in your amazing city speak better English than the folks in my hometown."

A chuckle ran through the crowd.

"Anyway, if you don't laugh, I'm going to chalk it up to 'lost in translation' a lesson learned. Speaking of lessons learned. Let's talk about the deficit of my education."

Mary paused as a stagehand dressed in black slid smoothly toward center stage, a stool in each hand. He placed them down, side by side, then pulled a water bottle from under his arm, loosened the cap before setting them on one of the stools, and slid back behind the curtains.

"Oh good." She lifted a thigh onto the stool, so she was half-sitting, half-standing. "I've had a busy day today. So this is nice. Okay, so about me. I grew up Catholic. Not the C&E Catholic, where you go to mass only on Christmas and Easter. We were good Catholics." She put the last words into finger quotes. "My Aunt Mary was a nun. And it was very strange to have a nun in the family, especially one who took the vow of poverty and silence. When she came over for dinner, she'd sit there and smoke. She'd eat what was scooped onto her plate. Then, if she wanted more of something, she'd lift her chin to point it out and make these puppy dog, pleading eyes." Mary acted it out. "And when she was full, she'd leave."

Mary paused as a chuckle ran through the room.

"But I guess the nun that had the most impact on my life was a woman by the name of Sister Inez. She's the one who taught my all-girls, state-required family life course. Here was a woman who—orphaned at age ten—grew up in a convent in Spain. As a fifty-year-old woman, she decided suddenly to leave her cloistered life where the only men she ever saw were the priest and, once a year, her dentist. She got on a plane, came to America, and started teaching language classes. And oddly, she was the one assigned to teach the girls at my school the state required sex ed information that she called 'Family Life.'"

Mary watched as the silhouettes of the giant men standing in the back of the room migrated to the tables the host brought them to.

Was that the team from this morning?

Was Halo with them?

Her heart beat faster.

"Sister Inez was a woman who had no understanding of

how sex worked. And even less understanding of the male body. In her Spanish convent, they shielded the nuns from the sins of the flesh, even in the paintings, there were no nudes. I will never know how and why she was the chosen teacher to prepare us young women for our marital beds." Mary reached over to take a sip from the water bottle. "So imagine, if you will, there I was in my science class, taking notes as the very innocent Sister Inez presented to us the private parts of a male body and its functionality."

Another sip, and she set the bottle down to free her hand.

"This is what Sister Inez told us about the male penis." Mary held up a peace sign and then pointed it toward the ground. 'A man has penises,' she said. *Two* of them." Mary tapped her middle finger. "One was for procreation." She tapped her index finger. "the other was for urination."

She raised her eyebrow. "Yes, I was taught, and honestly believed, that there would be two penises when I unwrapped the male package."

She let her head hang and shook it back and forth while the men in the room chuckled.

Raising her eyes again, she said, "I was married very early, straight out of high school." And lest Halo was in the room. "He's my ex- now. And I can't say that it isn't ultimately Sister Inez's fault. Our sex life got off on very bad footing. And I don't think my then-husband ever fully recovered from the experience." She adjusted herself on the stool. "Imagine on my wedding night, I am seeing a naked man for the very first time. I'm ready to consummate my vows." She held the two fingers and then pointed them down. The crowd already got it and laughed long and hard. "I understood that a man would be engorged while aroused. Sister Inez said that was how a woman could tell the difference between the penis meant for procreation and the penis meant for urination, and we wouldn't mistakenly put the peeing penis inside of us because that would lead to infections called STDs."

The guffaws grew louder.

"There he was, my new hubby. Very happy. Very excited about what was coming next. There was me, kneeling on the bed, looking down at him. And I realized my new husband only had one penis. I was in shock." She stopped and blinked at the audience. "Obviously, something was horribly wrong with him. Some terrible disfiguring accident that he hadn't told me about."

More laughter.

When Mary challenged herself to take the stand-up classes and say the things that she'd been taught not to say in public—things like sex and words like penis—it was a bit of a struggle. But when people laughed at the shared human experience, Mary had learned to really enjoy it. Connecting with an audience, receiving their energy in return that wasn't for "other people." It could be for her, too.

Wonder of wonders.

"And because my hubby was at full staff and ready to rock my world, I knew that whatever disfiguring horror had happened to him, he'd at least kept the penis meant for procreation. Win!" Mary held up a victory fist.

The laughs kept coming.

"Right, so there I am hunkered over, staring at his dick, and my expression had to be one of confusion. Horror even. How did this man pee? I wondered, trying to work through the situation in my mind. And I just remember looking up at him, wanting to convey sympathy, caring, and support. And so I said, "Oh, dear. I'm so so sorry. But it's gonna be OK. I'm sure this isn't as terrible as it looks."

The room roared with laughter.

"That's my time." Mary lifted the mic over her head.

"Thank you for your kind reception." She bowed, stood, and waved goodbye, turning to leave the stage, buoyed by their response.

Today had been weird, and having checked this off her to-do list, all Mary had to do was wait out the clock until midnight to get Deidre off her back.

The stage manager ran out on stage and grabbed one of her hands, dragging her back to center stage and taking the microphone from her.

Mary thought he might want her to take a second bow, but instead, he said, "Ladies and gentlemen, I think you all should know that Mary Williams, who just entertained you with her very funny story, happens to be the woman who scaled the pole, saving the young family in today's Old City fire."

Mary froze.

Recognition was absolutely something that she had *not* wanted to happen.

The whole audience rose to their feet. Their roar was a tsunami of energy that washed over her. Overwhelmed. Mary stood there, eyes unblinking, completely horrified to have this attention.

The spotlight swept the room so she could see the respect and gratitude.

What she saw brought her relief—a way to divest herself of this kind of attention.

The men at the back of the room, cheering her, were indeed the team that had saved her. Mary pulled the microphone to her mouth. "You are very kind. But I was merely one of a group of people trying to help. If you turn to the back of the room, ladies and gentlemen, you will see the heroic team that used their bodies to make a human ladder. My great thanks go out to each of them, as I could have done nothing alone. And without them, I would have been a victim of the fire."

As the wave of gratitude shifted to the men, Mary wobbled toward the stairs.

And there was Halo, his hands ready to catch her.

Without any hesitation at all, she collapsed back into his arms.

The only real surprise to Mary was that he whispered into her ear, “Oh, thank god, I was afraid I wouldn’t find you again.”

21

"Hey, you're shaking. Are you okay?" Halo bent to speak in her ear so she could hear above the continued applause for the rescue team—so well deserved.

No, actually, Mary realized she wasn't okay. She shook her head with a frown.

"Come on." He reached for her hand. "I know what might help. Why don't we go find Max, and you can get some dog medicine?"

As Halo led her out of her room, Mary turned and caught Deidre's gaze so she would know what was going on.

Deidre gave her an exaggerated wink and two thumbs up.

Mary turned to make sure that Halo hadn't seen that. Luckily, he was giving his own signal to the team.

As they moved away from the noise into the lobby, Mary asked, "Where's Max?"

"In my room. Nutsbe had a meeting, so he was doing dog-sitting duties." He stopped to look her in the eye. He did that a lot, Mary thought. It was like he was trying to read her expression and not just listen to her words. It felt intimate.

It felt …

Yeah, Mary had spent a lifetime speaking into the wind, hoping her then-husband was paying any attention at all. Invariably, she'd bring up a conversation, and her ex would gaslight her, saying she was crazy and that they had never talked about X, Y, or Z.

But Halo, Halo was fully present.

"If you're uncomfortable in my room, we can figure something else out." He reached for the elevator button, and the door slid open.

"Quiet is better, I think."

Flashing his keycard in front of the panel, then pressing the sixth-floor button, Halo said, "Max was devastated that you left without him when you got in the cab."

"Sweet Max." And that was the last they said until Halo tapped the door before swiping his card. The silence between them had been easy.

A man stood up from behind his computer. "Mary!" He looked over to Halo. "You found her."

"She happened to be downstairs." Halo moved over to the crate, where Max pawed at his latch. "Are you done with your meeting? We can leave."

"Good timing, I just got off the call." The man nodded toward Max. "He just used the toilet."

"Good job, Max." Halo opened the door, and Max pushed through, bounding over to Mary.

She bent down to let Max wiggle and kiss his way around her legs.

"My teammate, Nutsbe," Halo said with a hand toward the other guy.

"Hi there!" Mary got a hand free to offer a wave.

Nutsbe was gathering his things into a computer bag. "Hey, listen, I just got word from the hospital, Mary. The two boys were released and went home with family. They're perfectly fine."

Mary wavered, she was the heat rising from the desert highway, just a shiver in the air.

Halo wrapped his arms lightly around her waist, holding her steady. She felt him mouthing, "the mom?"

"The mother is in intensive care but they project a full recovery. They'll live. The building was all but destroyed. But there were no deaths."

"Whew." Mary looked up at Halo then took his hand so she could sink to the floor, using the bed for a backrest. "Whew," she said again.

"And back to business for just a moment then I'll get out of your hair." Nutsbe focused on Halo. "Your rental car is in the parking lot. I've programmed your shirt. You're all set for the bog tomorrow."

"Bog?" Mary tipped her head back. "I thought they were in Scotland."

"About an hour outside of Tallinn. It's gorgeous there," Halo said. "I went yesterday with the team, and I need to go back and introduce Max to the area and see how he does out there."

"Oh, I'd love to see that, and Deidre—my friend I'm traveling with—is nursing a bum knee from skiing. Do you think it's possible for me to come?" It was audacious, but why not ask? She looked from Halo to Nutsbe since Nutsbe seemed to be the organizer. "Or is this … Ha, Sorry about that. I'd think it was odd if you invited yourself to my place of work to see what I do after just meeting you. I'm sorry. Forget I asked."

"No, ma'am, I'm glad you did, actually," Nutsbe said. "Our job is to keep civilians safe in various scenarios. It might be interesting to have you go out with Halo and get your feedback.

I need to run this by our team lead, Titus Kane. But the team knows and highly esteems you."

"Isn't that nice?" A bemused smile softened Mary's face. "I'm not sure that I've been highly esteemed before."

Nutsbe grinned. "Your heroism will be told for generations, The Legend of Flagpole Mary." He clasped his bag. And pulled the strap over his shoulder. "We have a protocol in place that allows volunteers to join a research trip," he told Mary. "You'd need to sign a contract with us. It provides insurance should anything go wrong. It puts you under our protection. And you'd have to understand that Halo is working while he's out there and is held to a very," he cleared his throat, "strict set of conduct rules."

"Of course," Mary said.

"After I check with Titus, I'll text Halo with the response. If I get his okay, I can meet you downstairs in the morning with the paperwork." He reached into his thigh pocket and pulled out a pad and pen, handing them to Mary. "Can I get your legal name, home address, and local contact number? If you're able to go, I need them for the contracts. If Titus doesn't okay it, for whatever reason, we'd still like to have your information in our system because of today."

"Yes, of course." Mary reached for the pad and leaned over the nightstand to jot out the information. Nutsbe accepted it back and walked into the hall.

"Thanks, mate," Halo said, gently closing the door. Turning to Mary, he asked, "Are you comfortable being in this room? If you prefer, we could go to the lobby or our conference room downstairs, or—it's a beautiful night—we could sit in the park."

"Can I lay on your bed?" Mary asked. "Is Max allowed up?"

"Make yourself comfortable."

"Your team, they're American. And you're Australian?" Mary asked, sitting on the corner of the mattress and slipping off her shoes.

"Yes. Well raised in Australia, born in America."

"Your eyes are different," Mary budged farther onto the bed, settling her back against the headboard, her legs stretched long.

"I'm sorry?" Halo gave Max the hand signal to load onto the bed.

Max jumped up next to Mary, curling into place against her.

Mary wiggled a finger near the corner of her face. "Your eyes are different from the other men's. With the other guys, there's a hardness to them. I wonder if that's what happens when you go to war." Her fingers rubbed behind Max's ear. "What did you do for the military?"

"I was a Commando." Halo dragged a chair to the side of the bed near her feet.

"Commandos. What is that?"

"Australian special forces."

"Ah, okay, that makes sense." She popped her brows. "And whew! You're not an actor."

"Sorry?" He canted his head.

"Nothing." She batted a hand through the air. "Just let that go. Special Forces, you were in the thick of things."

He sat and untied his boots. "Ah. Well, I went to war. Twenty years of war."

"But…" Mary put her hand over her heart. "I'm sorry for the losses you must have experienced." Her brow drew together. "Commando. That was very dangerous."

"It had its moments." He shucked his shoes and socks. "I was lucky, though. I was the K9 handler."

"The others on your team didn't work with dogs?"

His brow drew together.

"I'm trying to understand why your eyes aren't hard."

"Pretty easy. Like I said, I was my Commando team's K9 handler. If I walked around with special forces energy, my dogs would pick up on that and get stressed out. Our dogs only work when they're having fun."

"Fun? In war?" Mary asked, adjusting the pillows behind her back.

"They don't understand war. They understand they're doing a job. And they want to please their handler. As the handler, I needed to make sure they were healthy and happy at work. Their job saved my brothers' lives. My life. So, so many times."

"War calcifies people." She sighed. "I'm an ex-military wife. I've seen it. There are ramifications for the families."

"This is, unfortunately, true. It had an effect on my family. I'm also divorced. It's me and Max."

"Max looks young."

"He turned two years last week."

"Happy birthday, baby." She scritched his ears. "How did he come into your life?"

Halo propped his feet on the bed next to Mary's. It felt comfortable. It felt like—Mary searched for a word, and all she could come up with was 'aligned.' It felt like they had already done all the trust-building. After all, she wasn't testing the guy to see if he'd show up and help her move something heavy. She'd literally put her survival in the man's hands, and he had been a solid partner in getting her from desperate to safe. She'd survived. Yeah, after today's fire, Mary couldn't imagine this man hurting her or allowing her to come to harm. There was a certain amount of peace that came with her conviction.

"I went with a friend on an errand to the shelter, where I met Max. From the moment I looked into his eyes, I knew that we were partners. I've been training him since he was a pup." Max lifted his head from Mary's lap and looked over at Halo.

"From the beginning, keeping Max's mind busy with training had been a challenge. But it's proven to be imperative. A bored Max can easily become a destructive Max. There is no kennel or lock yet from which Max can't devise his Houdini-like escape. And that led to one very bad puppy teething incident when I came home to find he'd eaten my leather couch."

Mary laughed. "Oh, but he was a little puppy, right?"

"He's still young and super bright, which makes for a challenging combo. If Max isn't learning, he's looking for his own fun. And sometimes that's destructive."

"Destructive like what?" Mary said, bending to plant a kiss on Max's head. "Besides your couch."

"He ate the rubber bumper off my mate's car."

Her brows flew up. "Serious?"

"He was mighty proud of himself when he had it all the way off." Halo reached over to the mini fridge and pulled out a water bottle, holding it up.

"Yes, thank you. That could become a very expensive habit, eating bumpers." She reached for the bottle and then settled back. "He was wearing a working vest today. I'm trying to put that together with his bringing me my clothes. What is his job? What are Malinois bred to do?"

"They're herd dogs, like shepherds."

"Then why do Navy SEALs use them?" She rolled the water bottle along her neck, appreciating the coolness and weight.

"High energy, amazing noses, highly trainable. They've got the speed and drive, the work ethic and loyalty that we need."

"The loyalty is apparent. And his job? What does he do? I mean, besides eating couches and cars."

"He's trained in tracking for search and rescue. He's also a tactical dog."

"Which means?" she asked.

"He can jump out of helicopters, fast rope down cliffs. He can take down the bad guy."

"A hero pup." Her hand slid down to pat Max's rump. "And you trained him to do all that? Impressive. Halo isn't your given name, is it?"

"No, I'm Basil St. John. Halo isn't a bad call sign. Could be worse. They could have focused on Basil and called me Herb or Spaghetti or something. Some guys got terrible names."

"Yeah? Give me an example."

"Well, you just met Nutsbe. His last name is Crushed."

"Nutsbe Crushed?" She laughed. "That's terrible! His poor mother."

"Interesting," Halo said. "I've only just met Nutsbe, but the few times I've mentioned his name to a woman, that's the reigning sentiment, 'his poor mother.' Curious."

"Hard to explain to a guy. On the other hand, I bet your mother's quite pleased that you came out of the military with the name Halo."

"She is, actually."

He leaned forward, his finger gently circling the string of bruises on the tops of her feet. "These weren't visible yet when you were in the street."

"Pole kisses," Mary said. "I get them every time I pole dance."

"Is that a popular sport where you're from?" Halo held her foot in his hand, massaging over her toes.

Normally, Mary would be reticent for a man to touch her feet unless she'd just stepped out of the bath. But oddly, it was a flash of thought and then gone. She'd just enjoy the sensation. "Pole dancing? Not really. No."

He turned her foot to look at the string of bruises up the inside of her leg from ankle to thigh. "These bruises in this pattern are from climbing the pole?"

"Yes, it happens every time."

"Does it hurt?"

"Being on the pole hurts a lot, yes. It feels like a whole-body Charlie horse. I'm not really holding the weight of my body on the pole with my strength. Let me put that a different way: while strength is required, it's not what's keeping me on the pole in my various configurations. It's my skin pressing and sliding against the metal until there's enough friction to keep my body up."

He winced. "If you're not doing it to earn a living, why would you do that to yourself? Sounds a bit masochistic."

"It's rewarding."

"I watched a video of you going up the pole and was wondering why you took off your clothes. But you're saying you need friction." His finger had been tracing circles around the bruises on her calf. He was slowly working his way up her leg.

"Exactly. And even then, if the pole was too slippery, no matter my strength or technique, I wasn't going to stay on or move up." She pushed her hair back behind her ear. "When I watched your guy powering up the pole, I knew it wasn't oiled or even polished, especially with his pants and shoes. I was running to help when I saw the pole tip. I figured I was lighter."

"And out of the mists came Mary."

"Oh, stop."

"I'm not giving you a hard time. I'm in awe." He slid the skirt of her dress higher on her legs and painted a warm palm along the bruises on her thigh. "So, fortunately, the pole wasn't oiled."

"Yeah, it had a good amount of texture, better friction." Mary was having a hard time focusing on the banality of this conversation.

Her mind stuck on the word friction; she wouldn't mind if that's where they were heading.

Right now, Mary wanted to scoot down on the bed, pull Halo's weight on top of her, and wrap her legs back around his waist like she had earlier in the day—not out of survival desperation, but just to feel the comfort of how their bodies fit together.

And yet, she wasn't entirely sure about the dynamics at play here, so she continued, "From the ground, it looked like the pole reached like a tree limb right out to the family. When I got up there and saw how far they were. That *mother.*" Mary tucked her chin as her ribs clamped down hard on her heart. "As a mom, I can tell you sometimes, when my kids were in danger, I became that proverbial mama bear and other times, my whole body shut down. It's a flip of the coin what my brain decides to do. I have seen it time and time again in the emergency department where I worked as a nurse."

"Today, you were the mama bear. I think that brains, for the most part, assess correctly. We act when it's best to act. Sometimes, survival depends on freezing in place. You have to trust your instincts. The mother was up there with so few choices and little hope except for someone to show up. And you did that."

She caught Halo's gaze. "Honestly, I was on the sidewalk watching things unfold," she whispered. "And then I saw those little boys' faces. They were *my* kids. *Mine.* My little boys up there with death breathing its dragon breath at their necks." She lifted her hand, turning it beside her head. "It was a switch that went off in my brain. And I believed they were my sons. There was *nothing* that would have stopped me from getting to them. And then, when I was up there and saw their faces, I realized they weren't mine. I didn't recognize those boys. But that didn't change anything."

She'd told this to Deidre earlier, and Deidre brushed on by the sentiment. Deidre hadn't been on that balcony and hadn't experienced what she and Halo had gone through.

Right now, the look in Halo's eyes told her that he understood. "Can I tell you a secret?" Mary whispered.

Halo put his hand over his heart.

"I was sent here to Tallinn to save them. Specifically. The time. The location. Sent here to climb the pole."

Halo held still.

"It's my birthday destination. Let me explain. I came here with my best friend, Deidre. She's a little more woo-woo than I am. A *lot* more woo-woo. Anyway, Deidre found this woman in Switzerland who looks at your star charts and decides where in the world you can travel on your birthday, a place that will change how you progress on your life's journey."

"Like a GPS coordinate?" Halo asked.

"More general, a city. Deidre dragged me along to Switzerland to get her birthday destination site. And the woman told me I was to go to Tallinn, Estonia, on my birthday. We were already in Europe, so we thought, why not?"

"On your birthday. Today."

"Yup. Be in Old City, Tallinn today." Mary held back that it was supposed to change all three parts of her life—her career, her love life, and her life's trajectory. Could this man be the change? If Mrs. V. was right to send her here—not that Mary was looking for a husband—but the solace of a man's arms, the strength of someone having her back. She'd never really had a relationship with a man who would be around. It could be him. Maybe.

Halo leaned in, painting a finger down the side of her face. "Happy birthday, Mary."

She closed her eyes and kissed him. It was a warm honey kiss, sweet and rich, decadent and filled with goodness. She'd never had a kiss feel that way before. Her heart was racing in her chest. With her lips on his, she maneuvered her way closer. His tongue laced with hers. Slow.

The kiss was glorious, but the angle somehow dug into a tender spot, and she grimaced.

"You're in pain. Of course, you are." His lips were so close that his words were a warm breath on her cheek. "What can I do?"

"Kiss my booboo and make me feel better?" Mary had said it playfully, but Halo took her quite literally.

He scooped under her knees and laid her out on the bed, crawling onto the mattress beside her. He lifted her foot to his lips. "Your poor foot." He kissed. "And the inside of your ankle." He kissed.

Mary's entire body heated, melted, and awakened.

Halo snapped his finger and pointed to the crate. Dutifully, Max jumped down and went to his bed.

Halo rested a finger under her chin, tilting her head so he could look her in the eye. "Can you tell me what you're thinking? What do you want to happen here?"

Mary hesitated. This next sentence was going to be the most spontaneous thing she'd ever said to a man who was a stranger just a few hours before. "I was wondering if you might have a condom with you?"

22

September Fifth

Tallinn, Estonia

Their day in the bog had gotten the green-light.

Mary was off to her room to get changed and would meet him in the lobby.

With Max by his side, he took the elevator to meet Nutsbe, thinking about what Mary had said after he'd made love to her. He had thought the experience was exquisite.

Perhaps because of the connection they'd made as they worked to not just save that young family but to save each other that made the sex such a rich, intimate, amazing feeling.

But when Mary left the room, she said, "Thank you again for our talk last night." She'd smiled. "And thank you extra for the very lovely distraction."

Halo wasn't sure what to make of that.

Was that what happened?

The sex was a stress relief? A distraction from bad thoughts?

If that's what it was for her, that's what it was. Halo couldn't make someone feel what he was feeling. He'd just thought that there was a deeper connection there. That something between them clicked into place when they were in survival mode together. That they'd forged a bond when he first caught her eye, and there was an acknowledgment that they needed each other to stay alive.

The very lovely distraction—that was a kick in the gut.

But Halo wasn't sure how American women phrased things. And, for sure, he wasn't going to press her. He was just going to let the day unfold.

"Morning." Halo lifted a hand when he saw Nutsbe at the table, computer open, papers stacked neatly to the side.

"Mary?"

"She's meeting me down here in a few minutes."

"Paperwork is ready for her signature." Nutsbe pointed to the chair across from him, and Halo sat down, signaling Max to lie under the table.

"You're new with Iniquus," Nutsbe said, "and I know you were told this in your initial training, but I'm going to do you a favor and hammer it home while it's just the two of us."

"Okay."

"Iniquus has a firm keep your zipper zipped policy. Command is serious about that. If Mary goes to the bog, she is under your protection and, therefore, your subordinate. There can be nothing physical that transpires between you. No kissing. No handholding unless you are offering assistance. There is a zero-tolerance policy. It will get you canned quicker than most anything."

"Yes, I quite understand," Halo said.

"No extracurricular activities of any kind. That is, no extracurricular activities unless sanctioned as a part of the mission."

Halo's brow drew together. "When would that happen?"

"It won't," Nutsbe said emphatically. "So this is any physical contact that you would not have engaged in when you were on a task force to protect the Australian prime minister. Stabilizing, lifting, carrying, palpating as a medic, yes. Any other reason a zero tolerance."

"Right. Zero," Halo said.

"There will be no reason under any circumstances that there would be room for a complaint or sexually inappropriate behavior. Could an individual give you consent, and you act on it? Negative. Why? Because they are yours to guard."

"Bloody hell, mate, I can cancel and just tell her it won't work."

"Not necessary, I don't want Mary disappointed. If she wants to go out to the bog with you and Max, we just need her signature, and I'll time-stamp it correctly. And you will explain to her the change in your demeanor. Look," Nutsbe leaned back in his chair, "you two were locked in on a very difficult and dangerous mission with children's lives on the line. I'm not unaware of the effects. Honestly, four men on my team met their wives or got engaged under such circumstances. It's the intensity and trust."

"Yes." Yes, that was precisely it. And others on the team had been through this, too. Interesting.

"No matter what happens around you," Nutsbe continued, "just like in the Commandos, it is put aside for the safety and wellbeing of your precious cargo. She goes into the bog one hundred percent. She comes out of the bog one hundred percent. We'll put an end time on the contract with her return to the hotel. So she needs to arrive at the hotel, get out of the car, and walk into the hotel alone. The contract ends."

"You're being very granular about this process."

Nutsbe leaned forward and lowered his voice. "Command ended a contract recently with a man who thought perhaps the strict rules of non-engagement didn't apply to him. While the woman made no complaints and attested to her consent, that was entirely beside the point. He knew it. He chose to ignore the consequences. The men who can pass through the vetting stage at Iniquus are few. We can't afford to have such departures. And since you're new, I want to hammer this home. Strict discipline is required, as is befitting a special operator. If you think you'll be tempted to lean in and kiss her, I'd leave her home, man. My best advice."

"Understood." Halo decided to take the tension down a peg. "I'm guessing this kind of little talk is why your team calls you mum?"

"Good morning, Mary!" Nutsbe smiled.

Halo looked around, and his heart skipped a beat as Mary came closer.

"Good morning, Nutsbe. Did you sleep well?"

"Nutsbe's a very nice guy," Mary said as they moved through the automatic doors toward the rental car.

"I think so." Nutsbe was right. Halo was going to have to keep a tight rein. His hand automatically reached for hers, and at the last second, he drew it back.

"He has a different patch on his uniform."

"He's on Panther Force, that's a tactical team. I'm Cerberus —that's a K9 team." Halo reached past her to open the door and held it as she climbed in.

With Max in the back seat and safety belts cinched into place, Halo set his phone—GPS open—into the ashtray, but that was for verification. He would try to rely on his shirt's directions.

One interesting thing Halo learned was that right now,

Russians have the capacity to hack Ukrainian drones and alter their GPS information. And likewise, it was possible to hack their shirts if the shirts were being routed via satellite. But if his shirt was offline, gathering the data from the device he carried with him, then he was safe from any interference.

They were silent as Halo got onto the highway, heading south out of the city.

"Tell me about Iniquus. You said that you were just hired?" Mary asked.

"Iniquus is looking at the geo-political world and upcoming threats. With extreme and unpredictable weather, we think our clients will find themselves in extraordinary circumstances that will require professional help. They're adding additional teams to meet the needs. I'm the first member of Team Charlie. Cerberus Team Alpha was over in Italy last week digging our clients out of the mudslide."

"I think I saw that in the news. The university students?"

"That's my understanding." Halo drove onto the highway where traffic was light, and the sound of the road was a steady hum.

"But the governments are there, right?" Mary swiveled in her seat so she was facing him. "They're training, too?

"Yes. Of course, and they do a great job. But they're focusing on everyone, and if you're our client—like you are today—we are focused uniquely on you."

Her chin pulled back. "You'd pass up a baby?"

"I didn't say that. I hope I never face that. We're mission-focused, bypassing all the other needs to get to our client."

"Well, I can understand that, but it still seems cold-hearted."

"Once we've fulfilled our contractual obligations, then we stay in the country and help if our help is needed and beneficial."

"Lives on the line."

"That's the job."

"Yeah, that explains the team at the fire. But why is Iniquus here? Estonia doesn't have a lot of natural disasters. I guess there could be manmade ones, like if the Russians pulled some shenanigans."

"Panther Force is providing security for an upcoming client event."

Leaving the city, the countryside widened in front of them.

They drove in an easy silence until Mary whispered. "Okay, this is going to be harder than I anticipated. I really want to hold your hand."

A grin spread over Halo's face.

He'd just been thinking the same thing.

23

HALO ANGLED THE CAR TO THE SLIGHT PRESSURE OF HIS SLEEVE on his right forearm. "Stop number one. Our client will be coming here to the waterfall for a picnic."

"Oh!" Mary said, looking over to where the river flowed over the lip of limestone in a picturesque shower. "This is lovely."

"At the top of the falls, the river's not deep, just over the ankles. We walked across it, and it was an interesting experience. Do you want to try?"

Following Halo's lead, Mary sat down on the flat rock, took off her shoes and socks, and then rolled her pants cuffs to her knees.

Standing on the water's edge, he held his hand out to her. "Here at the shoreline, it's a little slippery. Would you like my assistance?"

"I think that while my feet are in the water, it would be best that you held my hand so I felt safe." She smiled, and then her brows lifted. "Oh, it really is slippery."

"Two more steps."

They'd reached the part of the river covered with green grass-like plants that thrived under the crystal-clear cool waters.

"It's like walking on carpet, isn't it?" With Mary grasping his hands, they stood in the middle of the river, letting the water, cool and clean, swirl around their ankles and over the broad ledge.

Looking down at Mary, Halo realized how little he knew about her. He didn't even know if she was single.

Nutsbe hadn't said anything about the direction of Halo's conversation, just the direction of his hands. And his zipper. "On the stage, you said that you're divorced? I'm assuming you aren't in a relationship now?"

"You mean after I slept with you?" She laughed. "No, I'm not that kind of girl. But you're right to ask. I guess maybe we should have checked in with each other about that. I might have made character assumptions—nope, not a good way to say that. Let me try again. Are you involved with someone right now?"

"Besides you?" He chuckled. "No."

"Me? We're involved?" She said it under her breath; he almost didn't catch it.

"You wouldn't say?" He sent a glance her way, reading confusion in her eyes before he focused on the woods, raising his hand to point out a family of rabbits.

"I don't know what to say other than this week is happening very fast."

Was he the only one feeling this way? When he woke that morning, he'd looked over and felt such a sense of peace to find her beside him. It was, in its own way, like when he had seen Max and known they belonged together. It had been such a solid sensation. It had such a rightness about it that—Yeah, that was bloody unfair to this woman.

Halo decided to move the conversation back to basics. "And you have children? You mentioned you had sons?"

"Twins. They're twenty-one now. Both were diagnosed with ADHD when they were little. And to say that I was very busy and very exhausted all the time is putting it mildly."

"Military wife, that, too, isn't an easy go."

"No, it wasn't. It felt like Dan always had one foot in the marriage and one foot somewhere else." Squeezing Halo's hands, she lifted one foot and swished it back and forth through the current. "When the boys hit high school, the writing was on the wall for the death of my marriage. It was a bit terrifying. I had a high school education. I had been a mother and a volunteer. Busy, always busy, exhausted in my busyness, but there's not much to put on a resume—not for a job that makes enough money to pay the bills. So Dan—my ex—was staying in the military until he hit his retirement requirements at twenty years. I asked him to hold off on the divorce until then, let me get through college on spousal benefits, and at least have something in the way of a future. That's how it spun out. My friend Deidre, who I'm traveling with, went to nursing school with me."

She paused with her hand shielding her eyes and cast her gaze around before she looked at him again. Halo thought she might be trying to figure out what to share and how much was too much. As far as Halo went, he hoped she wouldn't censor herself. He found everything about Mary fascinating.

"When our kids graduated high school, we graduated with our nursing degrees. Deidre does surgical nursing now. I spent four years in the emergency department. This last May, my kids graduated from university and permanently flew away." She frowned. "I am officially an empty nester."

She turned and watched the water slide over the lip of rock. They stood that way for a long moment.

Turning to him, the grip on his hand a little tighter, Mary said, "I'm making progress on being an individual. I have my own little place with a garden. I just finished up my qualifications and am about to start my new job as a flight nurse."

"My nurse friends have the best stories." Halo smiled. "Did you have a lot of crazy things happen in the emergency room?"

"When I was at the store the other day, I saw they were already putting up Christmas decorations in the far corner when it's not even Halloween yet. Anyway, during the holiday season, we get a lot of tree-shaped objects stuck up people's—and by people, I mean men's—backsides. Sometimes, they're made out of material that breaks under pressure, and that's problematic, often surgical. Soon manufacturers are going to need to put warning labels on their seasonal décor."

"Ouch."

"That about sums it up."

They turned and, still hand in hand, walked up the river, watching as Max ran joyfully from one side to the other, bounding up the rocks and leaping back down.

"And your divorce? You have a child?" Mary asked. "Children?"

"A daughter. Stella. My ex-wife and I separated early in our marriage. She wanted to pursue a career that could only happen in Europe. She wanted Europe for our daughter."

"And you agreed?"

"I was deployed when she made the decision unilaterally."

"Oh, wow."

"We were in touch," Halo clarified. "She didn't sneak away. My career took me to Afghanistan. How could I tell her that her career needed to keep her in Australia?"

"I guess you couldn't. Did you think you would join them after your tour?"

"I had contracts to fulfill. And I was doing the thing that I felt in my heart I was supposed to be doing. I'm not a selfish enough man to keep her from her goals."

"But your daughter."

"Wasn't in Afghanistan. She was safe. Healthy. Well cared for. Great schools. Lovely friends. And I got to always be the good guy. Which to this day pisses her mother off."

"Mmmm."

"What does that mean?"

"I might be painting a picture that isn't true. Might be a cultural difference. How did you get to be the good guy?"

"I video-called Stella every opportunity I could. I read her books, listened to her day, told her jokes, and sang her songs."

"You sing?"

"Everyone can sing. Can I sing well? Well, enough that I made my daughter giggle."

"Got it." Mary seemed to tense. "Your wife was the disciplinarian, and you were the joy in her life."

He looked down and whispered, "In my job, I never knew if it was going to be the last time I talked to her. And I—"

"Halo, stop." She turned and looked at him sternly. "Don't."

"You were a soldier's wife."

"Navy wife, but I get it. It was on my mind every time I spoke with my ex. I thought: This could be the last time I talk to him. I was careful not to bring this up, not bring that up. It made for very superficial conversations. A little different, though." She turned and started walking again. "He really wasn't in the kinds of dangers others were in. Like you were in. My children's father was in a sub. We couldn't communicate a lot when he was deployed. When he was home, things were tense. I ran the household as a single parent. Not true. I co-parented with my friend Diedre. We've pretty much done everything together from the time our three boys were born a day apart."

"A litter of pups. I bet the dads were really glad, though,

knowing you two had each other's support when they weren't at home."

"When our husbands came home, they wanted things the way they'd left them. Not bad, mind you. Just he'd walk in the door, and all of my systems would suddenly be turned upside down. I lost control to him. He didn't have the same concerns that you did. He was fine with being the disciplinarian." There was an edge of resentment to her tone. "He wanted to make sure that if I had softened my boys' hearts while he was gone, he toughened them back up by the time he went back to sea." She shot a glance over to Halo. "That made him sound abusive. He wasn't. I don't think so, anyway. It's just that I got tired of it. We made a truce of sorts. It sounds like you and your ex found a different way of handling things." She turned back toward Max, who was trotting along with a massive branch in his mouth, making her laugh.

"I had my life in the military and Australia. But I also prioritized my relationship with Stella."

"You just moved to America. Had you thought of moving where she is?"

"Yes, and her mother and I agreed that I shouldn't do that. Stella's a teenager and being very teenagery, especially towards her mum."

"I know what that means."

"There's a bit of safety for Stella, I think, in the physical distance that allows us to stay emotionally connected. We've always had a mostly electronic relationship. My leaves from the military were always spent where she was, but it's mostly at arm's length. I'm not the disciplinarian—that was a mutual decision. I'm the steady wall for Stella to lean against. She hasn't shut down to me. Her mother thinks it's important that at least one of us can maintain that open connection."

"I'm happy and jealous for you. That's a great place to be in."

"Her mother doesn't have that luxury, and I see the toll. The frustration. Sometimes, it makes me feel selfish as hell to get the relationship with little of the burden. I'm sorry for your pain."

"Yeah."

And because a heaviness had draped itself over Mary's shoulders, he thought a change of location might help. "Is it all right that we head on now? I want to make sure there's enough daylight to move through the bog."

24

It was a quiet drive to the forest.

Companionably quiet.

Whatever shadow had crossed over Mary out in the river had lifted, and she was just enjoying, not feeling any pressure to entertain Halo. The absolute—and stunning—comfort of sitting beside him. Peace, Mary realized. What she was feeling was peace. And then she scanned back along her timeline to see why that feeling was so novel for her. And she couldn't remember a time when she'd actually felt peace, but instead, she'd spent time imagining what that *might* feel like.

When he pulled off the road, they were at a trailhead.

He pointed out the latrine, and she was glad of the relief. When she was done, Halo told Max to use the bathroom, and Max climbed up on the toilet seat and did his business. When he finished, Max looked confused that there wasn't a handle to flush.

"That's amazing," she said.

"Normally, he'd just go in the woods, but we need to practice his new skill in as many places as we can."

When Halo handed her a backpack that carried a water bottle, Mary said, "I can just put the bottle in my pocket."

"Iniquus requires backpacks with both straps clasped when on the bog." He waited for her to bring the straps around her chest, then waist, and then handed her a set of bog shoes. They reminded Mary of the kinds of plastic snowshoes her northern cousins used when they were little. These were about two feet long and a foot wide, rounded into a white plastic oval. And just like those darned boots and skis Mary had worn up on the glacier, her foot would slide into a toe binding and her heel would snap into place.

"Is that ominous about the backpack?" Mary asked, tucking the shoes under her arm to carry through the woods to the bog.

"Precautionary." He was putting Max on a lead, and she hadn't seen Max leashed anywhere else. What was that about?

Mary had hoped she'd have another excuse to ask Halo to offer a stabilizing hand, but as they moved onto the trail, she realized it was an easy hike.

They had moved far enough into the forest that Mary could no longer see the car. The trail she assumed he was leading her down wasn't that apparent, and he didn't have a GPS out.

"This is the right way?"

"I'm following my shirt," he said with a smile. "Here, feel the sleeve. Do you see how it's puffier on one side?"

"Yes."

"The shirt wants me to veer to the right here."

"Is that what Nutsbe was referring to when he said he'd programmed your shirt?"

"Exactly."

"Very cool. It might be interesting to have something like that when I'm out on a rescue. Where the patient is isn't always where the helicopter lands. Sometimes, we have to hike quite a distance, and then my hands are busy, and my attention is elsewhere."

"Congratulations on becoming a flight nurse. I can't imagine what it must be like for you to have gone through decades in a role then to suddenly need to reinvent yourself."

"I'm touching on the basics of the job I've always done, caring for others."

"Same but different is a nice challenge, hey? Tell me about your challenges." He looked down at her as she came to a stop. "That's such an interesting look on your face. What was that thought?"

"In all honesty?" Mary blinked, then turned to walk again. "Sure. I was stunned you asked, and I was just thinking, what the heck is this man doing with his probing questions of value? He's supposed to be regaling me with stories of how impressive he is—that's been my experience with men until now. You're throwing me off kilter." She laughed a bit nervously. "What are my challenges? Give me a second. No one's ever asked me that before."

Continuing down the path, he waited patiently while she was silent for a long time, gathering her thoughts.

Finally, she said, "Okay. Here's something. I'm no longer the coach. I'm the player. I used to look at my kids and try to find ways to expand their horizons—coach them along. I wanted them to have no limits for themselves and the possibilities that existed for them in their lives—a deep departure from the way I was raised."

"Small town Catholic. Yes, I heard your two-penis horror story as we came in last night. Hysterical in the retelling but baffling that you were put into that position. That's kind of, what, eighteenth century?" When Mary didn't respond, Halo said, "I interrupted you. My apologies."

"Apologies?" she whispered, then shook her head. That,

too, was new for her. When had a man in her life ever apologized for interrupting? "Uhm. Yes, I cheered the boys on through their first wobbly steps in whatever it was that they were trying. I encouraged them to try a lot of things so they could at least have some idea if they enjoyed it. I saw the world as a wide, exciting place for them."

She stopped speaking to see if he wanted to change the subject. And he seemed to be waiting to see what she had to say next.

So *very* unusual.

Mary cleared her throat. "When my children were young, I watched their sense of discovery and the power of accomplishment, and I lived vicariously through them, giving my kids all of the opportunities I could afford or could create. And when they left, those sparks of curiosity and novelty were gone, no fire in the belly. I had to learn how to light that for myself. It was an evolution of thinking. Most of my friends are older than me by about a decade because I got pregnant so young. I saw them settling into their after-nest lives, feeling comfortable. And that's lovely. I'm happy they're content, but that isn't what happened to me." It was about five silent steps down the trail until she found the word and was willing to admit to it. "I felt trapped. Stifled. Like moldy bread."

"Wow. Moldy bread," Halo said. "Sounds terrible."

"What I mean is that I needed something to make things fresh, thrust me out of my routine."

"Okay. How did you do that?" He extended a hand for her to step over a fat trunk that lay across their path.

She held his hand a few beats longer than necessary, then forced herself to let go. She didn't want to get him in trouble on her account. "These last four years, I've— no, this last year. The first three years out of my marriage, I was just learning how to work at a job and make decisions without considering other's tastes. It's this year that I'm trying to do things differently and see that I have endless opportunities. And that in and of itself is overwhelming."

"I agree that it's easier to order from a limited menu. And if you've sampled the lot, maybe head to a different restaurant."

"I like that metaphor. Yes. So I set out to make a list of twenty things to try—that's the breadth, and if I particularly like something, then I'd keep going to gain depth. As I set out on my twenty-things project, I told myself I could rearrange the hierarchy. But I had to follow through with the repetitions."

"Like what?"

"*Not* skiing."

"You said some of your bruises were from falling on the slopes."

"I was trying to be spontaneous. Which I am not by nature. And I was keeping Deidre company, and honestly, I was practicing being brave."

"What?" The surprise in his tone and on his face made her smile.

"I look at my older brothers and am in awe of them because they don't seem to have the piece in their brain that says, 'That's not for you.' They just do it," Mary explained. "I have everything they have except, like you know, testicles."

Halo laughed. "Do testicles, in particular, make a person think they can just do something?"

"I don't know. In my mind? It helps, I guess. Anyway, I decided to see what I could do about my own mindset of 'that's not for me.' I'm trying stuff out. And I created rules."

"Like—"

"I can't try it once and decide it's not for me. Twenty things that I try at least twenty times.

"Twenty is a lot."

"It is, especially when I don't like something."

"Why twenty? Random number you pulled from the air?"

"No. At the time I picked the number, I had been a responsible adult for twenty years. I figured, if I had the ability to make babies twenty years ago—and that's one of the scariest things I can imagine. You know, being completely responsible for another human being. Well then I could do something less scary, like stand-up comedy."

"You are hilarious. Good comic timing. They loved you last night." He stopped because Max had stopped. Max's nose was chuffing, and Halo was hard-focused in that direction.

"That depends on the routine," she said just above a whisper so as not to interrupt his concentration. "And it depends on the mood of the audience. I might be hysterical and have people peeing on themselves one night, and the next time I try—" She gave a thumbs down and a raspberry.

Max was focused back down the trail, and they were walking again. Mary could see where the trees would give way, and there was a broad expanse ahead of them. That must be the bog.

"I'm fascinated." Halo was grinning. "You've made people pee themselves?"

"You're so literal. Anyway, my big lesson with doing my schtick on the stage is that I need to appreciate a win. I don't have to be perfect. I have to show up. That's my mantra. Well," she shrugged, "it's what I'm trying to teach myself to do. Show up and give myself the opportunity. And grace."

"These twenty things are breadth over depth."

"Yes! At first, anyway." Mary felt good out here. If she lived in Estonia, the forest they'd just passed through with the little Alice in Wonderland red mushrooms and huge grandfather evergreens would be a place she went on her days off. "When I find something where I want to dive deep, I'm up for that."

"Okay, stand-up, that's one. Give me another."

"You mentioned singing with your daughter. I started voice lessons. I always wanted to be able to sing. And I did. I sang all the time. I just didn't sing well, and the people around me weren't appreciative that I kept searching for the right key."

"I get where you're going with this. In your mind, singing well was for someone else?"

This sounded to Mary's ear like an advanced relationship discussion. She and Deidre had both somewhat tried the dating circuit. Mary had a libido, after all, and sometimes it felt good to be in someone's arms. That meant she'd had first dates, lots of first dates. Some second dates. And third. The third was when she allowed for intimacy.

But on those dates, she was hitting up against that "she was too young to be so old" scenario.

The men in their late thirties—early forties were all divorced with kids. They were only available every other weekend. Their cash was low because of child support, so while Mary always paid her own way, she wanted to go do things that were a step above a fast-food budget, movies at the theater rather than on some guy's couch with microwaved popcorn.

All of them talked about light topics. None seemed to really want to get to know Mary as a human. Motherhood could be dehumanizing, and she really wanted to know what it felt like to have someone interested in hearing her story. What she was mulling and weighing.

This conversation—Halo's unfeigned engagement and interest—was so foreign to her.

Mary stood there, looking into intelligent brown eyes that seemed to see her as three-dimensional—it felt amazing and a little overwhelming.

She could swear these were the tentative steps of something solid and long-lasting. Yeah, in books Mary had read and movies she'd seen, this kind of conversation was the kind you had that led to … more.

"Mary?"

"Yes?"

"I was asking why Deidre signed you up to do stand-up comedy last night instead of singing. You're taking voice lessons, after all."

"Deidre grew up singing in a choir as a child and in a band in college. You heard her; she's amazing."

"We came in at happy birthday," he said.

"Oh, you missed out. So Deidre *sings,* and I sing along. There's a big difference. But it occurred to me, as I was making a list of things to try, that Deidre could sing because she had years and years and years of lessons, coaching, and practice. She didn't come out of the womb able to belt out a song the way she can. Granted, some people are born talents, but that's not what I wanted to focus on. I want to focus on the fact that I counted myself out without giving myself the opportunity to learn. I signed up for classes online."

"Not in person? You were afraid of breaking their eardrums?" His teasing didn't feel like it had a hidden knife in it the way Dan's had. Mary didn't mind Halo's teasing tone.

"I just thought having a little distance would be less intimidating."

"And you found someone?"

"I did, and it is the most ridiculous story you can imagine. I signed up for a trial service. I thought they'd pair me with some woman who had studied voice in college and was now—I don't know, a church choir director or a stay-at-home mom who needed to earn a couple of extra bucks."

"Not so?"

"This sweet young lady was teaching me. Just so kind and

lovely. After I met her online, I thought she was a college student, earning some extra bucks as a side hustle."

"Now, are we getting to the ridiculous part?"

"I decided to look her up online, and it turned out that she has a master's from *the* best music school in America. She lives in NYC and was about to perform for a national foundation. She was the lead in an opera that was on a very famous stage. That someone with a master's from anywhere was teaching me was—"

"A great opportunity?"

"Crazy, I think, is the right word."

"But why would you say that?"

"Because you start with training wheels," Mary said. "You get some basics under your belt. Have some fun. This was the kind of person you went to in order to polish for performances and competitions, to get ready for something big. All I wanted was to sing in the shower without driving people out of my house."

"Ah." He bent over and came up with berries on his palm. "Wild blueberries."

She tentatively tasted one. Not as sweet as she bought in the store, but finding them out here was fun.

"We should go ahead and get our bog shoes strapped on."

Mary breathed deeply, then sat on the ground to do as asked. "Yum! What is that smell? It's like lemons."

"That is called Labrador tea. It's part of the rhododendron family, a family that I have recently had a very bad experience with. Luckily, this one just smells good and is stress-relieving. That's what you're sitting on. It's everywhere."

Before Mary stood, she collected a bouquet of woody green leaves with tiny flowers. And buried her nose in them.

As they stepped forward, the ground under her shifted. It

was like trying to walk across an enormous waterbed. "As I get my bog legs, would you help me keep my equilibrium?"

"At your service, madam." He extended his hand.

Together, they stepped out into what was a foreign vista. The colors of chartreuse, wheat, and russet were other-worldly. The craggy trees no taller than Mary's shoulders could be found in sci-fi movie scenes.

It took a few minutes to get used to the ground undulating under her feet.

Max was hysterical how he lifted his paws high, as he pranced forward, his head rotating from side to side, sniffer going at warp speed.

"This water is acidic from the sphagnum moss, perfectly clean to drink, but it won't quench your thirst as it has no minerals," Halo explained. "It's too acidic for animals to survive in it. So no fish."

"Interesting." Mary shoved her bouquet of Labrador tea into a D hook on the backpack strap where it was near her nose. She thought she'd figured out that Iniquus required the backpack lest their client fall into one of the pools of water, and the guardians needed to grab something to pull them out.

"Unlike the fish, you can swim in the bog pools," Halo said. "The water feels quite unique. It's an amazing experience."

"No swimsuit. But then, again, we're here alone, and you've seen me naked. Would that get you in trouble?"

"I can't get naked. There's nothing to stop you from doing as you please."

25

When Halo told her it was all right for her to skinny dip, an image of her in the water flashed through her mind: She was a nymph floating luxuriantly—her pale skin against waters so flat and black that they mirrored the sky. At the same time, Halo stood and watched her with lustful thoughts and a hard-as-rock cock that they could act on once they got back to the hotel.

The air between them was electric, and a wave of horny swam through Mary's blood. She fully understood that when Halo cleared his throat and got them back on their previous subject, he was trying to divert her to a safer topic of conversation.

"Twenty things, twenty times, I have so many questions. So far, I've clocked that the twenty include standup, singing, and pole dancing. Pole dancing, while lifesaving, can also be a fluid and beautiful art form."

"Bruises the feet, rug burns on the inner thighs. It looks fluid, but the reality is smoke and mirrors. It's very difficult."

"Most things that look easy take an enormous amount of skill to make them look graceful and effortless," Halo agreed. "When in actuality, they are years of effort."

"When I first tried, it hurt, and I was really tempted to quit right off. And might have, except I'd promised myself twenty tries. Also, the women who were there weren't from my generation. They had a different worldview. They were inclusive and kind. They focused on their efforts and cheered on the others in the class. I thought I'd put up with a lot just to go and be around them and to learn from them. So much younger and so much wiser than I."

Halo said nothing.

She turned her head to breathe in the lemony scent. Halo was right; there was something very stress-relieving about this plant, and she wondered if she couldn't find some seeds to take home and fill her garden with this memory. "I realized pole pain is like stretching a muscle. Your brain wants to protect you, so it holds the muscle tight. Right? Over time, the brain begins to trust the move. Slowly, over months of consistent training, the brain lets go a little more and a little more until the stretch is allowed without resistance. And it was that way with pole pain. 'Get off the pole, it's painful!' my brain would scream. And to this day, it is still a bite. True. But so much less so. As my brain learns that I'm pretty safe with my moves, that nothing bad is happening, it stops screaming at me quite so loudly."

"Maybe you could teach me the rudiments when we're back in the States," Halo said.

There! He'd said it. He wanted to see her back home. Norfolk to D.C. was only four hours.

That thought was like champagne in her blood, bubbling up while she held her breath. Tension and excitement. It felt like she was underwater, and when she looked up, she could see the sun, knew there was air, and wanted so badly to pull herself toward that.

Was she ready?

Yes. Yes, she was. With Halo, she was.

"Did you ever bag on an idea?" Halo's question pulled her attention back from her champagne bubble thoughts. Mary was actually feeling a little strange—out of her body. She had to focus very hard to understand what he was saying.

"Like you went in willingly to a new experience, but you immediately thought—nope, I'm not doing this twenty times. Just not."

"Once." How brave was she? How much did she trust this man?

"What was that?"

"I … am uncomfortable sharing that." She held up her free hand as if bracing herself. "But I'm going to tell you because I'm practicing being brave about my truth rather than caring about your perceptions of me." She turned her head and took a deep breath of the lemon, enjoying the boost of calm.

"That's a challenge," he said kindly. "Will it make it easier if I promise not to judge?"

They were shifting their weight back and forth as they moved forward. "Is that a promise that is possible to keep?"

"No. You're right. Some judgment is always there, either pro, con, or neutral. Okay, would it help if I promised to listen with a charitable ear?" he asked.

"Interesting, okay. I don't think I need charity as much as I'm afraid of the pictures this might paint for you."

"Something about … no, I can't imagine what."

"I thought I might try to be a lesbian."

He canted his head. "Which means you aren't a lesbian but somewhere on the spectrum?"

"No. I'm hetero, pretty much through and through."

He licked his lips and looked like he was trying very hard not to smile. "But you thought you'd give it a go?"

"Well … no. Not in the way I can imagine you might be picturing it."

He gave her a wicked grin. “Are you sure? Because It’s a lovely picture I have going.”

“Stop.” She used her mother voice.

“Okay. So, How did you give being a lesbian a go?”

“I played thirty questions and stared into her eyes for fifteen minutes.”

“You’ll have to fill me in. I’m at a loss,” Halo said as they bobbled along the path, keeping to the higher, drier areas where they could. Pointing, he said, “That’s the pool I swam in if you want to try.”

“You’ll guard me?”

He put his hand on his heart. “With my life.”

And Mary giggled. This whole thing. All of it was outlandish. And she was feeling drunk on it. “Filling you in. There’s a list of thirty questions that they’ve studied scientifically. And they’ve proven that if you sit across from someone and answer each question, you will come to love them.”

“And the staring part?”

“Is part of the falling in love.”

“I see. And the science was wrong?”

“No, it was right,” Mary said. “I love her dearly—but like a sister. She’s fostering my foster cat while I’m away. It’s a mean cat, by the way. He hates human contact and hides all day long, only coming out to eat and use the litter box. Fostering cats was a first attempt on a twenty-try-it thing that I think—for me—will also be a hard no going forward. So I guess that’s two things that didn’t work out.”

Halo laughed.

“What?”

“Nothing.” He laughed again. “Sorry.”

“Stop snort-laughing and tell me what.”

Halo rested his hand on Max’s head.

Max was staring at Mary with a singular intensity, and Halo

followed the look from Max to her and back to Max as if he was trying to read some hidden communication. "It would be ungentlemanly," he said—something just a bit off in his tone.

Mary sniffed her bouquet, enjoying their banter. "I give you permission to be a momentary creep. Thirty seconds. Go."

"You thought maybe your thirty questions friend could take care of your pussy, and now she's taking care of your pussy."

"Okay, nice, you got that in with ten seconds to spare."

"Did you want me to finish the ten seconds?"

"Nope. Now, you're out of creep-time."

"Good thing."

"Yes, it is."

They had reached a little tree next to the pool that Halo had pointed out to her. It was on a slight rise that was a little less wet and mushy. She sat down and pulled off the bog shoes, then her pants.

"So not just twenty things but twenty things twenty times?" Halo whispered, taking a full step back, both hands on Max's lead as her shirt and then her bra found their way to the little pile.

"Except for being a lesbian, that was a single hour of questions."

"And then the staring."

"Exactly. And worth it." She sent a look over her shoulder and then slipped out of her panties. "Now, I love a new person. But I'm not doing anything physically intimate with her."

Halo turned his head, doing a sweep of the area. Mary thought he might be making sure that she wasn't naked in front of strangers. Or maybe he was trying to give her some privacy to get in the water.

"Was she sad?" Halo asked. "Because this woman already knew she enjoyed being with other women, right? Or were two hetero women trying to go lesbian together?"

Mary lay on the sphagnum moss, inching her way backward into the water. It felt like cool silk brushing over her skin. But it was still kind of scary in its opacity. She met her comfort zone when she folded her arms and rested her head on a pillow of glorious Labrador tea and sphagnum moss with her legs floating behind her. "She's a lesbian. And she loves me, but the chemistry isn't there for her either, so she's my—"

"Cat lady."

"Dear friend."

"Same thing." Halo smiled down at her.

"You know, in a way, you're right about that."

26

"OKAY, I'VE TALKED ABOUT THAT TO THE EXTENT OF MY comfort zone," Mary said. "Let's talk about something else. You said you'd just come in from Helsinki, Finland. Tell me something you learned there that you didn't know before."

Halo was watching Max. From his posture, something had him braced. Maybe he didn't like that Mary was in the water by herself.

"Sauna is pronounced *sownah*. And they would very much like everyone to pronounce it properly. According to our tour guide, it's the single Finnish word that most of the world knows." It was a natural thing to think about. He was at work fully clothed in his uniform, guarding a naked woman, the same as he had been back in Helsinki. It was a good reminder of the role he was playing right then.

"*Sowna*, okay."

He was glad she was facing downward, though, her bottom sinking under the water. Everything about Mary's body turned him on, and this was just an inappropriate time and venue. He'd admit it was a struggle to be professionally platonic around Mary. "Also, they are hardcore about their saunas. They are ubiquitous, and by that, I mean *everywhere* imaginable and unimaginable. For example, I was told that there's a fast-food chain that has a sauna in it. One can order a burger and go back and steam."

"Makes sense," she said, her words came slowly. "You replace the salt from your sweat with the salt on the fries."

"There's a Ferris wheel that has one of the cars as a sauna, so you can spin and sweat at the same time."

"With a lovely view," she said.

Max lay on the water's edge, the sphagnum moss giving a little under his weight. His gaze was glued on Mary, hard-focused. There was something about Max's response to Mary, starting when they first saw each other at the airport.

The only time Halo had seen Max respond like that before was at the shelter when Max uncurled from the corner of his crate as a tiny pup, caught Halo's eye, and began their lifelong bond.

And Halo trusted his dog.

Max had picked Halo out for a lifelong partnership. Had he picked out Mary, too?

There was a peace that settled into Halo's chest at that thought. And something else, a longing maybe or—yeah, the word "sentimentality" was coming to mind.

The bond Max felt, Halo got that. He felt it, too.

Halo just wasn't sure how to interpret the intensity and concern Max was displaying right now. Not environmental. It was something about Mary. He untied his boots, getting ready lest he need to go into the water after her. "Not sure about the view. Once you pour the water on the heating element in the sauna, the car fills with steam, hey?"

"And you can't get out," Mary said. "That actually sounds nightmarish for a sauna novice. I guess the pain thing would apply there. If you knew that the heat wasn't going to kill you, maybe it would be relaxing? I just can't imagine it. You could not get me on the sauna Ferris wheel. Could not."

"Here's another point. Public saunas, one wears swim togs. In private saunas, one goes in starkers." He pulled off his socks and stuck them into his boots to keep them dry.

"I've been in a ladies' sauna. We were all naked, going in wrapped in a towel. Then everyone just gives you mental privacy."

"Yes. Well, as far as I saw, there were no gender separations in the saunas." He unclasped his backpack.

"There's more to that story." She pushed away from the edge of the pool, rolling on her back and floating. Around her, the mirror-like surface reflected the marbled swirl of gray clouds overhead.

"As it turns out, many businesses have their own saunas to help their workers stay relaxed." When he was doing his planning this morning, he'd done the requisite weather checks, and the radar had been clear. Maybe Max was picking up something in the weather? Halo leaned back to assess. He remembered being on the mountain looking for Mrs. Haze. Halo had looked at the sky and didn't see anything ominous. Tripwire looked at the same sky and had furrowed his brow.

"Uh oh. That sounds like a private sauna situation." Mary smiled.

"Indeed. And as it turns out, when you are new to a team, it is polite—or so it was explained to us—for the office to host a sauna to welcome the new member." He pulled his phone from his thigh pocket, and as expected, he had no cell tower bars.

"Like, I don't know anyone here, so let's get naked and hang out in a very hot room kind of welcome?"

"Yes. Exactly. That." He pulled his sat phone from his pack, raised the antenna, and tried to call Nutsbe to get the current read on the weather and check in. But the cloud cover was too thick to make the connection.

Max's tongue was out, panting and chomping the way he did when he was stressed.

Glancing around and not seeing animals of any kind, Halo decided to unclasp the lead so the leather wasn't soaking in the water.

Max's behavior primed Halo's nervous system. He just didn't know why. His whole body was yelling for him to act, *act now*. But he saw nothing to act on.

"You were working close protection. Did you go into the sauna with your client, or were you outside of the door?"

"If I were outside the door, I wouldn't be protecting my client." She had floated toward the center of the pool, and Max was inching closer, front paws in the water, barely resting on the vegetation.

Mary raised her brows. "Did you do this naked?"

"When on duty, I'm required to be in full uniform."

"In the sauna."

"Quite warm." He decided to go ahead and get his pants off. If he were going in, the survival supplies in his pocket would weigh him down.

"With your naked client. Female?"

"I was with my client. And the rest of the office workers, both male and female."

"Hell of a way to get to know your boss."

"For my client, yes." He was picking over his words like produce, making sure that there were none in his basket with bruising or blemishes, nothing that would give away a client's private information. "Culturally a non-issue for the others, it was quite a shock to my client. They were very uncomfortable throughout but tried to mask it." He dragged his pants over his feet and piled them on top of his boots. Mary didn't seem to notice.

"And you were melting like butter." Was she slurring?

"That would be a fair description."

"Wow."

"Yes. It was quite wow, especially for an American. Other countries are less timid with nudity. Australians, in general, don't mind much. How are you doing in there? Everything okay?"

"It's nice." She offered up a contented smile. After a moment said, "Yeah, I don't know about myself. I don't think I've ever been in a situation outside of the gym or that females-only sauna I mentioned where I was challenged with just pulling off my clothes in front of strangers."

"You did to save that family."

"Not naked and no room for ego," she said as she started twirling around and around in the water like a ballerina. "To be honest, there wasn't even room for thought. My body began moving, and I began to freak out whenever I started processing things. So I did what I trained myself to do in the ER."

"Which was?" Her words sounded cogent and intelligent. But something wasn't right. Halo thought if he could keep her talking, he might figure it out. In his mind, he was working his way from the point where they got on the trail forward. Had he missed something along the way? What was happening here?

"Get out of the way of my brain. My brain had the training and a broader ability to observe and know the right action. This messed me up so much in school. I would answer the question, then second guess myself and change the answer when the correct answer was the first one all along, the one my brain sprang forward. But I guessed that if it came easy, it had to be wrong. Things needed to be hard. I worked on not doing that all through nursing school. But the test came when I was an emergency room nurse. With lives on the line, I had no time for second-guessing. Just let the brain do its work. That's the mantra."

"Let the brain do its work." He repeated as he thought that through. "Right, well, that's what we do, too. Lean into the training, don't second guess. Hesitate and die." He stood up and cast an anxious gaze around him. "And feel the fear later." Suddenly, the smell of ozone tickled his nostrils.

That wasn't good. Time to go.

Mary was treading water. "Oh, yum. Can you taste that?" she asked.

"Taste?" Smell ozone, yes. Taste?

She licked her lips. "Yes, your words taste like cinnamon chocolate." Her face crinkled with concentration. "Halo," she whispered. "Didn't you tell me there were no animals in the pools?"

"Yes, too acidic."

"There …" She paused. "There's …" Her face froze in horror. "Something wrapping around my legs."

"Our guide, Marilin, said that there were plants. Let me look it up." He reached for his bag and flipped to the book they'd been provided about the various things one might encounter on the bog. "Yes, just plants, Mary. But how about you come out?"

"Oh, wow. Look at you!" Mary called, her words filled with awe. "Look! I see why they call you Halo." She lifted a hand in the air to circle her head and slid down deeper into the black water. "The halo. The wings. *You* are my guardian angel."

Max stood up and was leaning in toward her. "Mary, come back over here now, please."

Her eyes opened wide, her brows to her hairline. She started screaming. "Snakes!"

Max bunched up his muscles and, on what little surface he had, was able to extend his leap out, arriving beside Mary.

The sound of horror rose through her throat and echoed across the landscape.

Halo, too, was in the water. Three powerful strokes brought him next to her.

Max had already caught hold of her messy bun and was swimming toward the edge, but that was the most he could do.

There was no land. There were no sides to press into and climb out. There was only water-saturated moss. It wasn't like a swimming pool rescue or a shore like a lake. Here, the water was deep, and there was nothing solid.

Halo commanded Max to release Mary's hair. The moment Max complied, Halo stuck his palm under his dog's bottom—kicking powerfully, a hand under Mary's head—he heaved Max toward a drier mound.

There was a scramble and splash, a bicycling of hind paws, but Max, with the momentum of Halo's push, was able to scramble himself up under the tree where things were a little drier and, therefore, a little more solid. There, he gave himself a shake.

Mary was thrashing and fighting something that terrified her. In her fright, she was pushing Halo under, drowning him.

Bobbing in the water, sucking in a breath every time he rose over the surface, Halo worked to straitjacket Mary with his arms. As he nudged her onto the moss, her weight forced the little floating island down below the water. It was inch by difficult inch that he moved her closer to the tree, up to Max, who whined and stomped and seemed frustrated that he wasn't helping.

Suddenly, the screaming stopped, and Mary reached for the tree trunk and pulled herself up. She sat there, dazed.

"Mary, it's Halo."

She looked into the pool where he was treading water.

She said nothing to him. She looked high as shit.

"Mary, when we were walking in here, did you eat a mushroom?" Halo patted over the moss as he asked, testing out a place to work on his own exit. Everything here had been agitated by Max and Mary, and now the edge was loose and pulled away like cotton candy.

He couldn't put any weight on it, or it would give way.

She blinked.

"Did you touch any of the red mushrooms?" he asked, enunciating each word.

"No mushrooms. No. Do you need help getting out of there?"

Was it reasonable that she seemed normal now? Did she not remember what she'd just done? In this moment, Halo almost thought he might be the one who was hallucinating. "I'd really like it, Mary, if you could sit there and get dressed. I think it's time to head back now."

He watched for a moment while she complied. Her face was slack, and her coloring too pale.

He was thinking through what he might know about this situation from his medic training. Obviously, something very wrong was going on.

Did she say that she'd tasted his words?

Until he was out of the water, Mary was going to be in more danger. Out and dressed had to be his objective. He remembered Marilin talking the team through the process. It was one of the things that Halo had wanted to try today while he was out on the bog—how to get him and his dog out of the bog water if the ground beneath them gave way and they found themselves in a pool.

He speculated that it was something like getting out of the water if you fell through the ice.

Halo bent his arms and zombie-crawled up onto the moss, arm over arm. It gave way beneath him. Once he had enough moss under his body to act as a type of raft, he kicked his feet. But that didn't work the way he'd expected.

With a quick check on Max and Mary, Halo closed his eyes. He went back to the moment when Thorn asked Marilin precisely how to get out if the pool's edge was too spongy. She specifically said not to take off the bog shoes. So, already, count him one down.

Marilin had demonstrated a kind of rolling crawl. With her image in his mind, Halo repeated her moves and was gratified to find himself lying in an area solid enough to support him.

It had been a complicated undertaking, and as he quickly dressed, Halo was glad that he had stripped down to a shirt and shorts. No wonder Marilin had to grab the blogger's backpack straps to save him. Walking along, and the ground sank away below him? Until Halo experienced having no exit, he didn't understand the difficulty of the situation.

As Halo tied his boots and slid his bog shoes back in place, Mary was hugging the tree with its four-inch trunk, petting it and having a little conversation about how the tree had spent its day.

And Max was looking at Halo with an expression that screamed, "Fix this!"

27

HALO CHECKED AGAIN TO SEE IF THERE WAS ANY communication connection.

And when he found none, he assessed.

Mary had been cogent enough to follow his instructions and was dressing while she had her conversation with the tree. Her movements were sloth-like and seemed to come from muscle memory. She didn't seem to be thinking or processing at all.

Pulling the backpack over her shoulders, Mary snapped the sternal strap in place, then pulled the tiny bouquet of Labrador Tea closer to her nose and sniffed deeply.

Halo looked down; the Labrador Tea groundcover spread as far as he could see.

Marilin had pointed out this plant, telling the team that it was relaxing and could make people lose track of time. "I show you," she'd said with a knowing smile. "Think in your mind a number of minutes you think that you have been in the bog." She paused. "Everyone has number?"

She looked at her watch. "Think your number. Okay, we have been here exactly two hours."

The men looked startled, and she laughed. "You see? Relaxed. Happy. Time flies."

Halo had set his alarm during his morning planning to ensure that he wouldn't succumb to the power of the Labrador tea, and he and Mary would leave the bog well before nightfall.

"So like that," Marilin waved a hand near her head. "It can be, how do you say? Like a hallucination."

Hallucination.

But Marilin had only been talking about losing the perception of time, right?

Halo grabbed his guidebook and flipped to the right page. Mary had been relaxed on their hike out, he thought. But then, she'd tasted his words, seen him as a guardian angel with wings, fought against some snake-like thing that attacked her in the water, and was now communing with a tree.

Rhododendron tomentosum, also known as Labrador tea, marsh tea, or wild Rosemary, is a small evergreen shrub with white flowers that bloom throughout the summer months. It is often found in bogs and woods with elevated humidity levels. The citrusy scent comes from ledol-containing volatile oils.

It is closely related to the genus Rhododendron.

Halo was developing an absolute aversion to the genus Rhododendron.

When smelling Labrador tea essential oils, the ledol can cause a sense of relaxation and well-being.

. . .

He looked at Mary again, resting her forehead on the scraggly tree trunk, barely thick enough to hold her weight. Relaxation, check.

The Labrador tea's toxicity depends on species and locality. Terpenoid ledol is found in all Labrador tea species. Labrador tea may cause physical symptoms such as dizziness, vomiting, and drowsiness.

DO NOT camp near Labrador tea. Persons with sensitivity to the volatile oils may be rendered unconscious.

Halo looked at Mary. Would he call her sluggishness drowsiness?

Grayantoxins are also found in Labrador tea. While rarely lethal, Grayantoxins can act as a hallucinogenic. In those with an allergy to the plant, this can be followed by hallucinations/delirium, seizures, paralysis, breathing issues, and death.

Wait – death?

It could well be the plant.

Halo had to wait for a moment for the terror that flooded his system to give him enough room to think. He found himself using his combat breathing to keep himself in the fight.

Halo pulled out his medical kit. Moving slowly so as not to startle Mary, he approached in a crouch.

Max had curled up against her, and he turned to focus on what Halo was doing. "Just going to check her out, buddy." If Max decided to guard her, things could turn bad very quickly.

"Turn bad?" he asked out loud as he pulled out a pressure cuff and stethoscope. As if this situation wasn't bad enough.

He culled through all the other things that Miriam had said. There was a viper in the bog. Though, she'd also said in the twelve years of her professional life as a naturalist she had never seen it. A gray snake with a thick black zigzag down its back. Halo began to check Mary head to toe, removing clothes and putting them back on, checking for any sign that she'd been bitten.

Nothing. Halo documented her vitals in his notebook as he worked.

He checked her pulse; it was weak and thready.

Her breathing was shallow.

Her skin clammy.

Her eyes were unfocused.

There had been nothing in the book about what to do if someone had an adverse reaction. But now he remembered Titus asking that question. Marilin said to get the person out of the area and let them breathe fresh air. An hour or so should have them feeling well again. But that was the headaches caused by sensitivity to the plant. Would that extend to a full-on toxic load?

So far, Marilin's instructions had been dead on.

"Mary, baby. Come, on, sweetheart, we're going to get out of here." He tugged her arm, and she fell loosely back against him. "Max, I'm going to leave you off lead. The last thing I need is for you to take off running and pull me over into a pool." Halo couldn't imagine Max doing that, especially while wearing a work vest, but Halo couldn't take any chances.

"I know what to do," Mary slurred, flapping her hand in the air. "When I went down the slope in Switzerland, I just sat on the back of my skis. Sit back and go. Scary. But down to the bottom." As she said that, she pushed into a squat on the back of her bog shoes. Her weight shifted to the back, forcing the back edge downward instead of flat, digging into the moss, creating a hole exposing the water beneath.

As she went in, her arms flailed wide.

Halo jerked Mary to the side to redistribute the weight over a larger area. And as he did, he realized that carrying Mary would put over three hundred pounds of combined weight into a concentrated area.

Could he find a solid enough path to get them out of there?

As he processed strategies, he was startled by the abrupt sound of his phone alarm going off.

That was his Labrador tea timer. Bog time was over.

Halo tapped it off. "Mary, I don't want to hang you upside down over my shoulders unless I have to. It's quite a ways to the wood line, even farther to the car and away from these plants. If you can hear me and understand what I'm saying, I need your help. I'm going to wear my backpack on my chest, and I'm going to carry you on my back. We're going to try it anyway." He maneuvered the pack forward and cinched the straps across his back. "I swear to you, love, that I'm going to get you safe. I just need you to help a little. I need you to wrap your legs around me like when we came down the wall from the fire. Okay? And I need you to keep breathing for me."

What he didn't say aloud was, *Please, please, please don't die.*

28

Halo struggled in ways he had never experienced before.

When he was a Commando, he'd often been in bad situations. There were times when he was fighting for the survival of his brothers, times when he was on a solo mission when his life was in his own hands. But here he was in a surreal landscape, navigating an ecosystem that he hadn't trained in, desperately afraid for the life of the woman he loved.

Loved.

From the point when she hung upside down, and their eyes met on the side of the burning building, Halo had been playing around with the sensation, testing it out, wondering about it.

But now, it was solid in his chest.

And it was coated with absolute fear that his skills wouldn't be enough to meet this moment.

As they moved forward, Mary had grown heavier as she sank into her stupor. Halo had trapped her arms under his front-facing backpack and laced his fingers under her bottom to keep her up on his hips, her head lolling on his shoulder.

Each step pressed his bog shoes deep into the moss. In his mind, he pictured Miriam fishing out the hiker. It sounded straightforward in the telling of the story. Having just tried to get out of a pool—without clothes, shoes, or another person attached to him—Halo now understood how heroic Miriam had been. How frightened. How brave.

Halo wasn't sure if the ground truly gave way beneath them either would survive. If he was going down, he planned to tip Mary backward, shove her away from him, and hope that Max could figure something out.

It was a harrowing thought.

But as the strategy came clearly to mind, he looked down at Max. And Max seemed to get the picture and understand his duty. Guard Mary.

Halo was following the pulses of his shirt. He had to veer this way and that to stay on the driest, highest ground. And he was glad that he had tested the navigation system before it became crucial, but also that the grandfather evergreen was up ahead, guiding him in.

His nostrils filled with the smell of ozone again.

And then the sky was slashed with the crackle of lightning.

"Holy hell. Come on now!" he called up to the sky.

Marilin said that this was a desperate circumstance, that if they were on the bog when they saw lightning, they were to get to the tree line as fast as they could.

He was already doing that.

The idea that he'd lose his line of sight, that the water would rise—all the ramifications of the situation sizzled along his nerves.

The air shuddered with the boom of thunder.

Stopping as briefly as possible, Halo wrangled each of them into the rain ponchos he'd yanked from the side pockets of his field pack as he yelled, "Go, Max! Go! Find the car! Go, Max! Fast track! Go!"

Halo couldn't divide his attention. He had to trust that, before the rain flushed away their scent trail, with the command to move at full speed, Max would be waiting for Halo at the vehicle. Safe.

So far, Max's training sessions had translated beautifully into real-world missions.

As the words left Halo's mouth, Max dashed in the correct direction. His light frame leaped across the expanse of bog, and he disappeared into the tree line.

The next crack of lightning split the clouds open, and the rain fell in a torrent.

Halo sent up a thank you to the engineers who had figured out this shirt because, just like on the Virginia mountainside, Halo could only see three feet ahead of him.

The tree line was gone.

The bog water was rising alarmingly fast.

Mary hung limp over his back. Flailing would make this impossible. "Just a little further, love, almost there," he called to her. And though his staggering movements kicked her bog shoes into his knees, he didn't want to take them off lest he need to set her down for some reason. Without the shoes, she'd sink out of sight, lost to the bog.

Keeping his focus on the three feet around him, the only space he could control, Halo made his way forward. When his foot landed on solid ground, it felt like a bleeding miracle.

Three more steps and the trunk of a tree let him know they'd made it out of the bog and into the forest.

The bog shoes came off and were left behind.

Marilin had said that the winds would be high enough that they could topple trees, but Halo had not imagined the sheer power that engulfed them.

The lightning intensified, giving him brief moments of clarity.

The tree limbs only somewhat softened the onslaught of rain.

But around him, Halo heard the crack of severed limbs and the thud of falling trees.

There was no safety in the woods.

He powered up the hill.

Was Mary starting to rouse? Since the rain began, Halo had felt like she was putting more energy into holding on to him. He was back in his childhood living room for a moment, watching the Wizard of Oz on the telly with his family. Dorothy lay in a stupor amongst the poppies. The good witch sent some kind of precipitation down to awaken her. Snow? Rain? And Dorothy had come back to her senses. Maybe this rain was cleaning the air of the volatile oils.

Moments later, Mary lifted her head from his shoulder.

"I've got you, love. Are you with me?" he called over the sounds of the storm.

"What's happening?" Her voice warbled in his ear.

"Just hang on a bit longer." Halo was putting all his energy into following the shirt, dodging the hazards, and getting them closer to the car. "I'll explain everything."

She wiggled in his arms. "Can you let me down?"

Halo didn't answer. If he set her down, he was afraid they would slow, and this situation was just too dire.

He'd felt fear on the battlefield, but that was completely different. He had a team, tactics, and a sense of the necessary steps to take for survival. But now, all he could think was that Mary needed medical assistance, needed help that he couldn't give. And his terror was that he wouldn't be able to keep her safe.

Her rousing enough to speak didn't abate that in his system.

The rain was less intense, and Halo tried to take advantage of the reprieve by moving as fast as he could. Another fear was that, just like in Virginia, being sopping wet in dropping temperatures put them at risk for hypothermia.

If I can just reach the car.

Halo turned his head to the left when he heard Max. It was his "Come here!" bark.

Should he trust Max or the shirt?

When Halo whistled for Max, the wind snatched the notes from his lips. He waited for a fleeting lull and sent the whistle out again.

A moment later, Max streaked into view.

Max sat in Halo's path, barked, and then bolted away again.

Halo kept moving toward the car, following the shirt. Mary was his priority. Max was skilled and strong; Halo needed to trust his dog.

Leaning forward to keep his balance on a sudden slope, Max darted back into view. Max had been lying on the bed of Labrador tea alongside Mary. Did it have toxic effects on dogs, too? Was Max hallucinating?

Max sat in Halo's path and dropped something from his mouth to the ground.

In the dim light and falling rain, Halo couldn't make it out.

Max picked it up and dropped it again.

Halo squinted down. "Max, hand it to me." Halo momentarily took his hand away from Mary's leg, and Max put a child's shoe in his hand.

Max had never brought him a random object, even when they trained for search and rescue. If an object was found with the missing person's scent, it was vital that it not be moved. Max had been trained to leave the object, find Halo, and signal a find. So, this behavior wasn't something that Halo understood. He lowered Mary to the ground, steadying her as she caught her balance and watched. She seemed okay to stand. He put his hand inside the shoe. And while wet through and through, it was still warm.

It was a tiny girl's shoe.

"What is it?" Mary asked as she dragged the shoe into her own hand. "Oh. Why is there a child's shoe in the woods?" Her words were still slurred.

There was a flash where the stakes came clear at once. He needed Mary to be safe and safe was not here. If this shoe meant a child was alone in the woods, Mary would not leave the woods without the child. Halo had no idea how Max had arrived in front of him with the shoe.

Max's bark was sharp and insistent. He started off in the direction he'd come from, traced back and repeated.

"We're going after him," Mary said, spreading her arms wide for balance. "Oh, I feel so strange."

"I bet you do." Halo caught her under the arm to keep her from sinking to the ground.

Rain dripping from the brim of his visored cap, Halo ran the scenarios.

"I'm going after him," Mary insisted, twisting toward Max and taking a wobbly step.

"Mary, I'm in charge of your safety."

"Halo, listen to me." She turned on him. "I may have fallen for you. I may even love you." She paused and seemed startled by her words.

Halo gathered them into his heart and would consider them later.

She pushed his arm away to stand on her own two feet. "But there's no way in this world I will ever allow any man to tell me what to do." A drunken finger was up, stabbing at him. "I can go, or I can sit. If I sit, you can go faster."

"I'm not leaving you. Not even for one second." She had

seemed cogent throughout, except for the hallucinations in the pool.

Maybe the ledol was affecting her muscular responses and repressed her system.

Maybe she was thinking clearly enough.

He had no idea. This scenario was rife with conflicting interests.

She was an Iniquus client.

In this situation, Halo was, first and foremost, acting as security with all the responsibilities that entailed.

It was a balancing act.

If a child was in danger, he wanted to be there to help. *Needed* to be there to help. But as he told Mary when she'd asked this very question earlier, he was a trained Commando. A mission was a mission with a singular focus and a singular outcome.

Lightning cracked, outlining the leaf-covered branches in a flash of white.

The thunder that followed vibrated his bones.

As the sound rolled off into the distance, Mary stepped toward Max. "I'm going." As Mary reached out to brace herself on a tree, the tree shifted, making her trip forward.

"Mary, you can't touch the trees." Halo wrapped an arm around her.

Okay, the decision was made. He'd go where she went.

"Max," Halo called, "show me."

29

WHEN MAX TURNED AND PLOPPED BESIDE THE TREE, HALO realized the mistake he'd made. He hadn't asked Max about his find. Undoubtedly, the shoe belonged to a child in the woods, or Max would not have been this anxious. What Halo didn't know was if the child was alive or dead.

Yes, Mary was a nurse, but he felt that her mental state was fragile. And after the trauma of yesterday's fire, finding a deceased child in the woods, under these circumstances…

Normally, he wouldn't try to shield her. She was a strong woman. But these were strange times. And Halo just wanted a look before she did.

"Mary, can you hold my pack for me?" he asked, shrugging it off. She reached from under the red poncho, taking hold, then slipping down to sit on a root. He signaled for Max to stay with Mary and he slid into place next to her.

Braced for the worst, Halo rounded the thick trunk.

There, in a hollow at the base of a tree, a child hid from the rain, shivering.

"Hey, there," he said in a singsong voice. "Hey, you look cold."

She shrank from him.

He turned his head. "Mary?"

Instantly, she was there. "Oh, look at you, you poor baby." Her hands went to the child, palpating and looking her over without moving her from the shelter of the tree. Mary leaned toward Halo's ear. "Tell me this isn't a wood fairy or nymph or something. This is like a four-year-old child, right? A child alone in a tree in the middle of the woods? Or is this a hallucination?"

"This is a child, Mary. Is she okay to move?"

"I think so." Their heads were held close as they yelled into each other's ears past the continuing roar of the torrent hitting the canopy of leaves. "But where did she come from? Surely, she's not in the woods by herself. Maybe her adult is hurt?"

Max came between them and sniffed at the child. "Good job, Maxi. I'm really proud of you, mate."

Halo reached for his pack and pulled out a picnic tarp, plastic on the outside and fleece-lined on the inside. He handed it to Mary while he pulled the bag back into place under his poncho.

"Do we have a plan?" Mary asked as she opened the covering under her own poncho, keeping the lining dry.

"I'm going to see if Max can't track back to where she came from. With this wind and rain, I'm not sure that's possible. If yes, we'll decide next steps then. If no, we'll get back to our car and get her to the authorities," he said, reaching for the child that Mary had swaddled.

The little one shivered in his arms. Wet and obviously exhausted, her eyes stared glassily at him, wary but too tired to put up any resistance.

"Here we go." Halo held the child under Max's nose. "Maxi, where did this baby come from? Trackback, Max. Trackback."

With the little one in one arm, Mary clasped in his other, Max's paws wide as he got his nose right down to the ground, Halo tried to keep up as Max wended his way through the forest.

By Halo's calculations, they moved about a half mile through the forest when they emerged on a roadway. Halo was slowed by Mary's feet, which moved her clumsily forward. He could feel her concentrating hard, trying hard, pushing herself.

The street was empty except for the tree that had fallen across the roadway that Halo's headlamp picked out of the darkness.

That was going to be problematic.

According to the pulses from his directional shirt, their car was up the road to the right. That meant the city was farther down the road to his left. He was in a rental car, and they had no comms.

It could be that Panther Force might send out a search heading to their last known location when he and Mary didn't return to the hotel after the storm. If they waited at the car, they'd be found. But obviously, with trees coming down, it wasn't optimal.

Max came back to check on them.

"I'm following, buddy. Keep going."

At the very least, this was in the direction of their car. With the engine on, he could get this baby's wet clothes off and get her warmed up. Mary could rest.

As they approached the tree, Halo realized that it lay across the hood of a car.

"Oh, no," he heard Mary exhale. She tried to coordinate her

feet to run forward but stumbled, stretching her hand toward the ground as Halo jerked to keep her upright.

"Slow and steady, Mary."

"Yes."

They circled around the enormous root ball to find the back door of a car standing wide. A child's car seat was wet, but it was the safest place to be while he checked the mum. He quickly strapped the child back into her place.

The airbag had deployed.

The woman unconscious, blood dripping from a cut on her head.

Halo snaked a hand forward to the front door, unlocking it. With his foot braced on the side, he was able to jerk the driver's side door open. He softly shut it again. "Mary, I'm going to walk you and Max around to the other side of the car and have you both get in with the child and keep each other warm, okay?"

"I'm an emergency nurse," she hollered over the wind.

"You are. Let's get you into the car for now so I can see what needs to be done for the mum, hey?" Mary probably understood that Halo wasn't trusting her abilities at that moment. After all, just a few minutes before, she wasn't entirely sure whether she was looking at a child or a fairytale creature.

Hand on the car, Halo rounded back to the unconscious woman's side, trying to block the wind and rain with his body while he moved through the steps of first aid.

"Mary, this woman is heavily pregnant."

She thrust herself forward. "Oh, no."

"And she's either urinated on herself or her water's broken," Halo called.

"Put your hand on her belly," Mary instructed. "Is it soft?"

"No, it feels like a soccer ball."

"A contraction, Halo. She can't have her baby out here in this storm."

Halo's mind had been racing since the moment they'd come up on the accident. How would he deal with an injured driver, a messed-up Mary, a small, wet, possibly hypothermic child, a dog, no comms, and perhaps even a roadside birth, all in the middle of a raging storm?

30

Mary felt ridiculous shivering in the wrecked car while Halo was out in the storm. He'd said that he needed to get the tree out of the road, and Mary was processing his ability to do that. She'd thought of Jack and the Beanstalk and that maybe Halo had something in his pocket he could eat to become a giant. Then, it would be easy.

She thought of Alice in Wonderland and the bottle she drank, and Mary had asked him if he had a power drink, but her words must have escaped him.

It was this very odd half-reality she was living in.

On the one hand, here she was, recognizing that she, Halo, and Max had once again been thrust into life-or-death circumstances, that things were very dire, that her right action was needed.

Her limbs weren't fully cooperating. She felt like she was drunk in her movements, though, her head didn't feel that way at all. She felt clear, cogent.

And yet, she also wasn't sure.

This all had a dream-like quality, and at moments, it was

more like a nightmare. The sounds and images were forming, and they were too improbable to be real. And just like in her sleep, Mary was telling them to go away; she was dreaming. And they did; they'd poof and go away.

Back in the woods, Mary had leaned into the tree hollow, and had run her hands over the shivering child, careful not to catch her hand on the wings. But those words had tasted wrong. And she'd asked if this was a fairy child.

Halo had looked both horrified and resolute.

Whatever magic was happening in these woods, Mary felt like it was thinning.

She was quickly waking up.

Halo wasn't sipping a magic potion to grow big. There was a practical way to get that tree off the car and out of the road.

He told her that Marilin, the expert he knew, explained that since trees falling down was part of the storm season, many of the locals had chainsaws in their trunks. He'd pressed a button on the dash, then turned to her. "Here's hoping."

She'd lifted crossed fingers.

Mary felt she should be helping but wasn't sure how. If she got out of the car, he'd be paying attention to her. In this rain with the chainsaw? That was too dangerous. The best thing to do was to follow Halo's instructions and hold the child, hug Max, and try to keep everyone warm.

Halo climbed into the front passenger seat, pulling a hand over his face to clear it of rain.

"Mary." He was turned to look her full in the face, assessing. "How are you doing?"

"Better, I think."

"I need that to be true." He bit his back teeth down, working his jaw, some kind of internal argument going on. "Here's the deal, we need our car. I'm not sure how far away it is. I'm not sure how dangerous it is to get you there."

"I'm not leaving the woman or child."

"Which means I need to leave you." He squeezed his hands around the headrest.

"I'll have Max, and Max will protect me."

"I have to trust that you won't get out of this car, Mary. You have to swear to me that no matter what you see or hear, your promise to me is bigger and stronger."

"I swear to you, I will stay in the car."

He looked from Mary to Max; they locked eyes, and Mary imagined that Halo was sending Max a movie explaining his duties. Max's whole body posture changed. His head swiveled to take in the interior, and he looked back at Halo. They were in agreement.

"Bloody hell," Halo said. He reached out and cupped his cold hands around her face. "Mary, I *love* you. I need you to do this for me."

"I will stay here with the doors shut. I don't want you to worry about me. I need you safe. I very much love you, too."

Halo paused. A grin spread across his face. He leaned in and gave her a kiss that seemed to seal their conviction. "Hell of a way to get to know you, Mary. Shit, woman, I need you to be okay. And I *need* you in my life."

Those words tasted sweet and flowed like warm honey in her veins.

Well, Mrs. V. had said that three things would change in one single location; two of them were love and her life trajectory. So far, it looked like Mrs. V. had been right. "Be safe for me, Halo. Swear it."

That man.

That man!

He astonished her with his capability and intelligence, with his gentleness and calm.

What had she put him through in the bog and the woods?

She'd ask him for details somewhere along the way. Mary had roused from her stupor, draped over Halo's shoulder as he piggybacked her through the storm.

Where had the storm come from?

At first, she thought it was part of the nightmare.

Part of the snakes and the dragons.

The sorcerers' cast spells of retribution on anyone in that realm when they found happiness in love.

When she woke up, Mary was partly embarrassed and partly amazed that she was being cared for and rescued from her circumstances. When had that ever happened before? It was so foreign to her that she'd fought with him in the woods. And was immediately contrite.

He had been right about his duty.

And perhaps not wrong to direct her.

Honestly, what would happen in the emergency department if a patient were incoherent and not fully clear about reality? Would the doctors follow a hallucinating patient's decisions? As Halo would say, "Not bloody likely."

Now, as the child clung around Mary's neck, Mary's hand patted the child's back, and her other hand rested on Max.

Sweet, heroic Max with the golden sniffer that tracked the child's path straight to the crash despite wind and rain.

The storm raged on.

EXCEPT FOR MARY'S racing thoughts, everything had been at a standstill in the car, cocooned by the sounds of the torrent.

And then the whirlwind began.

When the headlights blinked, and hazard lights flashed as Halo drove up beside them, Mary felt fully herself. Exhausted but fully back in her body, clear in her mind.

The effects of the bog had worn away with time and distance.

Halo was at the door, pulling out the child seat, then slammed the door shut again. He arrived at her side of the car, leaning in, pressing an ardent kiss onto her lips. "I love you. Thank you for being right where I left you."

Squatting by her side, Halo reviewed his plans for moving the mother, getting them tucked into the rental car, and driving them to the hospital. Did she agree?

"No comms yet? They can't send an ambulance?"

"No bars. How should I do this?"

He was partnering with her, not insisting. She, too, had expertise here.

"I agree. We'll do your plan. But I think, if you can take most of the mother's weight, I can add stability on her other side and take one of her legs."

"How long until the baby gets here?" he asked.

"Her contractions are a steady five minutes apart. But under these circumstances, all bets are off."

"Let's move then."

When Halo pulled the child from Mary's arms, walking away from the car to put her in her seat, she began screaming and fighting him. That child must be terrified. Unfortunately, there was zero time to calm and cuddle her. Their focus had to be single-mindedly on getting the mother to the hospital. It was a really bad sign that she'd been unconscious for as long as she had. And using Halo's medical equipment to make her assessments, Mary wasn't sure the woman would survive the drive.

They could try.

The most they could do was try.

With the little girl strapped in her seat and Max against the passenger side window, Mary sat in the middle so she could reach forward and get to the mom. Halo had placed the mother in the front with the seat pushed back as far as possible, then leaned her back as far as possible.

Mary hoped that by laying her out, they might slow her labor.

Was that a thing?

Was it the right thing?

Mary wasn't a labor and delivery nurse. They didn't take laboring women on the helicopter under any circumstances. In the hospital, she was the one racing in with a crash cart. These were very different skill sets.

"Drive, Halo."

And he threw them into gear and continued down the road. Slower than she would want. But Halo was balancing their speed—fast enough to get them to safety, slow enough not to risk that safety on the way.

Mary was clinging to good fortune—a functional car, a man who had expert driving skills. There was no reason to dwell on what-ifs.

There was plenty of big and bad and dangerous up the road.

They were basically driving blind.

The child, strapped into her seat, screamed and screamed without cease,

As near as Mary could figure, the kid—though old enough to get out of the seat and out of the door—was still very young. She had been quiet all the way through the forest, wrapped in a plastic tarp and held securely in Halo's arms. The screaming began when Halo took her from Mary to move her to the rental car.

And now, nothing would soothe her.

The entire route was dark.

The electricity was down.

If the mother didn't rouse, this was probably going to be a cesarean. And if the mother was to die en route, the baby would die, too. Mary didn't say that out loud, but she was sure Halo understood.

The wipers screeched back and forth along the windshield, doing little to improve the view.

Halo seemed to find his sweet spot between fast enough to make progress and slow enough not to get them into worse trouble.

Imagine getting in yet another accident on the way.

Halo's magic shirt was their guide. As they left the scene of the car accident, he'd used his handheld device to program in the nearest hospital. And if Mary watched closely enough, she could see the forearms swell and decrease.

Braced in that moment, Mary was startled when her phone rang.

Pulling her hand back from the woman's belly, she grabbed at the rucksack and clawed for her cell. They'd been out of communication for a while now. Perhaps they were close enough to Tallinn. "Hello?" she gasped.

"Mary? Nutsbe here. Who is that screaming?"

Mary turned to the child, still crying in her car seat, jangling Mary's overwrought nerves.

"Oh, thank god you're on the phone. Halo will explain."

"We can't get through to Halo."

"He's here. Maybe we have different servers," she said for absolutely no reason. This wasn't a time for a chat. "We have a situation. I'm putting you on speaker and holding the phone out so Halo can tell you what's going on."

The phone shook in Mary's hand. Her own nerves for being on the road like this under these circumstances. Her own worry about the mother and the reason why that child would not stop screaming.

The professionalism of their "affirmative" and "WILCO" helped.

"I have your shirt online," Nutsbe said. "You are four minutes out from the hospital."

"I'd like to keep this line open," Halo said.

"Standing by," Nutsbe responded.

Yes, it was nice just to know there was someone out there who was doing overwatch.

31

Running on generators, up ahead, Halo saw that they had lights on at the hospital where they were out in the rest of Tallinn.

Blocks away now, Halo knew Panther Force was there, ready to assist.

Here, the water was running deep, farther up his wheel rims than he'd like. And as he knew from many a mission past, you don't count the win until you cross the finish line.

That thought had formed just as Halo felt the car lift and his control vanished.

Mary braced, sucking in a lungful of air.

The car behind them plowed into them, pushing them forward until they, too, hit the vehicle in front. Luckily, they were barely moving. Out of his window, he saw the water churning.

He called the situation out for the team to hear over their open line.

"Moving."

And Halo knew that help was on the way.

He rolled down the windows lest the car roll or submerge,

taking advantage of the limited time that the electrical system would function.

The rain poured in.

"Oh, wow, Halo, it's up to the windows!" Mary called, leaning out.

"Get the child out of her seat."

If they went under, Mary, Max, and the baby could get out the windows. Halo and the mother were too big to even try. Max was a strong swimmer, but Halo didn't know about Mary's skills other than that she was comfortable enough to swim in the black waters of the bog. But she'd try to save the child, and that would put them both at risk. He had to get the windshield out.

Yelling his directives back to Mary to cover everyone in the back seat with her poncho, Halo reached for the tarp and wrapped it over the pregnant mother. He curled over the top of her.

Each time another car was swept up and pressed forward by the raging waters, they bumped and jostled.

"Titus. Halo, we've entered the building in front of you from the parallel roadway. We've made it to the apartment window on the second floor. We're rigging pully lines to the light pole at your eleven o'clock. We have you in sight, brother. Coming your way. Over."

"Copy." Halo braced one foot under the dash and, pulling his knee in for a sidekick, he started battering the windshield, aiming for the corners and side where the window was the weakest. The first cracks were a victory. He kept kicking as the window pressed outward, like taffy. Created to protect the passengers in an accident, Halo knew there was no breaking this glass; all he could hope for was peeling it free.

With each kick, tiny shards peppered over them.

Suddenly, there were thunks on his hood. The car dipped

forward. Gloved fingers wrapped into the progress he'd made and dragged the glass backward.

Gage's face came into view. "We're here. We're tying you in. The people behind you are going to knock into the car, but you're not moving forward anymore." He swept his hand around the edge of the empty windshield space, removing the last of the glass shards.

"Got the mother?" Gage called, passing a line into the car. "Let's get her out first. How's she doing?"

"No change." Halo clipped the carabiner in place. "The contractions are still five minutes apart."

"We have an exit strategy and a car waiting."

Hands, legs, feet, faces, there was a press of common effort as the unconscious woman was lifted free.

The water splashed and then gushed into the car.

Mary was thrusting the child forward.

Halo passed the tiny girl on to other hands.

"Come on, Mary, You're next."

But she grabbed Max's collar and shoved him toward Halo.

Another bang shifted the car, and while it held in place, it tipped to its side.

Halo fought the rush of water. Filling his lungs he dove and reached, searching for Mary, but she was gone.

He couldn't wrap his mind around the empty space.

A hand dragged Halo to the surface. "She's in the water," Gage yelled.

Halo scrambled out of the open windshield. Titus was on a line swimming toward Mary. Mary was digging in with one arm. Max had clamped his mouth onto Mary's other arm and was swimming toward the car with single-minded determination.

Titus made a one-handed grab for her wrist and pulled them both in.

Gage got his fingers through Max's collar, snapped a carabiner, tethering him to the line, and pulled Max onto the submerging car.

The water churned dark and angry. Halo was clamping into one of the lines, then dove into the water, clasping safety rigging for Mary. Until he was all the way in, he hadn't fully appreciated the strength of the flash flood. The debris burned as it abraded his skin. With Titus gripping under her arms, Halo wrangled Mary into the harness.

Gage hefted Titus from the water.

The two turned and dragged Halo and Mary onto the side of the car. "We've got you!"

Halo looked over at the distance to the window. The waters below. His eye followed the rigging, and he was grateful for his team's expertise.

With Max draped over his shoulders, Gage moved hand over hand to the window where Nutsbe waited with an assist. After handing Max off he climbed through the window.

Titus leaned in to talk into Halo's ear. "I'm going up to join Gage." He pointed at the second-story window where the rigging hooked in above the flood waters. Nutsbe leaned out, projecting a light down to illuminate the rescue. "Once we get up there, we're going to use the pully to get you two into the apartment. Mary's reserves were taxed by that swim. We'll pull you two up together. Hang tight for a second while I get across."

Titus swung hand over hand to the second-story window. "Ready?" Titus called out. "You two keep tight hold of each other."

Mary and Halo looked at each other. "Always," they said as one, then their lines tightened, and they were snatched into the air.

EPILOGUE

"ARE YOU KIDDING ME RIGHT NOW?" SAM ASKED FROM THE corner of the couch where she'd curled up. "Kyle's and my first meeting story is so sad compared to yours. Dangerous, romantic." She hugged herself. "I mean, when Kyle proposed, it was on the same beach where we met having cocktails with friends, and I thought that was so sweet. But there you and Halo were, dangling from buildings and braving raging floods."

Mary smiled at her future daughter-in-law as she rubbed a steady hand over Max's coat. Max had popped his head up and stared toward the door, his gray whiskers prominent in the reflected light. Halo must be home.

"When Kyle and I have our own children," Sam said, moving her computer with its Pinterest bridal boards display off to the side. "They'll grow up knowing their grandparents were heroes."

Mary felt the same pitter pat of her heart, the same smile sliding across her face as the door opened and her husband moved into the room. He had a package under his arm and a cake box in his hands as he kicked the door shut.

His eyes were locked on Mary, as they always did, until he

made his way over to her and gave her the kiss. It was the storming car kiss. It was the "I've made a commitment to your well-being and my love for you kiss. It was *their* kiss. The one that they greeted each other with and the one they gave as a promise each time they left.

"Y'all are so cute," Sam cooed.

Halo handed the cake box to Sam and then the package to Mary.

Halo's next kiss was for Max. "How you doing, old man?"

"Don't call him that!" Mary and Sam said together.

Mary reached for the cheese knife from the snack board on the coffee table to slice open the package, and Sam opened the cake box.

"It looks delicious, but what does 10 – 50 mean?" Sam asked.

"Our origin story that I was just telling you," Mary's hand wrapped Halo's as he rested it on her shoulder.

"We met ten years ago today," Halo said. "And Mary is turning fifty. We celebrate both."

"Yes!" Sam said. "Harrowing! Terrifying. I can't even imagine. Why hasn't Kyle told me your story?"

"Perhaps he's not a hundred percent sure that his mom could really do the things we said." Mary looked into the brown box and pulled out a piece of pottery, holding it up and turning it this way and that. "This is proof positive that it all did happen, though." She held it out to Halo to examine. "Every year, on the anniversary of the storm, Anneli, that's the little girl Max found in the woods, sends us a piece of handmade art." Mary dug further into the paper, pulling up a framed picture and folded stationery. "We get a picture and an update."

"So, the mom and the infant? They survived?" Sam asked.

Mary held up the photo for Sam to see. "The baby is now a ten-year-old boy. Toomas."

Max sniffed at the letter and then looked at Mary expectantly. "Let's see, Max."

Mary dug through the box and pulled out a dog toy. "They didn't forget you, buddy."

Halo accepted the letter from Mary, then walked around the back of the sofa to sit next to her and Max, wrapping his arm around them while he studied the photo.

"And how long between the time you got home from Tallinn to the time you were married?"

"Three weeks," Halo said. "The longest three weeks of my life."

"Wait!" Sam turned to Mary. "You said Mrs. V. predicted three changes in Tallinn. Obviously love. Obviously, life trajectory. But your career?"

"Iniquus knew of a group that needed a flight nurse in the D.C. area, transporting pediatric patients,'" Halo said. "And Mary was able to start right away. Of course, in the halls of Iniquus, she isn't Mary. She's Flagpole Mary and much revered."

"Stop teasing." Mary lifted her chin to accept Halo's kiss before turning back to Sam. "I will tell you, when Deidre called and told me we were flying to Switzerland to change our lives, I didn't believe her at all. Of the three places that she was offered, Deidre decided on changing her life trajectory. That's how she ended up contentedly delivering babies alongside her husband in Namibia. It's all because we followed our charts."

Mary and Halo's eyes caught and held.

"You see?" Sam said, "That's what I want for Kyle and me, that level of love and devotion. The happily ever after of it all."

"If you want that," Mary said, bending to kiss Max's head, "you'll need to make sure you have a dog with you that's as magical and amazing as our Max."

While this is

The END

of **Guardian's Instinct**,

more Team Charlie books are coming in 2024.

The next book in Iniquus World Chronology is

Nutsbe Crushed's story
Please join Cerberus Tactical K9 for a new K9 series of doggos
trained by Cerberus Tactical
starting with Beowolf.

Are you reading along with the Iniquus World?
Guardian's Instinct is book thirty-two!
It all started with
WEAKEST LYNX
If you're new to Iniquus, turn two pages to read chapter one.

READERS

I hope you enjoyed getting to know Mary, Halo, and Max. If you had fun reading Guardian's Instinct, I'd appreciate it if you'd help others enjoy it, too.

Recommend it: A few words to your friends, book groups, and social networks would be fantastic.

Review it: Please tell your fellow readers what you liked about my book by reviewing Rescue Instinct.

Discuss it! – I have a SPOILERS group on Facebook.

WEAKEST LYNX

THE LYNX SERIES BOOK ONE

1

THE BLACK BMW POWERED STRAIGHT TOWARD ME. HEART pounding, I stomped my brake pedal flush to the floorboard. My chest slammed into the seat belt, snapping my head forward. There wasn't time to blast the horn, but the scream from my tires was deafening. I gasped in a breath as the BMW idiot threw me a nonchalant wave—his right hand off the wheel—with his left hand pressed to his ear, still chatting on his cell phone. Diplomatic license plates. *Figures.*

Yeah, I didn't really need an extra shot of adrenaline—like a caffeine IV running straight to my artery—I was already amped.

"Focus, Lexi," I whispered under my breath, pressing down on the gas. "Follow the plan. Give the letter to Dave. Let him figure this out." I sent a quick glance down to my purse where a corner of the cream-colored envelope jutted out, then veered my Camry back into the noonday DC gridlock, weaving past the graffitied storefronts. I recognized that the near-miss with the BMW guy probably wasn't his fault. I couldn't remember the last ten minutes of drive time.

I watched my review mirror as a bike messenger laced between the moving cars on his mission to get the parcel in his bag to the right guy at the right time. Once he handed over his package, he'd be done—lucky him. Even though I was handing my letter off to Dave, the truth was that wouldn't be my endpoint. I wasn't clear about what an endpoint would even look like. Safe. It might look like I was safe, that I had my feet back under me. But that thought seemed like it was far out on the horizon, and right now, I was just looking for something to grab on to, to keep me afloat.

When I finally parked in front of Dave Murphy's mid-century brick row house, I sat for a minute, trying to regain my composure. I'd pushed this whole mess to the back burner for as long as I could but after last night's nightmare… Well, better to get a detective's opinion. Dave had handled enough crack-pots over his time with the DCPD that he'd have a better grasp of the threat level. Right now, even with all my training, I was scared out of my mind.

I glanced down at my hands. The tremor in them sent the afternoon sunlight dancing off my brand-new engagement and wedding rings. I felt like an imposter wearing them—like a little girl dressed up in her mother's clothes. *I'm too young to be dealing with all this crap,* I thought as I shoved my keys into my purse. I pulled my hair into a quick ponytail and stepped out into the February cold. Casting anxious glances up and down the street, I jogged up the stairs to bang on Dave's front door.

The screen squeaked open almost immediately as if he'd been standing there waiting for my knock. "Hey, Baby Girl," he said, stepping out of the way to let me in. Dave had been calling me Baby Girl since I was born because my parents couldn't decide on my name, and that was how I was listed on my hospital ankle tag.

"Glad I found you at home." I walked in and plopped down on the blue gingham couch. It had been here since I could remember. The fabric was threadbare and juice stained by his five-year-old twins. On a cop's salary, fine furnishings ranked low in priority. Right now—edgy and confused—I appreciated the comfort of familiarity.

Dave shifted into detective mode—hands on hips, eyes scanning me. "Long time, no see."

"Where are Cathy and the kids?" I asked.

"They've got dentist appointments. Did you come to tell us your news?" He lifted his chin to indicate my left hand and settled at the other end of the couch, swiveling until we were face to face.

"Uhm, no." I twisted my rings, suddenly feeling drained and bereft. What wouldn't I give to have my husband Angel here? The corners of my mouth tugged down. I willed myself to stay focused on the reason for the visit. My immediate safety had to take priority over my grief.

Dave raised a questioning brow, waiting for me to continue.

"Angel and I got married Wednesday. I'm Lexi Sobado now." My voice hitched, and tears pressed against my lids. I lowered my lashes, so Dave wouldn't see. But his eyes had locked onto mine, and he never missed much.

"Married? At your age? No introduction? No wedding invitation? Why isn't he here with you now?" Dave angled his head to the side and crossed his arms over his middle-aged paunch. "I'd like to meet the guy," he all but snarled.

Dave probably thought I'd come here because my husband screwed things up already. I pulled the pillow from behind my back and hugged it to me like a shield. "I'm sorry. I should have let you and Cathy know what was going on—I was caught up, and I just..." I stopped to clear my throat. "Angel and I got married at the courthouse, and no one came with us. Not even Abuela Rosa."

"Angel Sobado. He's kin to Rosa, then?"

I gave the slightest tip of a nod. "Angel is her great-nephew. I couldn't bring him with me today because he deployed with the Rangers to the Middle East Thursday. That's why everything happened so fast. He was leaving." The last word stuck in my throat and choked me.

Dave leaned forward to rest his elbows on his knees. Lacing his fingers, he tapped his thumbs together. "Huh. That's a helluva short honeymoon. Married Wednesday. Gone Thursday." Dave's tone had dropped an octave and gained a fringe of fatherly concern.

His compassion gave me permission to break down. But those Angel-emotions were mine. Private. Right now, I needed to hold myself in check long enough to get through my mission of handing off the letter. I shifted my feet back and forth over the rug as I glared at my purse.

"Might even explain the expression on your face," Dave said, narrowing his eyes. He slouched against the arm of the overstuffed couch.

Stalling wasn't going to make this any easier. I reached a hesitant hand into my bag, pulled out a plastic Zip-loc holding the envelope, and held it up for Dave. "The expression is because of this," I said.

Dave took the bag. After a brief glance, he hefted himself to his feet. Over at his desk, he pulled on a pair of Nitrile gloves, then carefully removed the letter.

DEAREST INDIA ALEXIS,

O my Luve's like the melodie

That's sweetly play'd in tune!
As fair thou art, my bonnie lass,
So deep in love, am I:
And I will love thee still, my dear,
Till a' your bones are white and dry:
Till a' your veins gang dry, my dear,
And your skin melt with the sun;
I will luve thee until your heart is still my dear
When the sands of your life shall no more run.
And fare thee weel, my only Luve,
And fare thee weel a while!
And I will come again, my Luve, so I can watch you die.

DAVE READ the words aloud then stared at me hard; his brows pulled in tight enough that the skin on his forehead accordioned. "What the—"

"Someone shoved the poem under the door to my room, and it's scaring the bejeezus out of me." I gripped the pillow tighter.

Dave peered over the top of his reading glasses. "Last night? This morning?"

"Wednesday morning." I braced when I said it, knowing it would tick Dave off that I didn't bring this to him immediately. Ever since my dad died, his buddies had stepped in and tried to take over the fathering job, even though I'd be turning twenty in a few days.

True to my expectations, Dave was red-faced and bellowing. "*Wednesday?* You waited two whole days to tell me you've gotten a friggin death threat?"

Yup, this was exactly the response Dad would have given me.

Dave jumped up, pacing across the room. Obviously, he

didn't think this was someone's idea of a joke. Fear tightened my chest at his confirmation. I had hoped he'd say, "No worries—someone is having fun pranking you," and then I could go on about my life without the major case of heebie-jeebies that tingled my skin and made me want to run and hide.

"It was our wedding day." I worked to modulate my voice to sound soft and reasonable. "I only had a few short hours before Angel had to take off. So yeah, I decided to focus on us instead of this." I motioned toward the paper in his hand.

Dave took in a deep breath, making his nostrils flare. "Okay." I could almost see his brain shifting gears. "When you first picked up the letter, did you get any vibes?"

"You mean, ESP-wise?"

He nodded stiffly, his eyes hard on me.

Vibes. That wasn't the word I would have chosen to explain my sensations. "I didn't hear anything. It was more like an oily substance oozing over me." I tucked my nose into the soft cloth of the pillow and breathed in the scent of cinnamon fabric freshener. "I vomited." My voice dropped to a whisper. "It felt like evil and craziness, and I can still smell that stench." A shiver raced down my spine.

Dave's lips sealed tightly; he was probably trying to hold back a litany of expletives. Finally, he asked, "That's all?"

"Yes."

"Did any of your neighbors notice anyone unusual lurking around? Did you check with management and run through the security tapes?"

"Dave, didn't you hear? My apartment building burned to the ground three weeks ago. I assumed you knew. It was on the news."

Dave's eyebrows shot straight up.

"I've been living in a motel the Red Cross rented out for all the families displaced by the fire. But to answer your question, no, nobody saw anything, and there were no cameras trained on my motel corridor." I curled my lips in to keep them from trembling. I was used to holding my emotions in check. I trained myself to present a sweet exterior, a costume of sorts, but right now, I was filled to overflowing, and my mask kept slipping out of place.

"Shit." Dave ran a hand over his face. "I had no idea. I'm letting your parents down. Apartment burned, married, husband gone, and now a death threat." His eyes narrowed on me. "Do you think that about covers all of your surprises for me today?"

I paused for a beat. "Yeah, Dave, I think that's it for today." Okay, even if he was like family, the way Dave was talking pissed me off. I was frightened. I wanted a hug and his reassurance. What I was getting was… Dave's brand of love. He wouldn't be this red-faced and agitated if he wasn't worried about me. Tears prickled behind my eyelids, blurring my vision.

"Hey, now. Stop. We'll get to the bottom of this. Did you already let Spyder McGraw know what's going on?"

I wiped my nose with the back of my wrist. "Spyder's still off-grid. I have no idea when he'll get home."

"Were you assigned a different partner while he's gone?"

"No, sir. I only ever worked for Spyder—he sort of wanted to keep me a secret." I still couldn't believe Mom had sat Dave down and told him all about my apprenticeship with Spyder McGraw. Under Spyder's tutelage, I was following my dream of becoming an Intelligence Officer, learning to out-think and out-maneuver the bad guys trying to hurt American interests. And like anyone heading toward a life in the intelligence community, my skills needed to go under the radar. Now that my mom had died, only four people—Spyder, the Millers, and Dave—knew that side of my life. I would prefer Dave didn't know.

"Still, did you consider bringing this to Spyder's commander? Iniquus would probably give him a heads up. Get a message to him."

"Iniquus is my last resort. Sure, Spyder told me to talk to them if I ever found myself in trouble." I sucked in a deep breath of air. "Bottom line? He never wanted them to know I worked for him, well, for them. Safety in anonymity and all that." My fingers kneaded the stuffing in the pillow. "Besides, I guess I was hoping this would all just go away."

Dave's eyes were hard on me. "You know better. Once some psycho's caught you on his radar, you're stuck there until someone wins."

"Okay, so I make sure it's me who wins."

"Exactly right." He considered me for a minute before he asked, "You've kept up with your martial arts training?"

"I have a sparring partner who's pretty good. We rent time at a Do Jang twice a week."

Dave lowered his head to read over the poem again. He put the letter and envelope back in the Zip-loc and placed it on his mantle. Pulling off his gloves with a snap, he looked down at them. "I hate these things. They give me a rash. Look, I'm going to take this down to the station and open a file. If you get anything else, I want you to bring it to me right away. Understood?"

"Yes, sir."

"This is the only poem, letter, communication of any kind you've gotten?"

I nodded. For the first time since I walked into Dave's house, I became aware of sounds other than our conversation and the thrumming blood behind my eardrums. A football game played on TV. I glanced over as the announcer yelled some gibberish about a first down, then moved my gaze back to Dave. "You must have taken graveyard shift last night," I said.

He picked up a remote, zapped off the TV, and sent me a raised eyebrow.

"It doesn't take a psychic. You look like an unmade bed."

Dave ran a hand over his dark hair, thick on the sides, sparse on top. He hadn't used a comb today or bothered to shave. He was hanging-out-at-home comfy in jeans and beat-to-hell tennis shoes. It looked like the only thing I was interrupting was the game re-run.

"Double homicide. Turned into a long night up to my ankles in sewage."

"Yum." I tried on a smile, but it was plastic and contrived.

Dave narrowed his eyes. "We need to move you. Pronto. It's priority one. You need to be someplace secure where I can keep better tabs on you."

"I've been looking since the fire, but I haven't found anything."

"Would you consider buying?" he asked.

"Yes, actually—I'm looking for a low-cost fixer-upper I can work on to help me get through this year without Angel." I followed Dave into the hallway. "Diversion, and all that."

"How about here, in my neighborhood? I could keep a better eye on you—and you won't be showing up at my door with a suitcase full of surprises." He grabbed his coat from the

closet and shrugged it on. "I'm taking you over to meet my neighbor. She has the other half of her duplex on the market." He looked over his shoulder at me. "You shouldn't be running around without a jacket." He handed me an oversized wool parka that smelled like raking leaves. He kicked a Tonka truck out of the way, and we moved out the front door.

On the front porch, I slid into the shadows and took in the length of the road—no cars, no barking dogs, everything quiet.

Dave glanced back. "Coast is clear."

I tucked the coat hood up over my ponytail. Screened by

Dave's broad back, I started across the street. Down the road, a car motor revved. I reached under my shirt and pulled out my gun.

THE WORLD of INIQUUS

Chronological Order

Ubicumque, Quoties. Quidquid

Weakest Lynx (Lynx Series)

Missing Lynx (Lynx Series)

Chain Lynx (Lynx Series)

Cuff Lynx (Lynx Series)

WASP (Uncommon Enemies)

In Too DEEP (Strike Force)

Relic (Uncommon Enemies)

Mine (Kate Hamilton Mystery)

Jack Be Quick (Strike Force)

Deadlock (Uncommon Enemies)

Instigator (Strike Force)

Yours (Kate Hamilton Mystery)

Gulf Lynx (Lynx Series)

Open Secret (FBI Joint Task Force)

Thorn (Uncommon Enemies)
Ours (Kate Hamilton Mysteries)
Cold Red (FBI Joint Task Force)
Even Odds (FBI Joint Task Force)
Survival Instinct - (Cerberus Tactical K9 Team Alpha)
Protective Instinct - (Cerberus Tactical K9 Team Alpha)
Defender's Instinct - (Cerberus Tactical K9 Team Alpha)
Danger Signs - (Delta Force Echo)
Hyper Lynx - (Lynx Series)
Danger Zone - (Delta Force Echo)
Danger Close - (Delta Force Echo)
Fear the REAPER – (Strike Force)
Warrior's Instinct - (Cerberus Tactical K9 Team Bravo)
Rescue Instinct - (Cerberus Tactical K9 Team Bravo)
Heroes Instinct - (Cerberus Tactical K9 Team Bravo)
Striker (Striker Force)
Marriage Lynx (Lynx Series)
A Family of the Heart Cookbook
Guardian's Instinct - (Cerberus Tactical K9 Team Charlie)

Coming soon, more great stories from the ex-special forces security team members who live, work, and love in a tightly knit family.

Beowolf
Blaze Ahead

Sheltering Instinct
Shielding Instinct

For more information visit

www.FionaQuinnBooks.com

ACKNOWLEDGMENTS

My great appreciation ~

To my publicist, Margaret Daly

To my cover artist, Melody Simmons

To my editor, Rossana Tarantini

To my readers -Dar K and Jennie Lopez who came up with the title for this novel

To my Beta Force, who are always honest and kind at the same time, especially M. Carlon,

To my Street Force, who support me and my writing with such enthusiasm and kindness.

To the real-world K9 professionals who serve and protect us.

Virginia K9 search and rescue teams for their work in our community, their dedication, and professionalism.

To all the wonderful professionals whom I called on to get the details right as I conducted my research, especially —

Meagan Longley – for taking me on a tour of her helicopter and spending time filling me in on the background information about life and work as a flight nurse, big congratulations to Meagan on her board certification!

My Estonian bog naturalist expert, **Marilin Pehka**, who introduced me to a unique and glorious world. She embodies the adventure.

My voice teacher extraordinaire – **Yvette Keong**, whose kindness and grace are gifts I wanted my character, Mary, to experience.

My talented pole teacher, **Morgan Obenchain**, whose physical strength and fearlessness hanging upside down, ten feet off the ground, helped me imagine the way for Mary to save the family from the fire.

To my Australian consultant **Katrina Player** and the generosity of her time and talent, making sure that Halo rang true.

Please note: This is a work of fiction, and while I always try my best to get all the details correct, there are times when it serves the story to go slightly to the left or right of perfection. Please understand that any mistakes or discrepancies are my authorial decision-making alone and sit squarely on my shoulders.

Thank you to my family.

I send my love to my husband, T. I love all of our adventures together—and for this book, the Estonian bog with the intoxicating scent of Labrador tea and the gorgeous city of Helsinki—they, and you, feed my creativity and enjoyment of life.

And, of course, thank *YOU* for reading my stories. I'm smiling joyfully as I type this. I so appreciate you!

ABOUT THE AUTHOR

Fiona Quinn is a six-time USA Today bestselling author, a Kindle Scout winner, Amazon Top 40, and an Amazon All-Star.

Quinn writes suspense in her Iniquus World of books, including Lynx, Strike Force, Uncommon Enemies, Kate Hamilton Mysteries, FBI Joint Task Force, Cerberus Tactical K9 Series Alpha, Bravo, and Charlie, the Delta Force Echo series, and now, an Iniquus cookbook!

She writes urban fantasy as Fiona Angelica Quinn for her Elemental Witches Series.

And, just for fun, she writes the Badge Bunny Booze Mystery Collection with her dear friend, Tina Glasneck, as Quinn Glasneck.

Quinn is rooted in the Old Dominion, where she lives with her husband. There, she pops chocolates, devours books, and taps continuously on her laptop.

Visit www.FionaQuinnBooks.com

Find & Follow Fiona Quinn on Social Media

facebook.com/FionaQuinn.52
x.com/fionaquinnbooks
instagram.com/fionaquinnbooks
bookbub.com/authors/fiona-quinn
goodreads.com/fionaquinnbooks

COPYRIGHT

Printed Chesterfield, VA, USA

eBook ISBN: 978-1-946661-84-5

Print Paperback ISBN: 978-1-946661-85-2

Print Hardback ISBN: 978-1-946661-86-9

Library of Congress Control Number: 2023923801

Cover Design by Melody Simmons from eBookindlecovers

Fonts used with permission from Microsoft

Printed in Great Britain
by Amazon